THE OFFICIAL

STAR TREK

QUIZ BOOK

MITCHELL MAGLIO

A WALLABY BOOK

PUBLISHED BY POCKET BOOKS NEW YORK

This book is dedicated to my nieces Beth Ann and Danielle, the brightest stars in my universe.

Another *Original* publication of Wallaby Books

A Wallaby Book published by
POCKET BOOKS, a division of Simon & Schuster, Inc.
1230 Avenue of the Americas, New York, N.Y. 10020

This book is published by Wallaby Books, A Pocket Books Division
of Simon & Schuster, Inc., under exclusive license from Paramount
Pictures Corporation, the Trademark Owner.

ISBN: 0-671-55652-5

First Wallaby Books Printing May, 1985

10 9 8 7 6 5 4 3 2 1

CONTENTS

TO: Admiral R. Falcone
   Dean of Cadets, Starfleet Academy
   San Francisco, Earth

FROM: Admiral M. Maglio
   Superintendent of Education, Starfleet Command
   New York, Earth

STARDATE: 8410.15

SUBJECT: FINAL EXAMS

Dear Bob:

As you know, this year's final exams will be based, in part, on the Captain's Log of the U.S.S. *Enterprise* (NCC-1701), Admiral James T. Kirk commanding. It is the feeling of Starfleet Command that the study of the day-to-day function of an actual starship is an essential element in the education of our cadets. I agree.

Enclosed is a hard copy of the Final Exam Quiz Book. Have your instructors place special emphasis on its contents, as the *Enterprise* log will account for 90% of this year's written exam.

Many thanks, Bob, for suggesting that we use the *Enterprise* logs as opposed to those of another starship. The *Enterprise* could never be accused of being a dull ship. Also, Jim Kirk was of enormous help in developing our new grading system. The new system is as follows:

50%–60%—Plebe	71%–75%—Lieutenant	86%– 90%—Captain
61%–65%—Cadet	76%–80%—Lt. Commander	91%– 95%—Commodore
66%–70%—Ensign	81%–85%—Commander	96%–100%—Admiral

If you have any questions, or comments, please contact me at Starfleet Headquarters.

Very Sincerely Yours,

Mitchell L. Maglio
Admiral, Starfleet Headquarters

"STAR TREK" HISTORY

1) "Star Trek" first aired on
   a. September 26, 1968   **b.** September 8, 1966
   c. October 1, 1970   **d.** December 3, 1966

2) "Star Trek" was created by
   a. Gene Roddenberry   **b.** Gene Coon
   c. D. C. Fontana   **d.** Mel Brooks

3) The pilot that sold "Star Trek" to the network was called
   a. "The Cage"   **b.** "The Man Trap"
   c. "Where No Man Has   **d.** "Charlie X"
      Gone Before"

4) The first "Star Trek" pilot was entitled
   a. "Where No Man Has   **b.** "The Omega Glory"
      Gone Before"
   c. "The Cage"   **d.** "The Menagerie"

5) During the first season, "Star Trek" was aired on
   a. Thursdays at 8:30 P.M.   **b.** Mondays at 8:00 P.M.
   c. Fridays at 9:00 P.M.   **d.** Sundays at 7:00 P.M.

6) The "Star Trek" theme was composed by
   a. Bill Conti   **b.** Alexander Courage
   c. John Barry   **d.** John Williams

7) "Star Trek" was canceled after
    a. 5 seasons   **b.** 2 seasons
    c. 4 seasons   **d.** 3 seasons

8) The character of Dr. McCoy is first seen in the episode called
    a. "Man Trap"   **b.** "Charlie X"
    c. "The Cage"   **d.** "City on the Edge of
                                         Forever"

9) The first Captain of the *Enterprise* was
    a. James Kirk   **b.** Matt Decker
    c. Robert April   **d.** Chris Pike

10) The man who created the costumes for "Star Trek" was
    a. Gene Coon   **b.** Bill Theiss
    c. Ray Reilly   **c.** Matt Jefferies

11) "Star Trek's" prop master was
    a. Alexander Courage   **b.** John D. F. Black
    c. Irving Feinberg   **d.** Nick Glasser

12) Captain Pike was played by
    a. John Colicos   **b.** Jeffrey Hunter
    c. William Windom   **d.** Robert Culp

13) The "Star Trek" letter campaign in 1967 was organized by
    a. David Gerrold   **b.** Gene Roddenberry
    c. NBC   **d.** Bjo Trimble

14) "Star Trek's" final episode was
    a. "The Empath"   **b.** "Whom Gods Destroy"
    c. "Turnabout Intruder"   **d.** "The Enemy Within"

15) The "Star Trek" episode nominated for an Emmy Award was
    a. "The City on the Edge of   **b.** "The Menagerie"
        Forever"
    c. "Mudd's Women"   **d.** "The Tholian Web"

16) "Star Trek's" only recurring guest character was
    a. Harry Mudd   **b.** Matt Decker
    c. Kor   **d.** Sam Kirk

17) Jim Kirk's middle name is
    a. Thaddeus   **b.** Tom
    c. Tiberius   **d.** Terrance

18) The *Enterprise* was built at
a. The San Francisco Naval Yards
b. Starbase II
c. The Brooklyn Naval Yards
d. The Vulcan Science Academy

19) The war between the Federation and the Klingon Empire was stopped by
a. Kirk
b. The Organians
c. The Thalosians
d. The Melkots

20) The first "Star Trek" pilot cost
a. $750,000
b. $1,000,000
c. $350,000
d. $630,000

21) "The Cage" was filmed in
a. 1965
b. 1964
c. 1966
d. 1967

22) "Star Trek" was originally produced by
a. Columbia
b. Republic
c. Desilu
d. Quinn Martin

23) The serial number on the saucer section of the *Enterprise* is
a. NCC-1301
b. NCC-2701
c. NCC-1701
d. NCC-1071

24) After the first pilot was screened, NBC wanted Roddenberry to drop the character of
a. Pike
b. Spock
c. Vina
d. Dr. Boyce

25) Captain Pike's navigator was
a. Number One
b. Spock
c. Carol Marcus
d. Joe Tyler

26) The Earth was almost destroyed (in the "Star Trek" universe) by
a. The Eugenics War
b. Klingons
c. Famine
d. Disease

27) The Federation and the Romulan Empire are separated by
a. The Klingon Empire
b. Melkotian space
c. The Neutral Zone
d. An energy barrier

28) The *Enterprise* was the first Federation ship to
  a. Use warp drive
  b. Leave the galaxy
  c. Encounter intelligent life
  d. Visit Vulcan

29) Jim Kirk was _____ when he took command of the *Enterprise*
  a. 40 years old
  b. 30 years old
  c. 34 years old
  d. 39 years old

30) Warp drive was invented by
  a. Richard Daystrom
  b. Zephram Cochrane
  c. Garth of Izar
  d. Jackson Roykirk

31) The Prime Directive forbids
  a. Aggressive action
  b. Interference with alien cultures
  c. Contact with Talos IV
  d. Passage through the Neutral Zone

32) After the 5-year mission of the *Enterprise,* Kirk became
  a. Chief of the Military
  b. Chief of Domestic Affairs
  c. Chief of Starfleet Operations
  d. An instructor at the Academy

33) The *Enterprise* is the first Earth vessel to establish
  a. Deep space colonies
  b. Diplomatic relations with the Klingons
  c. Visual contact with the Romulans
  d. The Prime Directive

34) Violation of General Order 7 is punishable by
  a. Imprisonment
  b. Court-martial
  c. Discharge
  d. Death

35) The *Enterprise* was designed by
  a. Ed Milkis
  b. Walt Jefferies
  c. Gene Coon
  d. Irving Feinberg

36) The greatest military leader in Federation history was
  a. Admiral Komack
  b. Garth of Izar
  c. Christopher Pike
  d. James T. Kirk

37) "Star Trek's" third season producer was
   a. Gene Roddenberry   b. Gene Coon
   c. Fred Freiberger   d. D. C. Fontana

38) The war between the Federation and the Klingon Empire was
   a. Won by the Romulans   b. Won by the Federation
   c. Never fought   d. Inconclusive

39) There were _____ episodes of "Star Trek"
   a. 76   b. 77
   c. 78   d. 79

40) McCoy's medical instruments were really exotic
   a. Salt shakers   b. Pill bottles
   c. Ear plugs   d. Snuff cases

41) This script was submitted as a possible second "Star Trek" pilot
   a. "The Man Trap"   b. "The Omega Glory"
   c. "Charlie X"   d. "The Corbomite Maneuver"

42) The *Enterprise* was originally going to be called the
   a. Constitution   b. Valiant
   c. Yorktown   d. Exeter

43) The first episode of "Star Trek's" second season was
   a. "Journey to Babel"   b. "Amok Time"
   c. "The Omega Glory"   d. "The Doomsday Machine"

44) *Star Trek—The Motion Picture* premiered in
   a. January 1978   b. December 1979
   c. June 1980   d. November 1977

45) During its third season, "Star Trek" aired
   a. Monday at 8 P.M.   b. Thursday at 9 P.M.
   c. Friday at 10 P.M.   d. Wednesday at 7 P.M.

46) Chekov's role in "Gamesters of Triskelion" was originally written for
   a. Sulu   b. Scotty
   c. Spock   d. McCoy

47) "Star Trek" was originally produced in association with
    a. Norway Productions   **b.** Apple Productions
    c. Lorimar Productions   **d.** MGM Productions

48) *Star Trek III: The Search for Spock* premiered in
    a. April 1984   **b.** May 1984
    c. June 1984   **d.** July 1984

49) During the filming of "Star Trek's" final episode, William Shatner came down with
    a. Stomach cramps   **b.** The flu
    c. Laryngitis   **d.** An ear infection

50) A model of the *Enterprise* hangs over the aerospace room of
    a. Museum of Broadcasting   **b.** The Franklin Institution
    c. The Smithsonian   **d.** Museum of Flight

"STAR TREK" TECHNOLOGY

1) The *Enterprise* is _____ long
  a. 840 feet   b. 760 feet
  c. 947 feet   d. 690 feet

2) The primary hull is how many decks thick?
  a. 11   b. 12
  c. 13   d. 14

3) The *Enterprise*'s maximum safe cruising speed is
  a. Warp 5   b. Warp 6
  c. Warp 7   d. Warp 8

4) One stripe, followed by one row of dashes on the sleeve of a Starfleet day uniform denotes the rank of
  a. Lieutenant   b. Ensign
  c. Commander   d. Lieutenant commander

5) The turbolifts are driven by
  a. Antigravs   b. Rockets
  c. Cables   d. Turbines

6) At full strength, a starship's shields can hold for
  a. A week   b. 20 hours
  c. 2 weeks   d. 24 hours

7) The range of a starship's transporter is
  a. 16,000 miles   b. 17,000 miles
  c. 18,000 miles   d. 19,000 miles

8) The secondary hull of the *Enterprise* is _____ decks thick
  a. 12   b. 14
  c. 11   d. 16

9) DY-500 class ships were built in
  a. The 20th century   b. The 21st century
  c. The 22d century   d. The 23d century

10) Deck seven of the *Enterprise* houses
  a. Officers' quarters   b. Food preparation
  c. Crew quarters   d. Sick bay

11) Masiform-D is a powerful
  a. Depressant   b. Stimulant
  c. Truth serum   d. Poison

12) Emergency transporter rooms can handle _____ people
  a. 6   b. 10
  c. 12   d. 20

13) The Constitution-class starship has _____ officers
  a. 7   b. 43
  c. 15   d. 100

14) Tractors beams have a range of
  a. 50,000 miles   b. 100,000 miles
  c. 150,000 miles   d. 200,000 miles

15) Recreation areas are located on deck
  a. 5   b. 11
  c. 8   d. 13

16) There are _____ Constitution-class starships in Starfleet
  a. 9   b. 10
  c. 11   d. 12

17) Warp 1 is the equivalent of
 a. The speed of light
 b. Twice the speed of light
 c. 3 times the speed of light
 d. 10 times the speed of light

18) A parsec is
 a. 5^2 light-years
 b. 5.8 light-years
 c. 3.26 light-years
 d. 4.39 light-years

19) Stokaline is a general
 a. Stimulant
 b. Radiation treatment
 c. Depressant
 d. Vitamin

20) The maximum gross weight of the *Enterprise* is
 a. 200,000 tons
 b. 190,000 tons
 c. 180,000 tons
 d. 170,000 tons

21) Research labs on a starship are located on decks
 a. 4 and 5
 b. 2 and 3
 c. 7 and 8
 d. 9 and 10

22) Standard orbit ranges from 1,000 to _____ miles
 a. 7,000
 b. 9,000
 c. 12,000
 d. 5,000

MATCHING

Match the following "Star Trek" devices to the episode they were featured in.

1) Agonizer

2) Ahn-woon

3) Cloaking device

4) Corbomite

5) Planet killer

6) Instrument of obedience

7) Subcutaneous transponder

8) Kligat

9) M-4

10) M-5

11) Mind sifter

a. "Errand of Mercy"
b. "For the World Is Hollow . . ."
c. "Patterns of Force"
d. "The Doomsday Machine"
e. "Friday's Child"
f. "The Ultimate Computer"
g. "Journey to Babel"
h. "Whom Gods Destroy"
i. "Requiem for Methuselah"
j. "The Deadly Years"
k. "Amok Time"
l. "Mirror, Mirror"
m. "The *Enterprise* Incident"

FILL-INS

1) Spock's destruct sequence is _____
_____ _____ _____.

2) The coded message that warns a starship away from a planet is _____.

3) The Borgia plant comes from the planet _____.

4) Class M planets are _____ type.

5) Starbase 12 is in the _____ system.

6) Phaser One has a blast radius of _____ meters.

7) DY 100 class ships were built in the _____.

8) DY 500 class ships were built in the _____
_____.

9) The coded order calling for the destruction of a planet is General Order _____.

10) The *Enterprise* has _____ phasers.

MATCHING II

Match the stripe pattern on the sleeve of a Starfleet day uniform with its corresponding rank.

1) One stripe/one row of dashes

2) One stripe

3) Three rows of stripes

4) One stripe/one row of dashes/one row of stripes

5) Four rows of stripes

6) Two rows of stripes

a. Lieutenant
b. Ensign
c. Commander
d. Admiral
e. Commodore
f. Captain
g. Lieutenant commander
h. Chief

ALIEN LIFE FORMS IN THE "STAR TREK" UNIVERSE

1) **The natives of Delta Theta III are**
   - **a.** Humanoid
   - **b.** Vulcanoid
   - **c.** Gaseous
   - **d.** Reptilian

2) **The Drella of Alpha Carinae V derive sustenance from**
   - **a.** Love
   - **b.** Hate
   - **c.** Jealousy
   - **d.** Pride

3) **Berengaria VII is a home for**
   - **a.** Centaurs
   - **b.** Dragons
   - **c.** Vampire bats
   - **d.** Unicorns

4) **Phylosians are a race of intelligent**
   - **a.** Fish
   - **b.** Cats
   - **c.** Reptiles
   - **d.** Plants

5) **The Mellitus cloud creature hails from**
   - **a.** Signia Minor
   - **b.** Alpha Majoris I
   - **c.** Alpha Trianguli III
   - **d.** Triton III

6) **Lokai is a native of**
   - **a.** Sigma Draconis
   - **b.** Ingram B
   - **c.** Cheron
   - **d.** Deneb

7) The natives of Gideon suffer from
   a. Disease
   b. Overpopulation
   c. Social upheaval
   d. Constant wars

8) Many Vulcan children own a pet
   a. Sehlat
   b. Tribble
   c. Mugato
   d. Sandbat

9) The father of Klingon thought was
   a. Kahless
   b. Kor
   c. Koloth
   d. Kang

10) Creatures of rock hail from
   a. Deneb
   b. Excalbia
   c. Antares
   d. Cheron

11) The natives of Antos IV practice
   a. Telepathy
   b. Empathy
   c. Astral projection
   d. Cellular metamorphosis

12) The humanoid females of Sigma Draconis VI are
   a. Eymorgs
   b. Troglytes
   c. Morgs
   d. Leetar

13) Vulcan merchants trade in
   a. Tribbles
   b. Spican flame gems
   c. Antarean glow water
   d. Kevas

14) Iotians have a tendency to be highly
   a. Aggressive
   b. Imitative
   c. Passive
   d. Curious

15) Kirk was once compared to this native of Deneb
   a. Sandbat
   b. Le-Matya
   c. Blood worm
   d. Slime devil

16) _____ are soft and shapeless
   a. Selahts
   b. Eel birds
   c. Regulan blood worms
   d. Mugato

17) Capellans use a throwing weapon called a(n)
   a. Shuriken
   b. Kligat
   c. Boomerang
   d. Ahn-woon

18) The _____ are a peaceful race, whose primary wealth comes from Dilithium crystals
  - **a.** Halkans
  - **b.** Capellans
  - **c.** Vians
  - **d.** Cheronians

19) The native of Gamma Canaris N is _____ in nature
  - **a.** Chemical
  - **b.** Carbon
  - **c.** Electrical
  - **d.** Radioactive

20) The Le-Matya is a feline predator from the planet
  - **a.** Vulcan
  - **b.** Rigel II
  - **c.** Omicron Ceti III
  - **d.** Earth

21) The population of Platonius originally came from
  - **a.** Andromeda
  - **b.** Sandara
  - **c.** Alpha Centauri
  - **d.** Murasahi 321

22) The head of the Romulan Empire is called
  - **a.** Emperor
  - **b.** Caesar
  - **c.** High Teer
  - **d.** Praetor

23) The Romulan home world has a _____ sun
  - **a.** Red
  - **b.** Binary
  - **c.** Yellow
  - **d.** Green

24) Tellerites are physically
  - **a.** Humanoid
  - **b.** Reptilian
  - **c.** Pig-like
  - **d.** Blue skinned

25) Vanna is a native of the planet
  - **a.** Canarus II
  - **b.** Earth
  - **c.** Rigel III
  - **d.** Ardana

26) Phineas Tarbolde of Canopus wrote
  - **a.** The Articles of the Federation
  - **b.** Let Me Help
  - **c.** Nightingale Woman
  - **d.** All I ask is a tall ship

27) Some of the natives of Ardana live in
  - **a.** Space
  - **b.** Villages
  - **c.** Prisons
  - **d.** The clouds

28) The natives of Dramia II dwell in
    a. Caves
    b. Trees
    c. The mountains
    d. Cities

29) The Providers are natives of the planet
    a. Omicron Delta
    b. Orion
    c. Triskelion
    d. Ingram B

30) The "thought creatures" who nurtured Charles Evans are called
    a. Organians
    b. Medusans
    c. Melkots
    d. Thasians

31) Christopher Pike was taking the *Enterprise* to
    a. Epsilon Indi
    b. Cheron
    c. Sarpeidon
    d. Vega IX

32) Sigma Draconis III rates B on the
    a. Evolutionary scale
    b. Richter scale
    c. Agricultural scale
    d. Industrial scale

33) Giant sandbats come from
    a. Deneb
    b. Maynark IV
    c. Regula
    d. Antos

34) The _____ are nonhumanoid masters of illusion
    a. Vians
    b. Melkots
    c. Metrons
    d. Talosians

35) Uletta comes from the planet
    a. Rigel IX
    b. Antos II
    c. Vendikar
    d. Zeon

36) The right of statement is a privilege of _____ society
    a. Klingon
    b. Romulan
    c. Orion
    d. Capellan

37) A space-traveling race of intelligent Lizards are the
    a. Andorians
    b. Tholians
    c. Gorns
    d. Horta

38) The highly evolved race that settled the dispute between the Federation and the Gorns is called the
- **a.** Melkots
- **b.** Organians
- **c.** Zetars
- **d.** Metrons

39) The leader of Capella IV holds the title of
- **a.** Provider
- **b.** High Teer
- **c.** Warrior chief
- **d.** Overlord

40) Natives of this planet are white on one side and black on the other
- **a.** Megas II
- **b.** Cheron
- **c.** Livitus IV
- **d.** Taurus II

41) The creature who is neither machine nor being is
- **a.** Sargon
- **b.** Ayelborne
- **c.** Landru
- **d.** The Guardian of Forever

42) The high priestess of Yonada is named
- **a.** Mea 3
- **b.** Elaan
- **c.** Natira
- **d.** Shahna

43) Troyians have _____ skin color
- **a.** Blue
- **b.** Green
- **c.** Yellow
- **d.** White/black

44) Yarnek's home planet is
- **a.** Excalbia
- **b.** Maynark V
- **c.** Tarsus IV
- **d.** Thasia

45) Camus II's civilization is
- **a.** Young
- **b.** Growing
- **c.** Old
- **d.** Dead

46) Aurelians are
- **a.** Pig-like
- **b.** Cat-like
- **c.** Bird-like
- **d.** Horse-like

47) Capellans are a race of
- **a.** Scientists
- **b.** Cave dwellers
- **c.** Philosophers
- **d.** Warriors

48) The ugliest race in the galaxy is
    a. Andorians   **b.** Tellerites
    c. Excalbians   **d.** Medusans

49) Andorians are known for their
    a. Antennae   **b.** Tails
    c. Pig-like features   **d.** Skin color

50) A race of salt vampires developed on the planet
    a. M113   **b.** Psi 2000
    c. X311   **d.** Albia 599

51) Ardana's chief export is
    a. Pergium   **b.** Dilithium
    c. Zienite   **d.** Villium

52) The natives of Alpha Proxima II are
    a. Humanoid   **b.** Vulcanoid
    c. Feline   **d.** Reptilian

53) The energy being that calls itself Rejac comes from the planet
    a. Tellar   **b.** Cheron
    c. Earth   **d.** Vulcan

54) Scalosians are highly
    a. Accelerated   **b.** Aggressive
    c. Advanced   **d.** Evolved

55) The Providers of Triskelion take the form of living
    a. Computers   **b.** Ships
    c. Brains   **d.** Rock

56) The father of Vulcan philosophy is
    a. Sarek   **b.** T'Pau
    c. Surak   **d.** Thelev

57) Tycho IV is the home of
    a. Zephram Cochrane   **b.** Flint
    c. The Providers   **d.** The vampire cloud

58) The inventor of the warp drive was born on
    a. Earth   **b.** Vulcan
    c. Alpha Centauri   **d.** Organia

59) The giant dry worm comes from the planet
- **a.** Ekos
- **b.** Scalos
- **c.** Antos IV
- **d.** Camus II

60) Planet 892-IV's civilization greatly resembles that of
- **a.** Vulcan
- **b.** Rome
- **c.** Talos IV
- **d.** Exo III

61) The natives of Exo III created a race of
- **a.** Giants
- **b.** Dwarfs
- **c.** Androids
- **d.** Warriors

62) One of the planets in the Minaran star system bred a race that is
- **a.** Telepathic
- **b.** Empathic
- **c.** Deaf
- **d.** Sociopathic

63) Regulus V is home to the giant
- **a.** Blood worm
- **b.** Vampire cloud
- **c.** Eel bird
- **d.** Slime devil

64) The only life native to Omicron Ceti III is
- **a.** Plants
- **b.** Fish
- **c.** Single cells
- **d.** Insects

65) The natives of Gamma Trianguli VI live in
- **a.** Fear
- **b.** Wonder
- **c.** Privation
- **d.** Paradise

66) The Fabrini are known for their great knowledge of
- **a.** Navigation
- **b.** Medicine
- **c.** Physics
- **d.** Law

67) Natives of Cheron can project
- **a.** Thoughts
- **b.** Illusions
- **c.** Force bolts
- **d.** Force fields

68) Colony beings come from the planet
- **a.** Sarpeidon
- **b.** Ingram B
- **c.** Garo VII
- **d.** Regulus IV

69) Hortas have a life span of approximately
- **a.** 20,000 years
- **b.** 30,000 years
- **c.** 40,000 years
- **d.** 60,000 years

70) The Malurian star system has a population of
    a. 16 billion   **b.** 4 billion
    c. 10 billion   **d.** 3 billion

71) Vulcans have a life span of
    a. 150 years   **b.** 200 years
    c. 250 years   **d.** 300 years

72) The Federation debates the admission of
    a. Coridanians   **b.** Thalpsus
    c. Platonius   **d.** Minara II

73) Garth's life was saved by the natives of
    a. Exo III   **b.** Antos IV
    c. Ekos   **d.** Sarpeidon

74) The natives of Camus II knew the secret of
    a. Immortality   **b.** The universe
    c. Time travel   **d.** Life energy transfer

75) Sarpeidons have unlocked the secret of
    a. Time travel   **b.** Dimensional travel
    c. Life energy transfer   **d.** Immortality

76 The only known race from the Andromeda galaxy is the
    a. Capellans   **b.** Cheronians
    c. Kelvans   **d.** Tholians

77) Neural is the home of the
    a. Great white bird   **b.** Horta
    c. Sikar   **d.** Mugato

78) Vians are highly evolved beings dedicated to saving one of the populated worlds of
    a. Chantara   **b.** Minara
    c. Maluria   **d.** Berengaria

79) Vulcans are very sensitive to
    a. Heat   **b.** Light
    c. Water   **d.** Cold

80) The body chemistry of natives of Rigel V is similar to that of
    a. Tellerites   **b.** Vulcans
    c. Humans   **d.** Andorians

81) The natives of Rigel IV are physically similar to
a. Tellerites
b. Vulcans
c. Humans
d. Excalbians

82) Orions are notorious
a. Liars
b. Pirates
c. Smugglers
d. Counterfeiters

83) The cave dwellers of Ardana are called
a. Troglytes
b. Diggers
c. Slavorrs
d. Stratans

84) A race made up of the life forces of several distinct beings is the
a. Tholians
b. Organians
c. Zetars
d. Thasians

85) The commander of the *Fesarius*, and a citizen of the First Federation, is
a. Tan Ru
b. Loskene
c. Trelane
d. Balok

86) At the age of 7, Vulcan children undergo the
a. Plak tow
b. Pon farr
c. Kahs-wan
d. Koon-ut kal-if-fee

87) The Vulcan word Nome means
a. Logic
b. All
c. Reason
d. Peace

88) The normal pulse rate for a Vulcan is
a. 90 beats per minute
b. 100 beats per minute
c. 212 beats per minute
d. 73 beats per minute

89) "Son" Worshipers are native to
a. Psi 2000
b. M113
c. KI 1100
d. 892-IV

90) Vendorians are
a. Telepaths
b. Energy creatures
c. Shape shifters
d. Empaths

91) Tellerites are immune to the effects of
a. Age
b. Fatigue
c. Alcohol
d. Reason

92) Tholians are creatures of
    a. Crystal   **b.** Energy
    c. Fire   **d.** Thought

93) Spock was almost killed by the poisonous plants of
    a. Venecia V   **b.** Corob II
    c. Theta III   **d.** Gamma Trianguli VI

94) Green slave girls come from
    a. Delta   **b.** Corinth
    c. Orion   **d.** Thalosia

95) Human males are aroused by a pheromone secreted by the females of
    a. Orion   **b.** Delta
    c. Elas   **d.** Troyius

96) The Kzin are
    a. Reptilian   **b.** Aquarian
    c. Feline   **d.** Vulcanoid

97) John Gill offered Nazi doctrines to the
    a. Zeons   **b.** Vians
    c. Cheronians   **d.** Ekosians

98) Gav is a native of
    a. Tellar   **b.** Andoria
    c. Sandara   **d.** Beta Origi

99) These beings don't like Klingons
    a. Organians   **b.** Orions
    c. Tribbles   **d.** Romulans

100) Intense heat is radiated by
    a. Triskelions   **b.** Excalbians
    c. Ekosians   **d.** Sarpeidons

101) The only planet in the galaxy forbidden to Federation ships is
    a. Taurus II   **b.** Talos IV
    c. Tarsus IV   **d.** Tumulus II

Match the following "Star Trek" characters with their home planets.

1) Gav

2) Mea 3

3) Li Yang

4) Bele

5) Maab

6) Sikar

7) Zarabeth

8) Loskene

9) Thelev

10) Rael

11) Garth

12) Nona

13) Trefayne

14) Daris

15) Mara

16) Marta

17) Kryton

18) Luma

19) Thann

20) Tomar

a. Vulcan
b. Izar
c. Sarpeidon
d. Scalos
e. Orion
f. Omega IV
g. Earth
h. Eminiar VII
i. Tellar
j. Cheron
k. Capella
l. Andoria
m. Tholia
n. Neural
o. Elas
p. Sigma Draconis VI
q. Organia
r. Minara II
s. Ekos
t. Klingon
u. Talosian
v. Vendikar
w. Kelva

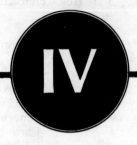

JAMES T. KIRK

1) Kirk's serial number is
   a. SD 932-7678-CEC   **b.** SC 937-0176-CEC
   c. SA 766-6756-CEC   **d.** SS 875-0072-CEC

2) Kirk was born in
   a. Georgia   **b.** Washington
   c. Iowa   **d.** Boston

3) Kirk is interested in
   a. Vulcan history   **b.** American history
   c. Archaeology   **d.** Russian history

4) Kirk graduated in the top _____ of his class
   a. 5%   **b.** 10%
   c. 2%   **d.** 4%

5) Kirk's first deep-space assignment was aboard the
   a. *Yorktown*   **b.** *Republic*
   c. *Exeter*   **d.** *Farragut*

6) Ben Finney was Kirk's shipmate aboard the
   a. *Lexington*   **b.** *Farragut*
   c. *Republic*   **d.** *Yorktown*

7) At Starfleet Academy, Kirk had a relationship with
   a. Janice   **b.** Ruth
   c. Areel   **d.** Edith

8) Kirk's nephew is named
   a. Peter   **b.** Sam
   c. George   **d.** Jim

9) Kirk was decorated with the Grankite Order of
   a. Valor   **b.** Bravery
   c. Leadership   **d.** Tactics

10) Kirk once contracted
   a. Xenopolycethemia   **b.** Rigellian fever
   c. Choriomeningitis   **d.** Kassaba fever

11) As of Stardate 8128.78, Kirk currently holds the service rank of
   a. Captain   **b.** Commodore
   c. Admiral   **d.** Rear Admiral

12) Kirk was given the Ribbon of Commendation from
   a. Axanar   **b.** Pentaries
   c. Gavilan   **d.** Orion

13) _____ _____ named his daughter after Kirk
   a. Leonard McCoy   **b.** Sam Gogley
   c. Bob Wesley   **d.** Ben Finney

14) Kirk was given a case of the bends in
   a. "The Empath"   **b.** "The Gamesters of Triskelion"
   c. "The Omega Glory" **d.** "The Devil in the Dark"

15) At Starfleet Academy, Kirk's personal devil was
   a. Ron Tracey   **b.** Finnegan
   c. Ben Finney   **d.** Garrovick

MATCHING

Match the women in Kirk's life (and they were many) to the episodes in which they appear.

1) Edith Keeler

2) Ruth

3) Areel Shaw

4) Shanna

5) Odona

6) Deela

7) Vanna

8) Janice Lester

9) Janet Wallace

10) Miramanee

11) Daras

12) Marlena Moreau

13) Lenore Karidian

14) Reena

15) Marta

16) Miranda Jones

17) Drusilla

18) Kelinda

19) Sylvia

20) Mea 3

a. "The Gamesters of Triskel-ion"

b. "Mirror, Mirror"

c. "Shore Leave"

d. "The City on the Edge of Forever"

e. "A Taste of Armageddon"

f. "Catspaw"

g. "Amok Time"

h. "The Mark of Gideon"

i. "Wink of an Eye"

j. "Journey to Babel"

k. "Turnabout Intruder"

l. "The Deadly Years"

m. "Court-martial"

n. "The Cloudminders"

o. "Patterns of Force"

p. "Whom Gods Destroy"

q. "By Any Other Name"

r. "Bread and Circuses"

s. "The Conscience of the King"

t. "Requiem for Methuselah"

u. "The Paradise Syndrome"

v. "Is There in Truth No Beauty?"

WILLIAM SHATNER

1) William Shatner was born in
   a. England
   b. France
   c. Canada
   d. Italy

2) Shatner graduated from
   a. N.Y.U.
   b. McGill University
   c. Ontario University
   d. Wittenberg University

3) Shatner graduated from college in
   a. 1950
   b. 1951
   c. 1952
   d. 1953

4) William Shatner received much of his training with the
   a. Stratford Shakespeare Company
   b. National Repertory Theater, Ottowa
   c. National Repertory Company, Rome
   d. National Repertory Company, London

5) On Broadway, Bill received critical acclaim for
   a. *Most Happy Fella*
   b. *Finnian's Rainbow*
   c. *The World of Suzie Wong*
   d. *Incident at Vichy*

6) Shatner's first motion picture was
   a. *Brothers Karamazov*
   b. *Judgment at Nuremberg*
   c. *White Comanche*
   d. *Lord of the Flies*

7) Bill made his Broadway debut in
   a. *Guys and Dolls*   b. *How to Succeed*
   c. *Tamburlaine the Great*   d. *Fiddler on the Roof*

8) Shatner did "Terror at 20,000 Feet" for
   a. "The Outer Limits"   b. "One Step Beyond"
   c. "Alfred Hitchcock Pre-   d. "Twilight Zone"
   sents"

9) Shatner's first television series was
   a. "For the People"   b. "The Lieutenant"
   c. "Star Trek"   d. "Barbary Coast"

10) After "Star Trek," Shatner starred in the short-lived television series
   a. "For the People"   b. "Barbary Coast"
   c. "Time and Again"   d. "T. J. Hooker"

11) Shatner currently stars in the hit television series
   a. "For the People"   b. "Barbary Coast"
   c. "T. J. Hooker"   d. "J. T. Estaban"

12) Shatner appeared with Spencer Tracy in
   a. *Seven Days in May*   b. *Adam's Rib*
   c. *Inherit the Wind*   d. *Judgment at Nuremberg*

13) William Shatner plays two roles in the motion picture entitled
   a. *White Comanche*   b. *Lord of the Flies*
   c. *House Calls*   d. *Dirty Words*

14) Leonard Nimoy and William Shatner first appeared together in an episode of
   a. "The Saint"   b. "Secret Agent"
   c. "The Man from   d. "Honey West"
   U.N.C.L.E."

15) William Shatner delighted audiences in the comedy hit
   a. *Revenge of the Nerds*   b. *Airplane II*
   c. *Mr. Mom*   d. *Animal House*

MR. SPOCK

1) **Spock's serial number is**
   a. S 179-276SP
   b. S 321-988ST
   c. S 322-774SS
   d. S 493-231V

2) **Spock's blood type is**
   a. O+
   b. O−
   c. T+
   d. T−

3) **Spock has been in Starfleet for**
   a. 10 years
   b. 12 years
   c. 18 years
   d. 20 years

4) **Under Captain Pike, Spock held the rank of**
   a. Ensign
   b. Lieutenant
   c. Lieutenant commander
   d. Commander

5) **When Kirk took command of the *Enterprise*, Spock was a**
   a. Lieutenant
   b. Lieutenant commander
   c. Chief
   d. Commander

6) **Spock has practically no**
   a. Pulse
   b. Respiration
   c. Blood pressure
   d. Rapid eye movement

7) Spock and Sarek did not speak for
    a. 18 years   **b.** 16 years
    c. 12 years   **d.** 10 years

8) Spock's blood is
    a. Iron-based   **b.** Silicon-based
    c. Silver-based   **d.** Copper-based

9) Spock was betrothed to T'Pring at age
    a. 5   **b.** 6
    c. 7   **d.** 8

10) Spock had a pet sehlat named
    a. Sherlock   **b.** Le-matya
    c. Plak tow   **d.** I Cahya

11) Spock is an accomplished
    a. Pianist   **b.** Violinist
    c. Cellist   **d.** Drummer

12) In "Journey to Babel" Amanda is
    a. 53 years old   **b.** 55 years old
    c. 58 years old   **d.** 60 years old

13) At 7 years of age, Spock underwent the
    a. Kahs-wan   **b.** Pon farr
    c. Plak tow   **d.** Fal tor pan

14) Spock's first commanding officer was
    a. April   **b.** Kirk
    c. Pike   **d.** Decker

15) Spock can control
    a. His heartbeat   **b.** His reaction to pain
    c. Brain waves   **d.** His bleeding

MATCHING

Match the Vulcan-related terms to the episode that featured them.

1) Neck pinch

2) Kahs-wan

3) Pon farr

4) Tal sahya

5) Death grip

6) Mind meld

7) IDIC

8) Nome

9) Inner eyelid

10) Kohlinahr

a. "The Savage Curtain"
b. "Is There in Truth No Beauty?"
c. "Yesteryear"
d. "The *Enterprise* Incident"
e. "The Enemy Within"
f. "The Corbomite Maneuver"
g. "Amok Time"
h. "Operation—Annihilate"
i. "Dagger of the Mind"
j. "Journey to Babel"
k. *Star Trek—The Motion Picture*

LEONARD NIMOY

1) Leonard Nimoy was born on
   a. March 16, 1934   **b.** March 26, 1931
   c. March 16, 1929   **d.** March 26, 1935

2) Nimoy graduated from
   a. Hunter College   **b.** N.Y.U.
   c. Boston College   **d.** Southern California University

3) Nimoy received his training with
   a. Grotowski   **b.** The Polish Poor Theater
   c. Ryszard Cheslak   **d.** The Pasadena Playhouse

4) Nimoy recorded an album called
   a. Vulcans   **b.** Leonard Nimoy Sings Cole Porter

   c. The Way I Feel   **d.** The Lonely Alien

5) Nimoy's first book was entitled
   a. You and I   **b.** Timelines
   c. We Three   **d.** A Vulcan's Guide to Earth

6) Leonard Nimoy played Narab in
a. "Captain Marvel" b. "Zombies of the Strato-
sphere"
c. "Superman vs. the Atom d. "Blackhawk"
Man"

7) Nimoy made his Broadway debut in
a. *Dracula* b. *Visit to a Strange Planet*
c. *Equus* d. *Incident at Vichy*

8) Nimoy's first television appearance was on
a. "Playhouse 90" b. "Dragnet"
c. "Your Show of Shows" d. "Space Patrol"

9) Nimoy currently hosts the series
a. "Nova" b. "Omni"
c. "In Search Of . . ." d. "Silver Screen"

10) Nimoy's first film appearance was in
a. 1950 b. 1951
c. 1952 d. 1953

11) Nimoy's first regular series was
a. "Space Patrol" b. "For the People"
c. "The Millionaire" d. "Star Trek"

12) Nimoy is currently touring in the one-man show
a. *Vincent* b. *Lenny*
c. *Lloyd* d. *Chaplin*

13) Nimoy's first directing assignment in a motion picture was
a. *The Conversion* b. *Star Trek III*
c. *American Nightmares* d. *Invasion of the Body
Snatchers*

14) Nimoy appeared in the film
a. *Tropics* b. *House on Garibaldi Street*
c. *Seven Days in May* d. *American Nightmares*

15) Nimoy's autobiography is entitled
a. *Leonard Nimoy* b. *Nimoy*
c. *Spock/Nimoy* d. *I Am Not Spock*

THE CREW OF THE U.S.S. ENTERPRISE

1) McCoy's father is named
- **a.** David
- **b.** Leonard
- **c.** John
- **d.** Robert

2) Scotty was first seen in the "Star Trek" episode
- **a.** "The Cage"
- **b.** "Where No Man Has Gone Before"
- **c.** "The Corbomite Maneuver"
- **d.** "The Man Trap"

3) One of Sulu's hobbies is
- **a.** Stamp collecting
- **b.** Old books
- **c.** Botany
- **d.** Military literature

4) Lieutenant Uhura's name means
- **a.** Light
- **b.** Beauty
- **c.** Love
- **d.** Freedom

5) In *Star Trek II* Chekov was the first officer of the
- **a.** *Enterprise*
- **b.** *Reliant*
- **c.** *Excelsior*
- **d.** *Grissom*

6) Kevin Riley was born on
- **a.** Earth
- **b.** Tarsus IV
- **c.** Taurus II
- **d.** Rigel V

7) In *Star Trek—the Motion Picture*, Janice Rand was assigned to
    a. Transporter duty   **b.** Engineering
    c. Sick bay   **d.** Security

8) McCoy was decorated with the
    a. Silver Palm   **b.** Legion of Honor
    c. Medinite Order   **d.** Oak Leaf of Axanar

9) M'Benga first appears in
    a. "Amok Time"   **b.** "All Our Yesterdays"
    c. "A Private Little War"   **d.** "Savage Curtain"

10) Scotty falls in love in
    a. "Wolf in the Fold"   **b.** "Space Seed"
    c. "A Piece of the Action"   **d.** "Lights of Zetar"

11) McCoy was married to
    a. Nancy Crater   **b.** Natira
    c. Diana McCoy   **d.** Barbara McCoy

12) Uhura is an accomplished
    a. Actress   **b.** Dancer
    c. Singer   **d.** Pianist

13) Riley lost his parents at the age of
    a. 9   **b.** 11
    c. 8   **d.** 4

14) Nurse Chapel gave up a career in
    a. Astrobiology   **b.** Astrophysics
    c. Alien anatomy   **d.** Vulcan medicine

15) Sulu first appears in
    a. "Where No man . . ."   **b.** "The Cage"
    c. "The Man Trap"   **d.** "Naked Time"

16) McCoy was born in
    a. Texas   **b.** North Carolina
    c. Kentucky   **d.** Georgia

17) Christine Chapel is now
    a. Retired   **b.** A doctor
    c. Chief Nurse of Starfleet   **d.** A research biologist

18) **Christine was once engaged to**
  a. Roger Corby
  b. John Gill
  c. Zephram Cochrane
  d. Bob Wesley

19) **Sulu is an accomplished**
  a. Boxer
  b. Gymnast
  c. Fencer
  d. Martial arts teacher

20) **McCoy was decorated by**
  a. Yonada
  b. Starfleet Command
  c. The Vulcan Medical Academy
  d. Starfleet surgeons

21) **Janice Rand first appears in**
  a. "Miri"
  b. "The Corbomite Maneuver"
  c. "The Man Trap"
  d. "Where No Man . . ."

22) **In *Star Trek—The Motion Picture*, Chekov's bridge station was**
  a. Navigation
  b. The library computer
  c. The helm
  d. Weapons control

23) **Kirk's first helmsman on the *Enterprise* was**
  a. Gary Mitchell
  b. Sulu
  c. Lieutenant Stiles
  d. Lieutenant Anders

24) **Uhura had her memory erased in**
  a. "Metamorphosis"
  b. "Devil in the Dark"
  c. "The Changeling"
  d. "Plato's Stepchildren"

25) **Nurse Chapel confesses her love for Spock in**
  a. "The Naked Time"
  b. "Dagger of the Mind"
  c. "Amok Time"
  d. "This Side of Paradise"

SERIES REGULARS

1) DeForest Kelly was born in
   a. Houston   **b.** Dallas
   c. Phoenix   **d.** Atlanta

2) Majel Barrett married Gene Roddenberry in
   a. 1969   **b.** 1968
   c. 1970   **d.** 1966

3) In World War II, Jimmy Doohan served in
   a. The U.S. Army   **b.** The Royal Canadian Air Force
   c. The U.S. Marines   **d.** The R.A.F.

4) George Takei made his film debut in
   a. *The Green Berets*   **b.** *Seven Days in May*
   c. *Ice Palace*   **d.** *Some Like It Hot*

5) Grace Lee Whitney made her Broadway debut in
   a. *Pajama Game*   **b.** *Guys and Dolls*
   c. *Fantasticks*   **d.** *Top Banana*

6) DeForest Kelly was married in
   a. 1945   **b.** 1950
   c. 1955   **d.** 1960

7) Majel Barrett's first film was
   a. *Inherit the Wind*   **b.** *West Side Story*
   c. *As Young as We Were*   **d.** *On the Beach*

8) James Doohan is a skilled
   a. Sailor   **b.** Carpenter
   c. Golfer   **d.** Pilot

9) George Takei was born in
   a. Boston   **b.** New York
   c. Los Angeles   **d.** Galveston

10) DeForest Kelly's first motion picture contract was with
   a. Paramount   **b.** Republic
   c. MGM   **d.** United Artists

11) Grace Lee Whitney appeared with Marilyn Monroe in
   a. *Bus Stop*   **b.** *The Seven-year Itch*
   c. *Some Like It Hot*   **d.** *The Misfits*

12) Majel Barrett was born in
   a. Detroit   **b.** Cleveland
   c. Boston   **d.** Miami

13) George Takei appeared with John Wayne in
   a. *The Green Berets*   **b.** *Sands of Iwo Jima*
   c. *Fighting Seabees*   **d.** *Big Jake*

14) DeForest Kelly's first film was
   a. *Maltese Falcon*   **b.** *High Sierra*
   c. *Fear in the Night*   **d.** *Gunfight at the O.K. Corral*

15) DeForest Kelly first worked with Gene Roddenberry in
   a. "Star Trek"   **b.** "The Lieutenant"
   c. "Police Story"   **d.** "For the People"

THE EPISODES

---------------- **"Obsession"** ----------------

1) As a Lieutenant, Kirk served aboard the U.S.S.
    a. *Exeter*   **b.** *Yorktown*
    c. *Farragut*   **d.** *Intrepid*

2) Kirk first encountered the cloud creature
    a. 5 years ago   **b.** 7 years ago
    c. 11 years ago   **d.** 13 years ago

3) In his first encounter with the creature, Kirk
    a. Fired at it immediately   **b.** Tried to communicate
                                 with it
    c. Froze up   **d.** Was severely wounded

4) Security Officer Garrovick holds the service rank of
    a. Ensign   **b.** Lieutenant
    c. Lieutenant commander   **d.** Commander

5) The creature is composed of
    a. Pergium   **b.** Ryetalyn
    c. Methane   **d.** Di-kironium

6) The creature comes from the planet
    a. Omega III   **b.** Tycho IV
    c. Argus X   **d.** Citar II

7) The *Enterprise* is to rendezvous with the U.S.S.
    a. *Yorktown*   **b.** *Lexington*
    c. *Farragut*   **d.** *Exeter*

8) The *Enterprise* is supposed to rendezvous and then to proceed to the planet
    a. Theta VII   **b.** Tycho IV
    c. Argus X   **d.** Memory Alpha

9) The creature drains its victims of
    a. Salt   **b.** Red blood cells
    c. White blood cells   **d.** Water

10) The creature attacks the *Enterprise* landing party on
    a. Theta VII   **b.** Argus X
    c. Tycho IV   **d.** Omega III

FILL-INS

1) The creature's molecular condition is _____.

2) _____ supposedly exists only in laboratories.

3) Kirk blames _____ for the death of his first commander.

4) When young Garrovick first encounters the creature, he _____.

5) Just before it kills, the creature gives off a(n) _____ odor.

6) The creature enters the *Enterprise* through the number two _____ _____.

7) The creature varies in _____.

8) Kirk destroys the creature with _____.

9) Garrovick's life is saved by _____.

10) The creature reproduces by _____.

TRUE/FALSE

1) Spock's blood is copper-based. _____

2) Garrovick's father was a Starfleet admiral. _____

3) The creature can travel at warp speeds. _____

4) Spock asks McCoy to explain "obsession." _____

5) The creature is not intelligent. _____

6) Spock is immune to the creature's attacks. _____

7) Scotty drives the creature out of the *Enterprise* by flushing the vent system with radioactive wastes. _____

8) Kirk does not recognize intuition as a command quality. _____

9) Kirk uses himself as bait for the creature. _____

10) Spock saves Kirk and Garrovick by switching to transporter circuit B. _____

"A Private Little War"

1) The *Enterprise* is in orbit around the planet
  a. Centra   **b.** Neural
  c. Vikos   **d.** Antos

2) Kirk first visited the planet
  a. 13 years ago   **b.** 11 years ago
  c. 15 years ago   **d.** 17 years ago

3) The local witch women are called
  a. Circe   **b.** Groton
  c. Sutu   **d.** Kanutu

4) Dr. M'Benga is a specialist in
  a. Rare diseases   **b.** Vulcan medicine
  c. Psychology   **d.** Internal medicine

5) The Mugato bite can be cured only with the aid of
  a. Canto root   **b.** Borgia root
  c. Mako root   **d.** Shoto root

6) Spock is injected with
- **a.** Vitalizer B
- **b.** Ryetalyn
- **c.** Tri-ox
- **d.** Cordrazine

7) The Klingons supplied the Villagers with
- **a.** Rifles
- **b.** Machine guns
- **c.** M-16s
- **d.** Breechloaders

8) Kirk is cured of the Mugato bite by
- **a.** McCoy
- **b.** M'Benga
- **c.** Tyree
- **d.** Nona

9) The Klingons first brought weapons to the Villagers
- **a.** 6 months ago
- **b.** 1 year ago
- **c.** 2 years ago
- **d.** 3 years ago

10) Kirk compares the conflict between the Villagers and the Hill People with
- **a.** World War I
- **b.** World War II
- **c.** The Civil War
- **d.** Vietnam

FILL-INS

1) Dr. M'Benga interned in a _____ _____.

2) The Mugato that attacks Kirk is killed by _____.

3) McCoy heats up some rocks with a _____.

4) On his first visit to the planet, Kirk lived with _____.

5) Kirk exchanges blood with _____.

6) Apella points out that it is hard to divide one _____.

7) Tyree is played by _____ _____.

8) In order to regain consciousness, Spock must be _____ repeatedly.

9) M'Benga is played by _____ _____.

10) Tyree orders _____ to track down the two villagers who killed his wife.

TRUE/FALSE

1) The Klingons are in violation of the Axanar Peace Treaty. _____

2) Spock's life is saved by a Vulcan healing trance. _____

3) Spock is revived by Nurse Chapel. _____

4) Kirk's phaser is stolen by Apella. _____

5) Kirk reasons that the only solution to his dilemma is to create a balance of power. _____

6) Kirk refers to the weapons as serpents for the Garden of Eden. _____

7) Tyree does not remember Kirk. _____

8) McCoy has never been to this planet before. _____

9) By the end of the episode, Spock is fully recovered. _____

10) Kirk is satisfied with his solution to the problem. _____

"The Mark of Gideon"

1) Gideon's atmosphere is
   a. Toxic to Vulcans
   c. Disease-free
   b. Thinner than Earth's
   d. Heavier than Earth's

2) The government on Gideon has consistently refused to allow
   a. Klingon ambassadors
   c. Any visitors
   b. Romulan ambassadors
   d. People to leave the planet

3) The planet's most pressing problem is
   a. Drought
   c. Plague
   b. Famine
   d. Overpopulation

4) The Gideon council forbids
   a. Sensor scans
   c. Kirk to visit the planet
   b. Any contact with the outside
   d. Contraception

5) The first beam-down coordinates given to the *Enterprise* are
  a. 020-875-079   **b.** 875-020-079
  c. 875-020-709   **d.** 020-785-709

6) The Gideon report to the Federation describes the planet as
  a. Overpopulated   **b.** A paradise
  c. Poor in natural resources   **d.** Warlike

7) When Spock first requests permission to search for Kirk, he is referred to
  a. The Federation Council   **b.** The Bureau of Starfleet Officers
  c. The Bureau of Planetary Treaties   **d.** The Gideon Council

8) Kirk once had
  a. Chorioproximia   **b.** Sythococcus novae
  c. Vegan choriomeningitis   **d.** Encentocarcinoma

9) The coordinates for the Gideon council chamber are
  a. 020-875-079   **b.** 875-020-709
  c. 875-020-079   **d.** 020-875-079

10) Spock finds Kirk
  a. On the "bridge"   **b.** In "engineering"
  c. In "sick bay"   **d.** In the "captain's quarters"

FILL-INS

1) Hodin is played by _____ _____.

2) Spock acknowledges that the purpose of diplomacy is to _____ _____ _____.

3) Odona is _____ daughter.

4) There are thousands of _____ outside the false *Enterprise.*

5) Spock contacts Admiral _____ at Starfleet Command.

6) Gideonites are virtually _____.

7) Hodin refers to Scotty as a very excitable _____.

8) Odona is played by _____.

9) Hodin's assistant is _____.

10) Odona claims to have lost _____ _____.

TRUE/FALSE

1) Kirk is the first Federation representative to be allowed on Gideon soil. _____

2) The natives of Gideon refuse to practice birth control. _____

3) The Gideon Council's report to the Federation was truthful. _____

4) At first, Kirk believes that he has never left the *Enterprise*. _____

5) Spock violates Fleet orders to search for Kirk. _____

6) Hodin wants Kirk to stay on Gideon. _____

7) Scotty beams up a representative from Gideon. _____

8) Odona leaves Gideon. _____

9) Kirk offers to stay on Gideon for a while. _____

10) McCoy accompanies Spock on his search for Kirk. _____

"The Changeling"

1) Nomad is responsible for the destruction of the
   a. Malurian system
   c. Omicron region
   b. Mutara system
   d. Talos system

2) Nomad was created by
   a. Robert Kirkson
   c. Kirk Robertson
   b. Kirk Jackson
   d. Jackson Roykirk

3) **Nomad believes that it was created by**
    a. A machine   **b.** Spock
    c. Kirk   **d.** McCoy

4) **Nomad was launched in**
    a. 1997   **b.** 2020
    c. 2231   **d.** 1976

5) **Nomad was damaged by**
    a. Another probe   **b.** Solar radiation
    c. Cosmic rays   **d.** A meteor

6) **Nomad's original programming was to**
    a. Return soil samples   **b.** Sterilize germ samples
    c. Contact new life   **d.** Plot stellar distances

7) **Nomad encountered and fused with the alien probe**
    a. Gu Ru   **b.** San Ro
    c. Tan Ru   **d.** Go Ju

8) **Chart 14A is a diagram of**
    a. The *Enterprise*   **b.** Nomad
    c. Earth's solar system   **d.** The Galileo

9) **Nomad "kills"**
    a. Sulu   **b.** Scotty
    c. Chekov   **d.** Uhura

10) **Nomad increases the ship's engine efficiency by**
    a. 69%   **b.** 32%
    c. 27%   **d.** 57%

FILL-INS

1) The auxiliary control room is on deck _____.

2) Nomad refers to his creator as the _____.

3) Nomad calls human beings _____ units.

4) Symbalene blood burn is a quick-acting _____.

5) Nomad signals the *Enterprise* using an old-fashioned
_____ _____.

6) The parent star in the destroyed star system is

_____ _____.

7) Kirk leaves Nomad with Lieutenant _____, in auxiliary control.

8) _____ _____ was considered to be brilliant, if erratic.

9) Nomad forces the *Enterprise* to travel at _____

_____.

10) The voice of Nomad was provided by _____

_____.

_____ **TRUE/FALSE** _____

1) Spock uses the Vulcan Mind Meld on Nomad.

_____

2) Kirk convinces Nomad that it is imperfect. _____

3) Scotty's life is saved by McCoy. _____

4) At the beginning of the episode, Nomad attacks the *Enterprise*. _____

5) Mr. Singh is a Lieutenant Commander. _____

6) Kirk refers to Nomad as "My son the doctor."

_____

7) Nomad can project a force field. _____

8) Spock has trouble breaking contact with Nomad.

_____

9) Nomad destroys itself. _____

10) Kirk and Spock reprogram Nomad. _____

"The Deadly Years"

1) The *Enterprise* is en route to
    a. Starbase 7   **b.** Starbase 8
    c. Starbase 9   **d.** Starbase 10

2) The *Enterprise* stops off at Gamma Hydra IV to
    a. Gather information   **b.** Offer medical help
    c. Evacuate colonists   **d.** Deliver supplies

3) Gamma Hydra IV recently had a close encounter with a
    a. Klingon ship   **b.** Meteor
    c. Comet   **d.** Romulan ship

4) The landing party contracts
    a. Radiation poisoning   **b.** Sythococcus novae
    c. Vegan choriomeningitis   **d.** Amyotrophic lateral sclerosis

5) Robert Johnson is
    a. 27 years old   **b.** 29 years old
    c. 30 years old   **d.** 33 years old

6) The current treatment for radiation poisoning is
    a. Cordrazine   **b.** Hyronalin
    c. Adrenalin   **d.** Tri-ox

7) The only member of the landing party not affected by the disease is
    a. Scotty   **b.** Chekov
    c. Sulu   **d.** Lieutenant Galway

8) Janet is a famous
    a. Biologist   **b.** Doctor
    c. Endocrinologist   **d.** Botanist

9) The Romulans have recently broken
    a. Code one   **b.** Code two
    c. Code three   **d.** Code four

10) The cure for the disease is
    a. Tri-ox   **b.** Hyronalin
    c. Adrenalin   **d.** Cordrazine

FILL-INS

1) Janet was married to Dr. _____ _____.

2) Janet's husband was a _____.

3) Commodore Stocker convenes an _____ _____ hearing.

4) The Romulans have not yet broken _____ _____.

5) Janet worked with plant life on _____ _____.

6) Kirk mistakenly refers to Gamma Hydra IV as _____ _____ _____.

7) McCoy tells Kirk that he has _____.

8) Stocker is played by _____ _____.

9) Spock asks for something to lower his sensitivity to _____.

10) The *Enterprise* crosses the _____ _____.

TRUE/FALSE

1) One of the symptoms of the disease is senility. _____

2) Kirk forgets signing a fuel-consumption report. _____

3) Kirk outwits the Romulans with the "Exnon Maneuver." _____

4) Each person develops the disease at the same rate. _____

5) McCoy refers to himself as an "old country doctor." _____

6) Stocker has had prior starship experience. _____

7) Stocker panics on the bridge. _____

8) Stocker offers command of the *Enterprise* to Sulu. _____

9) The *Enterprise* is attacked by Klingon warships. _____

10) Vulcans have longer lifespans than humans. _____

"Journey to Babel"

1) Coridan has a wealth of
   a. Pergium
   c. Dilithium
   b. Ryetalyn
   d. Trititanium

2) Sarek gave Spock his first instruction in
   a. Logic
   c. Mathematics
   b. Astronomy
   d. Computers

3) Spock and Sarek haven't spoken for
   a. 12 years
   c. 16 years
   b. 14 years
   d. 18 years

4) Gav is murdered by a technique called
   a. Ahn-woon
   c. Tal shaya
   b. Cro-troy
   d. Kal-if-fee

5) Sarek suffers from a
   a. Back condition
   c. Liver condition
   b. Respiratory ailment
   d. Heart condition

6) Spock once had a pet
   a. Sehlat
   c. Le-Matya
   b. Tribble
   d. Cruton

7) The Tellerite ambassador is
   a. Gav
   c. Thelev
   b. Shras
   d. Kryton

8) Before retiring, Sarek is in the habit of
   a. Eating
   c. Meditating
   b. Reading
   d. Walking

9) Sarek is
   a. 100.397 years old
   c. 97.876 years old
   b. 102.437 years old
   d. 105.998 years old

10) Sarek's blood type is
   a. T negative
   c. Q negative
   b. T positive
   d. Q positive

FILL-INS

1) Sarek takes _____ for his condition.

2) Amanda is played by _____ _____.

3) Sarek is portrayed by _____ _____.

4) The Andorian ambassador's aide is really an _____.

5) Kirk is stabbed by _____.

6) Sarek is attacked by _____.

7) The K-2 factor indicates _____ _____.

8) The *Enterprise* is attacked by _____ pirates.

9) _____ have 6-inch fangs.

10) Amanda describes Spock's pet as a fat "_____ _____."

TRUE/FALSE

1) Spock gives his father a transfusion. _____

2) McCoy injects Spock with a blood stimulator, used on test subjects from Rigel V. _____

3) Coridan admission is opposed by Vulcan. _____

4) Tellar favors Coridan admission. _____

5) Sarek had retired before the Coridan incident. _____

6) Sarek's disease first flares up on the *Enterprise*. _____

7) Spock and Sarek join minds. _____

8) Spock and Sarek resolve their dispute. _____

9) Sarek married Amanda because "it seemed the logical thing to do." _____

10) McCoy finally gets the last word. _____

"Spock's Brain"

1) Spock's brain is stolen by
   a. Luma   **b.** Kara
   c. Kanda   **d.** Sola

2) The alien starship operates on
   a. Ion power   **b.** Impulse power
   c. Rocket power   **d.** Warp power

3) The *Enterprise* follows the alien starship to
   a. Sigma Draconis VI   **b.** Sigma Draconis V
   c. Sigma Draconis IV   **d.** Sigma Draconis III

4) Sigma Draconis is a
   a. Class D star   **b.** Class G9 star
   c. Class M star   **d.** Class F star

5) The development of Sigma Draconis III parallels that of Earth in the year
   a. 1970   **b.** 1877
   c. 1485   **d.** 12 B.C.

6) Sigma Draconis IV parallels Earth of the year
   a. 1580   **b.** 1830
   c. 1930   **d.** 2030

7) The males on Sigma Draconis VI are called
   a. Eymorg   **b.** Eytrog
   c. Morg   **d.** Trog

8) The men refer to the women as givers of pain and
   a. Reward   **b.** Pleasure
   c. Delight   **d.** Agony

9) McCoy can keep Spock's body alive for
   a. 12 hours   **b.** 24 hours
   c. 36 hours   **d.** 2 days

10) The *Enterprise* heads toward Sigma Draconis at
   a. Warp 10   **b.** Warp 8
   c. Warp 6   **d.** Warp 5

FILL-INS

1) Kara's intelligence is increased by the _____.

2) The women refer to Spock's brain as the _____.

3) Kara insists that Spock's brain will live for _____ years.

4) Spock communicates with Kirk over his _____.

5) The women place pain bands around the crew's _____.

6) The landing party is freed from the pain bands by _____.

7) The underground complex is maintained by _____.

8) Kara is played by _____ _____.

9) Sigma Draconis VI is in a _____ age.

10) The operation to restore Spock's brain takes _____ hours.

TRUE/FALSE

1) Spock assists in the restoration of his brain. _____

2) The connections in Spock's brain are closed with a sonic separator. _____

3) A human can use the educational device only once. _____

4) Kirk stuns Kara with his phaser. _____

5) Luma offers to help the landing party. _____

6) The women call themselves Eymorg. _____

7) The women's complex runs on nuclear power. _____

8) Kirk, once again, violates the Prime Directive. _____

9) Spock finds Kirk's voice pleasing. _____

10) Spock compares the conditions on Sigma Draconis VI to those on old Earth. _____

_____ "The Conscience of the King" _____

(Or; "If Star Trek Be the Fruit of Life, Play On!")

1) At the beginning of the episode Kirk is attending a performance of
- **a.** *Othello*
- **c.** *Hamlet*
- **b.** *Macbeth*
- **d.** *Julius Caesar*

2) Thomas Leighton is a famous
- **a.** Actor
- **c.** Research scientist
- **b.** Starship captain
- **d.** Doctor

3) Leighton claimed that he could end the famine on the planet
- **a.** Cheron
- **c.** Tarsus IV
- **b.** Signia Minor
- **d.** Babel

4) Kodos was the governor of
- **a.** Talos II
- **c.** Gamma Delta II
- **b.** Psi 2000
- **d.** Tarsus IV

5) Kodos killed _____ colonists
- **a.** 4,000
- **c.** 5,000
- **b.** 6,000,000
- **d.** 1,000,000

6) Kodos has a daughter named
- **a.** Martha
- **c.** Juliet
- **b.** Lenore
- **d.** Edith

7) Lenore compares Kirk to
- **a.** Macbeth
- **c.** King Arthur
- **b.** Caesar
- **d.** Richard

8) The *Astral Queen* is commanded by
- **a.** John Daily
- **c.** Bob Wesley
- **b.** John Gill
- **d.** Ron Tracy

9) Kirk has Riley transferred to
- **a.** Engineering
- **c.** Communications
- **b.** Weapons
- **d.** Life sciences

10) **The actors put on a performance of** _____ **for the crew**

    a. *Macbeth*   **b.** *Hamlet*
    c. *Richard III*   **d.** *King Lear*

FILL-INS

1) Kodos is played by _____ _____.

2) Karidian's company is funded by the _____
_____ _____ _____.

3) Riley is poisoned with _____.

4) Kodos committed his crimes _____ years ago.

5) Of the 9 eyewitnesses who actually saw Kodos, only
_____ and _____ are still alive at the end
of the episode.

6) In *Hamlet,* Kodos plays the role of _____
_____.

7) Lenore goes _____.

8) Kodos is killed by _____.

9) Lenore tells Kirk to "beware the Ides of _____."

10) Kirk and Lenore have an interlude on the _____
deck.

TRUE/FALSE

1) Karidian was not Kodos. _____

2) Kodos killed the 7 eyewitnesses. _____

3) Thomas Leighton had discovered a new synthetic food.
_____

4) Lenore believes that her father is still alive. _____

5) Riley plans to kill Kodos. _____

6) The weapons locker is on H deck. _____

7) Several decks of the ship are almost destroyed by a phaser
overload. _____

8) Benecia is on the *Enterprise*'s planned travel route.
_____

9) The supply ships arrived at Tarsus IV sooner than Kodos had expected. _____

10) Spock believes that Karidian is Kodos. _____

_____ **"The Naked Time"** _____

1) At the beginning of the episode the *Enterprise* is in standard orbit around
  a. Camus II   **b.** Psi 2000
  c. Beta Origi   **d.** Stratos

2) The *Enterprise* is sent to the planet to
  a. Observe its break-up   **b.** Establish a colony
  c. Open diplomatic relations   **d.** Observe the native culture

3) Spock is accompanied to the planet's surface by
  a. Jim Kirk   **b.** Doctor McCoy
  c. Joe Tormolen   **d.** Lieutenant Riley

4) Spock finds the outpost crew
  a. At work   **b.** Ready to leave
  c. Drugged   **d.** Dead

5) The landing party brings back _____ to the ship.
  a. Bodies   **b.** A disease
  c. Rock samples   **d.** A survivor

6) McCoy establishes Spock's pulse rate as
  a. 242   **b.** 90 over 50
  c. 0   **d.** 300

7) The disease causes
  a. Rapid aging   **b.** Intense pain
  c. Heart trouble   **d.** Hidden traits to surface

8) Spectroanalysis rules out death by
  a. Hemorrhage   **b.** Drugs
  c. Fever   **d.** Age

9) "The Naked Time" was written by
  a. D. C. Fontana   **b.** Gene Roddenberry
  c. John D. F. Black   **d.** Isaac Asimov

10) Kevin Riley is played by
  a. John Cayton   **b.** Bruce Hyde
  c. John Colicos   **d.** Walter Koenig

FILL-INS

1) "The Naked Time" was directed by _____ _____.

2) Sulu chases crewmen through the corridors with a _____.

3) Riley sings _____ _____ _____ _____ _____, _____ over and over again.

4) Lieutenant Uhura calls for Alert _____ _____.

5) When Kirk is infected with the disease, he compares the *Enterprise* to a _____.

6) The disease passes from person to person through _____.

7) Nurse Chapel's first name is _____.

8) The *Enterprise* regresses in _____.

9) The engines are shut down by _____ _____.

10) Nurse Chapel catches the disease from _____ _____.

TRUE/FALSE

1) Joe Tormolen commits suicide. _____

2) Implosion is a common means of reigniting the ship's engines. _____

3) Kirk enjoys Riley's singing. _____

4) Jim Kirk longs for a beach to walk on. _____

5) McCoy tries the cure for the disease on Sulu first. _____

"Let This Be Your Last Battlefield"

1) Lokai and Bele come from the planet
   a. Delta Vega   **b.** Omicron II
   c. Rigel V   **d.** Cheron

2) The *Enterprise* is en route to
   a. Ariannus   **b.** Deneb IV
   c. Coridan   **d.** Orion

3) Bele's planet is
   a. A member of the Federation   **b.** Part of the Klingon Empire
   c. Uncharted   **d.** In Orion space

4) Bele's planet was destroyed by
   a. Disease   **b.** Race hatred
   c. A meteor shower   **d.** The Klingons

5) McCoy injects Lokai with a
   a. Depressant   **b.** Stimulant
   c. Truth serum   **d.** Metabolic stabilizer

6) Lokai demands
   a. A fair trial   **b.** Sanctuary
   c. Transportation   **d.** A platform

7) Bele has been chasing Lokai for
   a. 10,000 years   **b.** 50,000 years
   c. 100,000 years   **d.** 1,000,000 years

8) Bele's planet is in
   a. The northern part of the galaxy
   b. The southern part of the galaxy
   c. The western part of the galaxy
   d. The eastern part of the galaxy

9) Lokai's planet lies at
   a. 403 mark 5
   b. 403 mark 6
   c. 403 mark 7
   d. 403 mark 8

10) Spock compares the history of Bele's planet with that of
   a. Vulcan
   b. Earth
   c. Rigel V
   d. Deneb II

FILL-INS

1) Bele is the commissioner of _____ _____.

2) Lokai is white on the _____ side.

3) Bele is white on the _____ side.

4) The Federation has no _____ treaty with _____.

5) Bele first appears on the *Enterprise* _____.

6) Kirk threatens to _____ the *Enterprise.*

7) Bele takes over the ship's _____ controls.

8) Bele's ship was sheathed in materials that rendered it _____.

9) Bele and Lokai can project _____.

10) Bele believes that Lokai's people are _____.

TRUE/FALSE

1) The *Enterprise* encounters Bele before Lokai comes aboard.
_____

2) Bele and Lokai are resistant to phaser fire. _____

3) No one is left alive on Bele's planet. _____

4) The Federation refuses Bele's request for extradition.
_____

5) Lokai convinces Kirk to help him. _____

6) From 30 seconds to zero no command in the universe can abort the *Enterprise*'s destruct sequence. _____

7) Vulcans were once highly emotional. _____

8) Bele's people were freed thousands of years ago.
_____

9) Lokai intends to lead a revolution. _____

10) Bele and Lokai finally resolve their differences.
_____

"All Our Yesterdays"

1) Beta Niobe is about to
  a. Go nova
  b. Become a red giant
  c. Become a white dwarf
  d. Become a black hole

2) The *Enterprise* is in orbit around
  a. Beta Niobe
  b. Sarpeidon
  c. Delta IV
  d. Omicron Ceti III

3) The Library is run by
  a. Computer
  b. Androids
  c. Mr. Atoz
  d. Mr. Han

4) Before traveling through time, one must be processed through the
  a. Time portal
  b. Transporter
  c. Government
  d. The atavachron

5) Kirk is accused of
- **a.** Witchcraft
- **b.** Alchemy
- **c.** Vampirism
- **d.** Murder

6) Information in the Library is kept on
- **a.** Computer cards
- **b.** Computer tapes
- **c.** Film
- **d.** Disks

7) Zarabeth was exiled to the planet's
- **a.** Dark ages
- **b.** Stone age
- **c.** Ice age
- **d.** Neolithic age

8) Zarabeth was exiled by
- **a.** Atoz the Terrible
- **b.** Zor Khan
- **c.** Khan Singh
- **d.** Khalis

9) Zarabeth offers Spock some
- **a.** Wine
- **b.** Salad
- **c.** Soup
- **d.** Meat

10) Spock reverts to his ancestors of
- **a.** 5,000 years ago
- **b.** 6,000 years ago
- **c.** 7,000 years ago
- **d.** 8,000 years ago

FILL-INS

1) The librarian uses _____ as aides.

2) Kirk hears a scream coming from outside the _____.

3) Kirk is helped to escape by the _____.

4) Zarabeth's cave is heated by _____.

5) McCoy suffers extreme _____.

6) Zarabeth died _____ years ago.

7) McCoy accuses Zarabeth of _____.

8) McCoy and Spock must pass through the portal _____.

9) Zarabeth's kinsmen were involved in a plot to kill _____.

10) Kirk threatens to break his guard's _____.

TRUE/FALSE

1) Unprocessed time travelers will very quickly die. _____

2) Spock falls in love with Zarabeth. _____

3) Zarabeth returns to the *Enterprise* with Kirk. _____

4) Zarabeth's crime was in choosing her kinsmen unwisely. _____

5) Zarabeth was involved in a plot to kill the dictator of her planet. _____

6) Zarabeth is played by Mariette Hartley. _____

7) Spock eats meat. _____

8) Atoz helps Kirk find his friends. _____

9) The planet's entire population fled into the past. _____

10) Atoz uses a stun device on Spock. _____

"Charlie X"

1) Charlie is transferred to the *Enterprise* from the cargo ship
   a. *Epsilon*   b. *Exeter*
   c. *Antos*   d. *Antares*

2) The captain of the cargo ship is named
   a. Ramart   b. Decker
   c. Nelson   d. Tom Nellis

3) Charlie was found on the planet
   a. Talos IV   b. Regulus
   c. Thasos   d. Axanar

4) Charlie was marooned for
   a. 5 years   b. 13 years
   c. 2 years   d. 7 years

5) The first woman Charlie sees is
  a. Nurse Chapel   **b.** Lieutenant Uhura
  c. Helen Noel   **d.** Yeoman Rand

6) The galley chief puts meatloaf in the food processors and takes out
  a. Roasts   **b.** Nothing
  c. Chickens   **d.** Turkeys

7) Charlie's last name is
  a. Evans   **b.** Grayson
  c. Ryan   **d.** Thomson

8) The *Enterprise* is taking Charlie to
  a. Starbase 2   **b.** Earth
  c. Rigel II   **d.** Earth Colony 5

9) Spock tries to teach Charlie
  a. Computers   **b.** Chess
  c. Self-defense   **d.** Vulcan philosophy

10) The *Antares* has a crew complement of
  a. 10   **b.** 100
  c. 20   **d.** 30

FILL-INS

1) Charlie makes all the _____ on the *Enterprise* disappear.

2) When Uhura tries to raise the Earth outpost, she receives a

_____.

3) Charlie forces Spock to _____ _____.

4) Charlie gives Janice a _____ _____.

5) Janice introduces Charlie to Yeoman Third Class

_____ _____.

6) The Thasians contact the *Enterprise* on _____

_____ _____.

7) Charlie X was written by _____ _____.

8) Charlie survived alone on Thasus since the age of
_____.

9) Charlie is portrayed by _____ _____.

10) Spock checkmates Charlie in _____ moves.

_____ TRUE/FALSE _____

1) Charlie turns Tina into a lizard. _____

2) The *Antares* is destroyed by an enemy attack.
_____

3) Kirk tries to explain the facts of life to Charlie.
_____

4) Charlie changes the faces of playing cards into pictures of Lieutenant Uhura. _____

5) The Thasians are a warlike race. _____

_____ "Dagger of the Mind" _____

1) At the beginning of the episode, the *Enterprise* is trying to beam cargo down to the
    a. Tantalus Colony   **b.** Planet Mongo
    c. Attom Colony   **d.** Omicron Colony

2) The transporter operator is
    a. Kyle   **b.** Defalco
    c. Berkeley   **d.** Sandoval

3) The cargo sent *up* to the *Enterprise* is bound for
    a. Vulcan   **b.** New York
    c. Regulus   **d.** Stockholm

4) Simon van Gelder smuggles himself aboard the *Enterprise* in
    a. A shuttle craft   **b.** A packing case
    c. Disguise   **d.** A crowd

5) The director of Tantalus is
    a. Dr. Corey   **b.** Philip Boyce
    c. Dr. Adams   **d.** Dr. Carstairs

6) Spock uses the Vulcan mind meld on
    a. Kirk   **b.** Van Gelder
    c. Lethe   **d.** McCoy

7) Kirk is accompanied to the planet's surface by
    a. Dr. McCoy   **b.** Yeoman Rand
    c. Dr. Helen Noel   **d.** Lieutenant Uhura

8) Adams controls people through the use of
    a. Hypnosis   **b.** Drugs
    c. A mind sifter   **d.** A neural neutralizer

9) Kirk first meets Helen Noel at
    a. A Christmas party   **b.** Starfleet Academy
    c. Wrigley's Pleasure Planet   **d.** A New Year's party

10) Morgan Woodward (van Gelder) also appears in the "Star Trek" episode
    a. "Arena"   **b.** "The Doomsday Machine"
    c. "The Omega Glory"   **d.** "Patterns of force"

FILL-INS

1) Dr. Adams is played by _____ _____.

2) Helen escapes from her cabin through a _____.

3) Adams forces Kirk to _____ _____ with Helen.

4) Dr. Adams dies of _____.

5) Lethe stayed on Tantalus as a _____.

6) The Colony's force shield prevents _____ and _____.

7) "Dagger of the Mind" is directed by _____ _____.

8) Van Gelder's first act on returning to Tantalus is to _____.

9) Van Gelder has terrible pain whenever he tries to _____.

10) Adams is famous for his new methods in the area of _____.

TRUE/FALSE

1) Helen makes Kirk feel hungry. _____

2) Kirk uses the neural neutralizer on Adams. _____

3) Lethe was once a sadistic criminal. _____

4) McCoy assigns Helen Noel as Kirk's assistant. _____

5) McCoy is a great admirer of Dr. Adams. _____

"The Man Trap"

1) **At the beginning of the episode the *Enterprise* is orbiting**
   a. Psi 2000
   b. M113
   c. M232
   d. Organia

2) **Their mission was one of**
   a. Routine medical examination
   b. Scientific study
   c. Military tactics
   d. Rescue

3) **On the surface of the planet is an archeological dig, headed by**
   a. Dr. Parker
   b. Donald Corey
   c. Robert Crater
   d. John Crater

4) **Many years ago, Nancy Crater had been in love with**
   a. Kirk
   b. Spock
   c. Scotty
   d. McCoy

5) **Nancy's pet name for McCoy was**
   a. Pookums
   b. Plum
   c. Poopsy
   d. Precious

6) **Kirk and McCoy are accompanied to the planet's surface by**
   a. Joe Tormolen
   b. Lieutenant Mike Maranno
   c. Crewman Darnell
   d. Lieutenant Kyle

7) **"The Man Trap" was written by**
   a. D. C. Fontana
   b. George Clayton Johnson
   c. Gene Coon
   d. Merideth Lucas

8) McCoy claims that Nancy
   a. Hasn't been eating
   b. Seems strange
   c. Doesn't know him
   d. Hasn't aged

9) Both Bob and Nancy ask Kirk for
   a. Salt
   b. Medical help
   c. Relief
   d. Money

10) The borgia plant contains
   a. Strychnine
   b. Alkaloid poison
   c. Acid
   d. Arsenic

11) Sulu has a plant named
   a. Sam
   b. Janice
   c. Dunsel
   d. Beauregard

FILL-INS

1) Mysteries give Kirk _____.

2) Janice suggests that Green go _____
   _____ _____.

3) Janice Rand brings a meal to _____.

4) The creature must have _____ to survive.

5) Bob Crater compares the creature to the _____.

6) Darnell's face is covered with strange _____.

7) Before killing, the creature _____ its victims.

8) Kirk orders Sulu to go to Alert _____.

9) Spock's strength is _____ against the creature.

10) The creature goes to _____ for help.

TRUE/FALSE

1) The creature kills four crewmen. _____

2) The creature kills Bob Crater. _____

3) "The Man Trap" aired during "Star Trek's" second season. _____

4) The creature is not intelligent. _____

5) The creature is the last of her kind. _____

6) The creature is finally killed by Spock. _____

7) Nancy speaks to Uhura in French. _____

8) The creature has a habit of sucking its index finger. _____

9) Kirk suggests that McCoy take the red pills to help him sleep. _____

10) In the final scene, the creature tries to kill McCoy. _____

"Mudd's Women"

1) At the beginning of the episode, the *Enterprise* is pursuing
   a. Another starship
   b. A class J cargo ship
   c. An ore freighter
   d. A shuttle craft

2) The craft flees into
   a. An asteroid belt
   b. A solar system
   c. A black hole
   d. Romulan space

3) Mudd goes under the alias of
   a. Joe McPherson
   b. Leo Walsh
   c. Herm Gossett
   d. Jim Hanley

4) Mudd's current line of business is
   a. Smuggling
   b. Gambling
   c. Providing wives for settlers
   d. Selling slaves

5) Harry's full name is
   a. Harcourt Fenton Mudd   **b.** Harold Fenton Mudd
   c. Harry Mudd   **d.** Harrington Fenworth
                             Mudd

6) There is a lithium mining operation on
   a. Omicron Ceti III   **b.** Axis X
   c. Rigel XII   **d.** Antares IV

7) Mudd's master's license was revoked on stardate
   a. 1032.6   **b.** 1116.4
   c. 112.9   **d.** 3023.7

8) Dilithium crystals are worth 300 times their weight in
   a. Silver   **b.** Gold
   c. Diamonds   **d.** Rubies

9) The leader of the mining operation is
   a. Herm Gossett   **b.** Ben Childress
   c. Finnegan   **d.** Ben Crater

10) The women use
   a. Steroids   **b.** The Venus drug
   c. Tri-ox compound   **d.** The paradise drug

FILL-INS

1) The women's trust names are _____, _____, and _____.

2) Childress is accompanied to the *Enterprise* by _____.

3) In this episode, the computer functions as a _____.

4) Mudd's women are married to the miners by _____.

5) The Venus drug is in reality a _____.

6) The *Enterprise* needs _____ crystals.

7) In return for the crystals, Childress wants _____.

8) Eve tells Childress to clean his pans by _____.

9) Mudd hides the Venus drug in his _____.

10) Kirk offers to appear at Mudd's trial as a _____.

TRUE/FALSE

1) Mudd is played by Roger C. Carmel. _____

2) The *Enterprise* can maintain her orbit around Rigel indefinitely. _____

3) Rigel is struck by magnetic storms. _____

4) Eve's last name is *Macuren*. _____

5) Mudd contacts Rigel on subspace frequency 33. _____

6) Childress finds Eve playing solitaire. _____

7) Eve stays with Childress. _____

8) Harry Mudd appears in another episode of "Star Trek." _____

9) The Venus drug is legal. _____

10) Spock is unaffected by Mudd's women. _____

"Miri"

1) **At the beginning of the episode, the *Enterprise* receives a(n)**
   a. Invitation
   b. Challenge
   c. Gift
   d. Earth-style SOS

2) **The planet is an exact duplicate of**
   a. Earth
   b. Vulcan
   c. Orion
   d. Mars

3) **Miri is played by**
   a. Tracy Gray
   b. Susan Oliver
   c. Kim Darby
   d. Jeanne Bal

4) **The planet's science compares with Earth's in the**
   a. 1950s
   b. 1960s
   c. 1970s
   d. 1980s

5) **Kirk finds a broken**
   a. Bicycle
   b. Skate board
   c. Baseball bat
   d. Tricycle

6) **The children call themselves**
a. Babies
b. Kings
c. Grups
d. Onlies

7) **The children call games**
a. Foolies
b. Playtime
c. Games
d. Challenges

8) **Miri develops a crush on**
a. Kirk
b. Spock
c. Scotty
d. McCoy

9) **The adults had been conducting an experiment in**
a. Germ warfare
b. Cancer research
c. Life prolongation
d. Immunization techniques

10) **The children age 1 month for each**
a. 5 years
b. 100 years
c. 50 years
d. 200 years

FILL-INS

1) Kirk finds Miri hiding in a _____.

2) Jahn is played by _____ _____
_____.

3) Janice Rand is _____ years old.

4) McCoy orders a _____ from the *Enterprise.*

5) Spock is a _____ of the disease.

6) McCoy believes the serum that will cure the disease is based
on the _____ _____.

7) The children contract the disease upon entering
_____.

8) Janice asks Jim to look at her _____.

9) Near the end, the disease causes _____.

10) The children have enough food for _____
_____.

TRUE/FALSE

1) Kirk leaves a medical team behind with the children. _____

2) Kirk tells Janice that he loves her. _____

3) The children are playing school when Kirk finds them. _____

4) Spock tests the vaccine on himself. _____

5) Miri keeps busy by helping Kirk with the filing. _____

6) One of the first symptoms of the disease is the appearance of blue blotches on the skin. _____

7) The children beat Kirk. _____

8) Miri was directed by Gene Roddenberry. _____

9) The adults are called grups. _____

10) Miri helps Jim find Janice. _____

"Amok Time"

1) "Amok Time" was written by
   a. Harlan Ellison
   c. Isaac Asimov
   b. Theodore Sturgeon
   d. Robert Bloch

2) Nurse Chapel brings Spock
   a. News from home
   c. A bowl of plomeek soup
   b. A medical report
   d. A fresh uniform

3) The Vulcan mating is referred to as
   a. Pon farr
   c. Tal Shaya
   b. Kahs-wan
   d. Kohlinahr

4) At the beginning of the episode, the *Enterprise* is bound for
   a. Altair VI
   c. Aldebaran
   b. Vulcan
   d. Starbase II

5) The Vulcan marriage ceremony is called
   a. Doo-Sha-Wha
   c. Ahn-woon
   b. Nai-Hatchi-Kata
   d. Koon-ut-kal-i-fee

6) Spock's family has held their land for
 a. 1,000 years   b. 5,000 years
 c. 10,000 years   d. 2,000 years

7) T'Pring wishes to marry
 a. Stonn   b. Spock
 c. Kirk   d. Sonak

8) McCoy knocks Kirk out with a
 a. Neural paralyzer   b. Karate chop
 c. Phaser   d. Nerve pinch

9) The lirpa is the Vulcan equivalent to a Terran
 a. Sling   b. Bola
 c. Battle-axe   d. Bow

10) Altair VI has only recently begun to recover from
 a. Civil war   b. Planetary disease
 c. Political strife   d. Interplanetary conflict

FILL-INS

1) In ancient times, Vulcans _____ to win their mates.

2) The battle between Kirk and Spock is to the _____.

3) T'Pring is played by _____ _____.

4) Vulcan's air is _____ than Earth's.

5) If Spock doesn't reach Vulcan, he will _____.

6) Live long and _____.

7) The Vulcan male is accompanied to the marriage ceremony by his _____ _____.

8) The plak tow is the _____ _____.

9) Kirk speaks to Admiral _____.

10) Kirk assumed that Vulcans chose their mates _____.

TRUE/FALSE

1) Sarek and Amanda attended the marriage ceremony. _____

2) T'Pau is astonished when Spock speaks while in the plak tow. _____

3) Kirk disobeys orders in order to bring Spock to Vulcan. _____

4) T'Pring can divorce Spock only by the kal-if-fee. _____

5) Kirk is the victor in the battle with Spock. _____

6) Tri-ox compound aids in breathing. _____

7) A neural paralyzer simulates coma. _____

8) Kroykah is the Vulcan word for *stop*. _____

9) T'Pring wishes to marry Kirk. _____

10) T'Pring must become the property of the victor of the kal-if-fee. _____

"Arena"

1) The *Enterprise* is in orbit around the Earth colony on
   a. Delta Vega
   b. Indi Epsilon
   c. Cestus III
   d. Corox II

2) The colony is commanded by Commodore
   a. Travers
   b. Stone
   c. Stocker
   d. Wesley

3) The colony's lone survivor is
   a. Lieutenant Kelowitz
   b. Lieutenant Harold
   c. Wesley
   d. Lieutenant Stanton

4) The colony was unknowingly placed in a space sector claimed by the
   a. Romulans
   b. Klingons
   c. Metrons
   d. Gorns

5) The *Enterprise* is stopped dead in space by the
    a. Organians   **b.** Melkots
    c. Metrons   **d.** Gorns

6) Kirk's gunnery officer is
    a. Chekov   **b.** Lieutenant Harold
    c. Lieutenant Hansen   **d.** Lieutenant Lang

7) The Earth colony did not have time to
    a. Prepare defense   **b.** Raise her shields
    c. Call the *Enterprise* for   **d.** Counterattack
    help

8) Kirk and his opponent are placed on
    a. A planetoid   **b.** An asteroid
    c. A spaceship   **d.** A planet

9) Kirk reinvents
    a. The bow   **b.** The rifle
    c. Gunpowder   **d.** The handgun

10) The aliens provide Kirk with a
    a. Phaser   **b.** Tricorder
    c. Medi-kit   **d.** Recorder/translator

FILL-INS

1) Gorns are _____-like creatures.

2) Metrons are highly advanced _____.

3) Kirk defeats his opponent with a homemade
_____.

4) Kirk injures his _____ in a _____
_____.

5) The yellow powder that Kirk uses in his weapon is
_____.

6) Kirk uses _____ for projectiles.

7) The aliens intend to destroy the _____ of the contest.

8) Kirk refuses to _____ his opponent.

9) The Metron is played by _____ _____ .

10) Kirk's opponent is amazingly _____ .

_____ **TRUE/FALSE** _____

1) Kirk attacks his opponent with a club. _____

2) Spock helps Kirk find a weapon. _____

3) The Metrons intended to destroy the ships on both sides of the dispute. _____

4) Kirk acknowledges that his opponents may have some valid grievances. _____

5) Kirk ignites his weapon with a piece of flint. _____

6) Kirk has an instinctive loathing for his opponent's life form. _____

7) The *Enterprise* sends a search party after Kirk. _____

8) Sulu's relief helmsman is Lieutenant Hansen. _____

9) Lieutenant Commander Kelowitz is a security officer. _____

10) Kirk is caught in a snare. _____

_____ **"Tomorrow Is Yesterday"** _____

1) The *Enterprise* is photographed over
   a. Ohio   **b.** Nebraska
   c. Texas   **d.** Kansas

2) John Christopher holds the rank of
   a. Captain   **b.** Commander
   c. Major   **d.** Colonel

3) John Christopher's serial number is
   a. 7615978   **b.** 9124343
   c. 9813388   **d.** 4857932

4) Christopher's airforce base is in
   a. Kansas   b. Ohio
   c. Nebraska   d. Texas

5) Christopher's code name is
   a. Bluejay 4   b. Firefall 1
   c. Red tiger   d. Yellowbird

6) Christopher will have a son named
   a. John, Jr.   b. Robert Sean
   c. Sean Jeffery   d. Philip James

7) Christopher's son will lead Earth's first
   a. Mars landing   b. Earth/Saturn probe
   c. Jupiter colony   d. Venus probe

8) Kirk's computer calls him
   a. Baby   b. Dear
   c. Sweet lips   d. Lover

9) Christopher is stationed at the
   a. 305th Air Base   b. 507th Air Base
   c. 498th Air Base   d. 207th Air Base

10) Before traveling back in time, the *Enterprise* was headed for
   a. Starbase 7   b. Starbase 8
   c. Starbase 10   d. Starbase 9

FILL-INS

1) The *Enterprise* pulled into Cygnet IV for repairs on her _____ system.

2) The code name for Christopher's air base is _____.

3) If Christopher is not returned home _____ will be changed.

4) Christopher's plane is destroyed by a _____ _____.

5) The *Enterprise* is thrown back in time by a _____ effect.

6) Christopher always wanted to be an _____.

7) The *Enterprise* returns home by using the Sun's
_____ _____.

8) Christopher's son will hold the rank of _____.

9) The security commander of the air base is Colonel
_____.

10) Christopher flunked _____ training.

_____ **TRUE/FALSE** _____

1) John Christopher will make no significant contribution to history. _____

2) Christopher photographs the *Enterprise* with his wing camera. _____

3) Kirk is taken prisoner by base security. _____

4) Christopher is not surprised to find women on a starship.
_____

5) Christopher agrees to remain silent about the future.
_____

6) The *Enterprise* picks up a news story about the first manned moon shot. _____

7) Kyle gives an air base policeman a bowl of vegetable soup.
_____

8) The people of Cygnet IV felt that the *Enterprise* computer system lacked personality. _____

9) Christopher has never seen a Vulcan before. _____

10) The *Enterprise* goes back in time before returning home.
_____

"Catspaw"

1) The *Enterprise* is in orbit around
   a. Delta Vega   **b.** Antos IV
   c. Pyris VII   **d.** Ekos III

2) Kirk, Spock, and McCoy encounter three
   a. Klingons   **b.** Cats
   c. Bats   **d.** Witches

3) Sylvia's power source is a jeweled
   a. Wand   **b.** Amulet
   c. Ring   **d.** Necklace

4) The aliens are
   a. Telepaths   **b.** Empaths
   c. Fire starters   **d.** Shape shifters

5) Korob's wand is
   a. Magic   **b.** A matter transmuter
   c. Decorative   **d.** A teleportation device

6) Sylvia desires
   a. Information   **b.** Peace
   c. Sensation   **d.** Eternal life

7) Sylvia traps the *Enterprise* in a
   a. Space warp   **b.** Dimensional warp
   c. Force field   **d.** Time warp

8) Sylvia transforms herself into a giant
   a. Tiger   **b.** Lion
   c. Cougar   **d.** Cat

9) Sylvia makes zombies of McCoy and
   a. Kirk   **b.** Spock
   c. Scotty   **d.** Farrell

10) Korob is killed by
   a. Kirk   **b.** Sylvia
   c. Spock   **d.** Sulu

FILL-INS

1) Sylvia is seduced by _____.

2) Korob is played by _____ _____.

3) "Catspaw" was written by _____ _____.

4) Korob is crushed under a _____.

5) Sylvia is portrayed by _____ _____.

6) Korob and Sylvia live in a _____.

7) The nearest starbase is _____ days away.

8) Korob's power device amplifies _____ _____.

9) Kirk and Spock are imprisoned in a _____.

10) Without her power source, Sylvia _____.

TRUE/FALSE

1) Sulu is in Sylvia's power. _____

2) Spock is familiar with Halloween. _____

3) McCoy helps Kirk and Spock to escape. _____

4) Korob and Sylvia are humanoid. _____

5) Sylvia is insane. _____.

6) The *Enterprise* is warned away by Jackson. _____

7) Sylvia controls the *Enterprise* through a talisman. _____

8) Sylvia and Korob use science to achieve their "magic." _____

9) Sylvia and Korob go back to their home planet. _____

10) Sylvia gave McCoy and Scotty functional phasers. _____

"The Doomsday Machine"

1) Decker commanded the U.S.S.
   a. *Exeter*
   b. *Constellation*
   c. *Yorktown*
   d. *Intrepid*

2) The planet killer destroyed solar systems
   a. L-370 through L-374
   b. M-100 and M-101
   c. Q-385 through R-101
   d. A-555 through A-559

3) Decker is played by
   a. Tige Andrews
   b. William Windom
   c. Ted Cassidy
   d. Nick Glasser

4) Decker's science officer was named
   a. Gray
   b. Masada
   c. Johnson
   d. Pearson

5) Kirk compares the planet killer to
   a. The atom bomb
   b. The neutron bomb
   c. The antimatter bomb
   d. The hydrogen bomb

6) The planet killer came from
   a. Outside the galaxy
   b. The Klingon Empire
   c. The Romulan Empire
   d. Mongo

7) The Doomsday Machine sustains itself on
   a. Solar energy
   b. Cosmic rays
   c. Planets
   d. Stars

8) Decker takes command of the *Enterprise* under Starfleet regulation
   a. 303, section A
   b. 202, section H
   c. 405, section C
   d. 104, section B

9) The planet killer uses a force beam of
   a. Gamma rays
   b. Antimatter
   c. Charged particles
   d. Pure antiproton

10) The planet killer is on a direct heading for
   a. Earth
   b. Altair
   c. Rigel
   d. The Klingon Empire

FILL-INS

1) The *Constellation's* serial number is _____.

2) Scotty rigs the *Constellation* to _____.

3) Spock reports that the *Enterprise*'s warp engines will be out for one _____ _____.

4) Decker takes command of the *Enterprise* from _____.

5) Decker's first name is _____.

6) Decker beamed his crew down to the _____ planet in the system.

7) The planet killer's hull is made of _____.

8) Vulcans never _____.

9) Spock orders Decker to proceed to _____ _____.

10) "The Doomsday Machine" is an adaptation of the classic novel _____ _____.

TRUE/FALSE

1) If a starship's engines explode, an explosion of 97.835 megatons will result. _____

2) Spock establishes that there is more than one planet killer in the galaxy. _____

3) Decker commits suicide. _____

4) Phasers cannot pierce the hull of the Doomsday Machine. _____

5) The planet killer sets up local communications interference. _____

6) Decker is court-martialed for losing his ship. _____

7) McCoy certifies Decker as mentally unfit for command. _____

8) The first attack on the *Enterprise* knocks out her transporter. _____

9) The *Enterprise* breaks free of the planet killer by using reverse thrust. _____

10) The planet killer had been built primarily as a bluff. _____

_____ **"Devil in the Dark"** _____

(Otherwise titled: "Can a Vulcan and a Horta Find True Happiness Through Horta-culture"*)

1) The *Enterprise* responds to a distress call from
   a. Rigel IX   **b.** Janus VI
   c. Indiri III   **d.** Sol III

2) Pergium is an essential element in
   a. Phaser systems   **b.** Warp drive engines
   c. Transporters   **d.** Life support systems

3) The Horta is resistant to
   a. Heat   **b.** Phaser one fire
   c. Cold   **d.** Disrupter fire

4) The first person killed by the Horta is
   a. Schmitter   **b.** Vanderberg
   c. Apell   **d.** Giotto

5) The Horta steals the main circulation pump from the
   a. PDQ reactor   **b.** Pergium reactor
   c. Fusion reactor   **d.** Atomic reactor

6) On the 23d level, the miners found oddly shaped
   a. Tunnels   **b.** Caves
   c. Plants   **d.** Silicon nodules

7) The miners had inadvertently destroyed the Horta's
   a. Home   **b.** Mate
   c. Eggs   **d.** Mind

8) The Horta is a life form based on
   a. Carbon   **b.** Hydrogen
   c. Krypton   **d.** Silicon

*I don't think the Great Bird of The Galaxy is ever going to forgive me for that one. M.M.

9) **Every 50,000 years, almost the entire Horta population**
   a. Dies   **b.** Hibernates
   c. Spawns   **d.** Migrates

10) **Kirk communicates with the Horta through**
   a. Sign language   **b.** A universal translator
   c. Spock   **d.** The computer

FILL-INS

1) Kirk's security chief is named _____.

2) The Horta is the _____ of her race.

3) The first thing baby Hortas do is _____.

4) The head administrator is chief engineer _____.

5) Ed Apell describes the Horta as _____ and
_____.

6) The first thought Spock receives from the Horta is
"_____."

7) Spock believes the Horta has impeccable _____.

8) McCoy says that he's a doctor, not a _____.

9) Giotto is knocked out by _____.

10) McCoy uses silicon building materials as a _____
for the Horta.

TRUE/FALSE

1) The odds on Kirk and Spock both being killed during the
hunt are 2,228.7 to 1. _____

2) Hortas are by nature aggressive. _____

3) The Mother Horta finds human appearance pleasing.
_____

4) Kirk holds off the Horta with his phaser. _____

5) Kirk won't let the miners kill the Horta. _____

6) Spock helps the Horta and the miners reach a modus vivendi. _____

7) The Horta found Spock's ears attractive. _____

8) There were approximately 200 people involved in the hunt for the Horta. _____

9) Kirk asks Spock to go help Scotty with the reactor. _____

10) The Horta calls her nest the Chamber of the Ages. _____

_____ **"The Menagerie"** _____

1) **At the beginning of the episode, the *Enterprise* receives a subspace message diverting them to**
    a. Starbase 12   **b.** Earth Outpost 4
    c. Regula 1   **d.** Starbase 11

2) **The commander of the complex is**
    a. Commodore Stocker   **b.** Commodore Mendez
    c. Commodore Decker   **d.** Admiral Mendez

3) **Pike was crippled while inspecting**
    a. A starship   **b.** A scoutship
    c. A class J cargo ship   **d.** A starbase

4) **Chris Pike holds the rank of**
    a. Captain   **b.** Admiral
    c. Starship Fleet Captain   **d.** Commodore

5) **Pike was exposed to**
    a. Delta rays   **b.** Berthold rays
    c. Gamma rays   **d.** Beta rays

6) **Spock served with Pike for**
    a. 3 years, 4 months, 2 days   **b.** 6 years, 3 months
    c. 11 years, 4 months, 5 days   **d.** 10 years, 1 month, 20 days

7) **Kirk and Miss Piper have a mutual friend named**
    a. Areel Shaw   **b.** Helen Johannsen
    c. Carol Marcus   **d.** Nancy Crater

8) Pike's heart is
   a. Artificial
   b. Transplanted
   c. Quick-cloned
   d. Battery-driven

9) Pike will live
   a. 10 years
   b. A normal life span
   c. 6 months
   d. 2 years

10) Spock tells the crew that Kirk was
   a. Assigned to another ship
   b. Detained
   c. Assigned medical rest leave
   d. Given shore leave

11) General Order 7 forbids contact with
   a. Aminar V
   b. Talos II
   c. Talos III
   d. Talos IV

12) The *Enterprise* is pursued by
   a. Another starship
   b. A destroyer
   c. A shuttle craft
   d. A scout ship

13) If Spock reaches Talos, he faces
   a. Execution
   b. Court-martial
   c. Discharge
   d. Reassignment

14) Spock is placed under arrest by
   a. Kirk
   b. McCoy
   c. Scotty
   d. Mendez

15) The flashback sequences in "The Menagerie" were originally from the "Star Trek" pilot
   a. "The Omega Glory"
   b. "The Cage"
   c. "Court-martial"
   d. "Shore Leave"

16) The *Enterprise* first visited Talos IV
   a. 10 years ago
   b. 20 years ago
   c. 13 years ago
   d. 2 years ago

17) Mutiny requires a trial board of
   a. 12 jurors
   b. 2 command officers, 2 junior
   c. 3 command officers
   d. 3 admirals

18) The ship that crashed on Talos 31 years ago was
    a. The S.S. *Potemkin*   **b.** The S.S. *Columbia*
    c. The S.S. *Essex*   **d.** The S.S. *King*

19) Ship's doctor under Captain Pike was
    a. Philip Boyce   **b.** Mark Piper
    c. Leonard McCoy   **d.** Mark Winston

20) The *Enterprise* had originally been lured to Talos by
    a. Strange life-form readings   **b.** Odd radioactivity levels
    c. A false distress signal   **d.** An invitation

21) The *Enterprise* had been heading for
    a. The Vega Colony   **b.** Babel
    c. Earth   **d.** Mars

FILL-INS

1) "The Menagerie" was written by _____
_____.

2) "The Menagerie" was the only _____
_____ "Star Trek" episode.

3) "The Menagerie" won the coveted _____ award.

4) Talosians have the power of _____.

5) On Talos IV, Pike meets a woman named _____.

6) It is said that no human male can resist an _____
_____.

7) When Spock touched the Talosian plant life, he
_____.

8) The Talosians observe that humans are remarkably
_____.

9) Spock deduces that the Talosians live _____.

10) The Talosians use their illusions as a _____.

11) Pike is captured to serve as _____
_____.

12) The *Enterprise,* under Captain Pike, had a crew complement
of _____.

13) At his trial, Spock enters a plea of _____.

14) The Talosians find Pike's intelligence extremely
_____.

15) Number One was played by _____
_____.

16) The Talosians discover that humans have a unique hatred for
_____.

17) Under Pike, Spock held the rank of _____.

18) The Talosians were forced underground by _____.

19) Talosians _____ the illusions they create.

20) Number One sets a laser to _____.

_____ **TRUE/FALSE** _____

1) The Talosians cure Pike. _____

2) Spock is found guilty of mutiny. _____

3) Kirk is relieved of command. _____

4) Mendez accompanies Kirk to the *Enterprise.*
_____

5) Vulcans are incapable of telling a lie. _____

6) The Talosians fed Pike steak and potatoes. _____

7) Pike had recently killed a warrior on Rigel VII.
_____

8) Pike is still on the active list. _____

9) Kirk had met Pike once before. _____

10) Pike was Kirk's instructor at the Academy. _____

11) McCoy has Spock taken to the brig. _____

12) The Talosians are a dying race. _____

13) Pike captures the Keeper. _____

14) The Talosians offer to care for Pike for the rest of his life.
_____

15) Vina has died since Pike first visited Talos. _____

16) "The Cage" was turned down by NBC. _____

17) Spock mind melds with Pike. _____

18) When Pike flashes the indicator on his chair once, he means "No." _____

19) Pike's mind is as sound as anyone's. _____

20) Pike joins Vina upon his return to Talos. _____

_____ **"What Are Little Girls Made of?"** _____

1) The action takes place on
  a. Tarsus IV   **b.** Exo III
  c. Antos   **d.** F111

2) Roger Korby has been lost for
  a. 5 years   **b.** 10 years
  c. 3 years   **d.** 1 year

3) Rok was created by
  a. Corby   **b.** Brown
  c. The Old Ones   **d.** Andrea

4) Nurse Chapel once had a promising future in
  a. Teaching   **b.** Administration
  c. Bionics   **d.** Bio-research

5) Roger Korby's assistant was
  a. Brown   **b.** Matthews
  c. Rok   **d.** Andrea

6) Andrea was created by
  a. The Old Ones   **b.** Brown
  c. Korby   **d.** Rok

7) Kirk has a brother named
  a. Bill   **b.** George
  c. Bob   **d.** David

8) Kirk's brother wanted to be transferred to
  a. Exo III   **b.** Earth Colony II
  c. Beta Oragi   **d.** Tantalus

9) Rok considers humans
    a. Superiors   **b.** Friends
    c. Inferiors   **d.** Deadly

10) Korby plans to take the *Enterprise* to
    a. Earth   **b.** Vulcan
    c. Mutara   **d.** Midas V

FILL-INS

1) Kirk calls Spock a _____ _____.

2) Korby commits _____.

3) Korby has been called the _____ of archeological medicine.

4) Rok imitates _____ voice.

5) Survival must cancel out _____.

6) Andrea is not programmed for _____.

7) Rok is played by _____ _____.

8) Kirk's life is saved by _____.

9) Korby damages his _____.

10) The android double is discovered by _____.

TRUE/FALSE

1) Andrea is in love with Kirk. _____

2) Rok kills Korby. _____

3) Chapel offers to betray Korby. _____

4) Spock is dismayed at Kirk's use of the term *half-breed.* _____

5) "What Are Little Girls Made Of?" was written by Robert Bloch. _____

6) The Old Ones died off in a war. _____

7) Five years ago, Korby almost died. _____

8) Brown is destroyed by Rok. _____

9) Korby confesses his love for Andrea. _____

10) Rok does not know how long he has tended the machinery. _____

_____ **"The Galileo Seven"** _____

1) The *Galileo* is lost in
    a. The Mutara nebula   **b.** The Crab nebula
    c. Murasaki 312   **d.** The Coalsack

2) The *Enterprise* is en route to
    a. Earth Outpost 3   **b.** Starbase 2
    c. Markus   **d.** Makus II

3) The *Galileo* crashes on
    a. Psi 2000   **b.** Taurus II
    c. Anton III   **d.** Picon IV

4) The *Enterprise* is to deliver medical supplies to plague victims on
    a. Rigel   **b.** New Rome
    c. New London   **d.** New Paris

5) The *Enterprise* has standing orders to investigate all
    a. Alien activity   **b.** Novas
    c. Quasars   **d.** Pulsars

6) Ferris holds the rank of
    a. Commodore   **b.** Ambassador-at-Large
    c. Admiral   **d.** Galactic High Commissioner

7) The *Enterprise* has another shuttle craft called the
    a. *Columbus*   **b.** *Constitution*
    c. *Searcher*   **d.** *Astral Queen*

8) The creatures' shields are made of
    a. Wood   **b.** Stone
    c. Leather   **d.** Metal

9) The creatures make use of a
    a. Steel-tipped spear   **b.** Folsom point
    c. Bow and arrow   **d.** Slingshot

FILL-INS

1) The *Galileo* is _____ feet long.

2) "The Galileo Seven" was aired during "Star Trek's" _____ season.

3) The *Enterprise* leaves Makus at _____ _____ speed.

4) Kirk is counting on _____ to find the *Galileo*.

5) Scotty uses _____ as an alternative fuel source.

6) Spock retrieves _____ body.

7) Spock observes that there are always _____.

8) The *Galileo* burns up on _____.

9) The *Galileo* is exposed to violent _____.

10) There are _____ survivors of the *Galileo*.

TRUE/FALSE

1) The *Galileo* is thirty feet long. _____

2) Yeoman Mears is killed by the creatures. _____

3) Spock jettisons the *Galileo*'s fuel supply. _____

4) Taurus II is a class D planet. _____

5) The crew of the *Galileo* is found by a search party. _____

6) Kirk orders all sensors directed aft. _____

7) Spock orders his men to shoot to kill. _____

8) Spock believes that logic is a firm basis for command. _____

9) Spock refuses to allow Boma to be buried. _____

10) One of the survivors of the *Galileo* is Lieutenant Boma. _____

"Bread and Circuses"

1) The *Enterprise* picks up wreckage from the survey ship
   a. *Grissom*
   b. *Beagle*
   c. *Aurora*
   d. *Columbus*

2) The *Enterprise* follows the wreckage to the planet
   a. Rylos IV
   b. 357-III
   c. Planet II of system 798
   d. Planet IV of system 892

3) The survey ship was commanded by
   a. R. M. Merik
   b. Ron Tracey
   c. J. J. Estaban
   d. Commander Garrovick

4) The leader of the Sun Worshippers is
   a. Flavius
   b. Claudius
   c. Septimus
   d. Tiberius

5) Septimus had been a
   a. Governor
   b. Warrior
   c. Proconsul
   d. Senator

6) The most successful gladiator on the planet was
   a. Septimus
   b. Flavius
   c. Markus
   d. Merikus

7) Kirk tells Scotty to go to code
   a. Green
   b. Yellow
   c. Red
   d. Blue

8) Claudius observes that Kirk should have been
   a. Tortured
   b. Shot
   c. A Roman
   d. Left alone

9) Kirk, Spock, and McCoy are finally saved by
   a. Flavius
   b. Merik
   c. Septimus
   d. Claudius

FILL-INS

1) Merik failed a _____ test.

2) There were _____ survivors of the survey vessel.

3) The Sun Worshippers follow the Sun (son) _____
_____.

4) Earth's Rome had no _____ _____.

5) Scotty receives a _____.

6) The Roman network is called _____
_____.

7) The planet has had no war for _____ years.

8) The slave provided for Kirk is named _____.

9) The Roman gladiatorial games are _____.

10) The gladiator show is called "_____
_____ _____ _____."

TRUE/FALSE

1) Kirk is tortured by his slave. _____

2) Claudius wants Kirk to bring his people down to the planet.
_____

3) Merik kills Claudius. _____

4) Kirk's code forbids Scotty from taking any overt action.
_____

5) Claudius professes to respect Merik. _____

6) Claudius offers Kirk some roast kid. _____

7) Claudius knows nothing about the Federation.
_____

8) The Romans no longer practice slavery. _____

9) A psychosimulator test can be failed by a split second of indecision. _____

10) Septimus wants to have Kirk killed. _____

"Omega Glory"

1) The *Enterprise* is in orbit around
   a. Markus III   **b.** Omega IV
   c. Markus II   **d.** Omega III

2) The *Enterprise* discovers the dead starship
   a. *Exeter*   **b.** *Intrepid*
   c. *Yorktown*   **d.** *Potemkin*

3) Tracey's crew was killed by
   a. A sneak attack   **b.** Life support failure
   c. A disease   **d.** Each other

4) Galloway is wounded by a
   a. Kohm lance   **b.** Yang lance
   c. Phaser   **d.** Knife

5) Tracey believes he has discovered
   a. Immortality   **b.** Ultimate power
   c. A new life form   **d.** Great wealth

6) Galloway is killed by
   a. Cloud William   **b.** Wu
   c. Tracey   **d.** Chin Wha

7) The society on Omega was destroyed by
   a. Nuclear war   **b.** Biological war
   c. Interstellar war   **d.** Interplanetary war

8) Ron Tracey holds the rank of
   a. Captain   **b.** Admiral
   c. Commodore   **d.** Commander

9) The Yang leader is
   a. Wu   **b.** Cloud William
   c. Red Cloud   **d.** Chin Wha

10) Kirk reads to the Yangs from the
   a. Bible   **b.** Declaration of Independence
   c. Bill of Rights   **d.** Constitution

FILL-INS

1) The _____ _____ _____
_____ _____ comes every 11 years.

2) Tracey has violated the _____ _____.

3) The reading on the landing party's blood is _____
_____ _____.

4) McCoy says he may be able to cure the _____
_____.

5) Spock finds _____ _____ among the Yang
dead.

6) The Yangs are descended from _____.

7) The natives live longer because it's _____.

8) Freedom is a Yang _____ _____.

9) Tracey says that Spock has no _____.

TRUE/FALSE

1) The Ee'd Pleb Nista is the Pledge of Allegiance.
_____

2) Cloud William calls Kirk a great God servant.
_____

3) The rescue party is led by Scotty. _____

4) The highest of the holies is the Bible. _____

5) Tracey compliments Kirk on his bridge crew.
_____

6) Tracey defeats Kirk in battle. _____

7) Kirk is thrown into a cell with two Kohms. _____

8) Cloud William swears that the Holy Words will apply to all
the people. _____

9) Tracey drove off a Yang attack several days before the ar-
rival of the *Enterprise.* _____

10) Kirk is unconscious for 7 hours and 8 minutes.
_____

_____ **"Spectre of the Gun"** _____

1) The *Enterprise* is warned off by a
   a. Subspace message   **b.** Buoy
   c. Starship   **d.** Klingon ship

2) The landing party finds themselves in
   a. Tombstone   **b.** Dodge City
   c. Abilene   **d.** Mexico

3) The landing party is to be
   a. Questioned   **b.** Honored
   c. Killed   **d.** Imprisoned

4) The year is
   a. 1896   **b.** 1875
   c. 1864   **d.** 1881

5) Kirk is
   a. Bob McClowery   **b.** Billy Claiborne
   c. Ike Clanton   **d.** Frank Clanton

6) The sheriff's name is
   a. Paladin   **b.** John Behan
   c. Doc Holliday   **d.** Wyatt Earp

7) Chekov is mistaken for
   a. Morgan Earp   **b.** Ike Clanton
   c. Billy Claiborne   **d.** Tom McClowery

8) Kirk and the landing party are to take part in
   a. Custer's last stand   **b.** War of 1812
   c. The Civil War   **d.** The gunfight at the O.K. Corral

9) The "man who kills on sight" is
   a. Wyatt Earp   **b.** Morgan Earp
   c. Virgil Earp   **d.** Doc Holliday

10) McCoy tests his gas grenade on
   a. Kirk   **b.** Spock
   c. Scotty   **d.** Chekov

FILL-INS

1) Chekov is "killed" by _____ _____.

2) The sheriff suggests that Kirk _____ the Earps.

3) The town is surrounded by a _____ _____.

4) Spock tells Kirk that history cannot _____ _____.

5) The gas invented by McCoy is _____.

6) The buoy communicates _____.

7) Scotty is taken for _____ _____.

8) McCoy borrows supplies from _____ _____.

9) A local girl is in love with _____.

10) The Earps are not _____.

TRUE/FALSE

1) Spock convinces the landing party that all they have seen is an illusion. _____

2) Kirk kills Wyatt Earp. _____

3) The laws of science don't function on the Melkotians' planet. _____

4) The landing party is saved by a rescue party. _____

5) Kirk decides not to open relations with the Melkotians. _____

6) Spock uses a Vulcan mind meld on McCoy. _____

7) The landing party overcomes the Earps with their fists. _____

8) The Melkotian buoy is destroyed by the *Enterprise*. _____

9) Kirk's memories are used to create the illusions on Melkot. _____

10) Kirk wants revenge for Chekov's "death." _____

"Court-martial"

1) Ben Finney is the ship's
    a. Security officer   **b.** Records officer
    c. Morale officer   **d.** Com-tech

2) Kirk ordered Finney to report to
    a. The escape pod   **b.** The ion pod
    c. The solar pod   **d.** Sick bay

3) The *Enterprise* is repaired at
    a. Starbase 9   **b.** Starbase 10
    c. Starbase 11   **d.** Starbase 12

4) The commander of the starbase is Commodore
    a. Mendez   **b.** Wesley
    c. Decker   **d.** Stone

5) Kirk is put on trial for
    a. Malicious intent   **b.** Cowardice
    c. Culpable negligence   **d.** Murder

6) Finney and Kirk once served together on the
    a. *Republic*   **b.** *Farragut*
    c. *Archon*   **d.** *Excelsior*

7) The *Enterprise* visual log shows that Kirk jettisoned the pod during
    a. Red alert   **b.** Double red alert
    c. Condition green   **d.** Yellow alert

8) Sulu's relief helmsman is
    a. Lieutenant Stiles   **b.** Lieutenant Kyle
    c. Lieutenant Hansen   **d.** Lieutenant Greene

9) Finney is hiding in
    a. Engineering   **b.** Sick bay
    c. A Jefferies tube   **d.** His quarters

10) Finney has a daughter named
    a. Susan   **b.** Areel
    c. Jamie   **d.** Janice

FILL-INS

1) Areel Shaw is the attorney for the _____.
2) Areel holds the service rank of _____.
3) Sam Cogley is played by _____ _____.
4) Cogley cites the Fundamental Declarations of the _____ _____.
5) Stone offers Kirk a _____ assignment.
6) Kirk won the Gold Leaf for the _____ _____ _____.
7) Ben Finney is defended by _____ _____.
8) Finney named his daughter after _____.
9) Spock was decorated with the _____ _____ _____.
10) Kirk proves that Finney is not _____.

TRUE/FALSE

1) Finney has hated Kirk for years. _____
2) Finney once failed to report an open circuit. _____
3) Kirk is greeted warmly by old friends at the starbase. _____
4) Kirk demands his court-martial. _____
5) Spock discovers a flaw in the computer's memory banks. _____
6) The prosecution builds its case on "Kirk *vs.* the computer." _____
7) Cogley gives Kirk a book. _____
8) Stone is not on Kirk's trial board. _____
9) Kirk asks Areel to defend him. _____
10) Areel works in the Judge Advocate's Office. _____

"The Squire of Gothos"

1) The *Enterprise* is in space quadrant
   a. 702   **b.** 609
   c. 904   **d.** 305

2) The *Enterprise* is 8 days away from
   a. Earth Colony 1   **b.** Colony Beta 6
   c. Colony Gamma 1   **d.** Earth Colony 4

3) Trelane's observations of earth are inaccurate because of an error in
   a. Time   **b.** Space
   c. Instrumentation   **d.** Judgment

4) Trelane wishes to be called
   a. Squire   **b.** Sir
   c. Lord   **d.** Prince

5) Trelane's food has no
   a. Form   **b.** Substance
   c. Color   **d.** Taste

6) Gothos is a planet of magnitude
   a. 1-E   **b.** 1-V
   c. 1-R   **d.** 1-B

7) Trelane is a
   a. Thief   **b.** Child
   c. Lunatic   **d.** Killer

8) Kirk offers Trelane
   a. A tour of the *Enterprise*   **b.** Dinner
   c. His life   **d.** A hunt

9) Trelane has the power of
   a. Illusion   **b.** Telepathy
   c. Matter transmutation   **d.** Life and death

10) Trelane is told that he will not
   a. Be allowed to leave   **b.** Be hurt
      Gothos
   c. Be allowed to keep   **d.** Be allowed to make any
      Yeoman Ross   more planets

FILL-INS

1) Lieutenant DeSalle's first name is _____.

2) Trelane is portrayed by _____ _____.

3) Gothos's atmosphere is _____.

4) Trelane kidnaps Sulu and _____.

5) The *Enterprise* is on her way to deliver _____ to _____.

6) Karl Jaeger is a _____.

7) Jaeger's service rank is _____.

8) Kirk destroys Trelane's _____ _____.

9) Trelane's father is played by _____ _____.

10) Trelane assumes that Kirk acquired Uhura in one of his _____ of _____.

TRUE/FALSE

1) Trelane appears to Kirk as an English judge. _____

2) Trelane compares Yeoman Ross to Cleopatra. _____

3) The search for Kirk is led by Spock. _____

4) Yeoman Ross's first name is Teresa. _____

5) Trelane exposes Kirk to Gothos's atmosphere. _____

6) DeSalle's bridge station is navigation. _____

7) Trelane fancies Spock's company. _____

8) Kirk and Trelane duel with daggers. _____

9) Trelane apologizes for his bad conduct. _____

10) Kirk strikes Trelane in the face. _____

"Assignment Earth"

1) The *Enterprise* travels to the year
   a. 1970   **b.** 1968
   c. 1966   **d.** 1969

2) Gary Seven's designation is
   a. Agent 204   **b.** Supervisor 194
   c. Supervisor 206   **d.** Agent 347

3) Gary has traveled at least
   a. 3 parsecs   **b.** 500 light years
   c. 10 parsecs   **d.** 1,000 light years

4) Medical analysis shows that Gary is
   a. A shape shifter   **b.** An alien
   c. Human   **d.** A telepath

5) Gary's "cat" is
   a. Rhubarb   **b.** Isis
   c. Stellar   **d.** Cleopatra

6) The conditions on twentieth-century Earth closely parallel those on
   a. Omega III   **b.** Rigel II
   c. Omicron IV   **d.** Delta V

7) Gary's computer is a(n)
   a. Alpha II   **b.** Beta V
   c. Delta III   **d.** Gamma X

8) Agents 201 and 347 were killed
   a. In a fire   **b.** During transport
   c. On a mission   **d.** In a car accident

9) Roberta has a small mole on her
   a. Leg   **b.** Arm
   c. Shoulder   **d.** Face

10) Gary detonates the warhead at
   a. 202 miles, ascending   **b.** 205 miles, descending
   c. 104 miles, descending   **d.** 50 miles, ascending

FILL-INS

1) Gary is a class _____ supervisor.

2) The *Enterprise* avoids detection by using her
_____ _____.

3) Spock is strangely drawn to _____.

4) Gary Seven is played by _____ _____.

5) Roberta is _____ years old.

6) Gary's stunner pen produces _____.

7) Gary's all purpose pen is called a _____.

8) Roberta Lincoln is portrayed by _____
_____.

9) The *Enterprise* travels back in time using the
_____ _____ _____ factor.

10) Roberta was born in _____.

TRUE/FALSE

1) Isis is a shape shifter. _____

2) Gary's vault/transporter is behind the bookcase.
_____

3) Gary sneaks onto the McKinley rocket base.
_____

4) The mission of the *Enterprise* is to observe Earth's history.
_____

5) Gary's address in New York is 811 East 68th Street.
_____

6) The launch director at the rocket base is Col. Nesvig.
_____

7) Gary controls the rocket using his computer's exciever circuits. _____

8) The warhead is headed for the Eurasian continent.
_____

9) "Assignment: Earth" was a pilot that didn't sell.
_____

10) Gary and Roberta teamed up for many interesting experiences. _____

_____ "Return of the Archons" _____

1) The *Enterprise* is in orbit around
    a. Gamma IV   **b.** Beta III
    c. Rigel VII   **d.** Delta IV

2) The planet is located in *space sector*
    a. 5-9   **b.** 7-3
    c. 6-11   **d.** 4-13

3) The Red Hour is
    a. 5 P.M.   **b.** 6 P.M.
    c. 7 P.M.   **d.** 8 P.M.

4) The Red Hour signals the beginning of
    a. Communion   **b.** Absorption
    c. The holidays   **d.** Festival

5) The landing party finds lodging at
    a. Tamar's boarding house   **b.** Marplon's boarding house
    c. Tula's boarding house   **d.** Reger's boarding house

6) Landru's will is enforced by the
    a. Enforcers   **b.** Teachers
    c. Lawgivers   **d.** Punishers

7) Tamar is betrayed to Landru by
    a. Marplon   **b.** Hacom
    c. Tula   **d.** Reger

8) Lindstrom is the ship's
    a. Biologist   **b.** Sociologist
    c. Psychologist   **d.** Anthropologist

9) Kirk is saved from absorption by
    a. Tamar   **b.** Marplon
    c. Tula   **d.** Reger

10) Landru is a(n)
    a. Man   **b.** Energy being
    c. Computer   **d.** Illusion

FILL-INS

1) Sulu and _____ are absorbed first.

2) People who are controlled by Landru are of the _____.

3) The underground operates in units of _____.

4) Landru died _____ years ago.

5) Landru is played by _____ _____.

6) The *Enterprise* is struck by _____ _____.

7) Landru manifests himself in the form of a _____.

8) Reger is immune to _____.

9) Kirk and Spock are led to Landru by _____.

10) Landru is destroyed by _____.

TRUE/FALSE

1) McCoy is absorbed. _____

2) Kirk is absorbed. _____

3) Spock is immune to absorption. _____

4) Landru communicates with his people telepathically. _____

5) Lindstrom stays behind on the planet. _____

6) Kirk's life is saved by Tula. _____

7) Hacom is a member of the underground. _____

8) Lindstrom is absorbed. _____

9) Landru knocks Kirk out by using ultrasonics. _____

10) Landru destroyed the original Archons. _____

"The Lights of Zetar"

1) The *Enterprise* is en route to the library complex on
  a. Theta VII   **b.** Omicron IV
  c. Memory Alpha   **d.** Atoz I

2) Mira was born on
  a. Earth   **b.** Martian Colony III
  c. Rigel IV   **d.** Omicron Ceti III

3) Mira's father was
  a. Chief of Starfleet opera-   **b.** A starship captain
     tions
  c. Chief Surgeon—Starfleet   **d.** Chief Engineer—Starfleet

4) The library is open to
  a. Research scientists   **b.** Planetary leaders
  c. All Federation planets   **d.** Starfleet personnel

5) The Zetars consist of
  a. 5 distinct life units   **b.** 10 distinct life units
  c. 20 distinct life units   **d.** 30 distinct life units

6) Mira's mother is named
  a. Mira   **b.** Shannon
  c. Lydia   **d.** Nancy

7) The Zetars damage the library's
  a. Phasers   **b.** Shields
  c. Memory core   **d.** Life support

8) The Zetars' victims die of
  a. Suffocation   **b.** Brain hemorrhages
  c. Heart attacks   **d.** Stroke

9) The Zetars communicate through
  a. Telepathy   **b.** Mira
  c. Any given crewman   **d.** A universal translator

10) Mira foretells
  a. Kirk's death   **b.** McCoy's death
  c. Scotty's death   **d.** Spock's death

FILL-INS

1) The researchers at the library are found _____.

2) The library has no _____.

3) This is Mira's _____ deep space assignment.

4) Mira has been assigned to _____ _____.

5) Mira is played by _____ _____.

6) McCoy gives Mira a standard _____ analysis.

7) The Zetars attack different _____ centers.

8) When the Zetars attack the *Enterprise,* Sulu cannot _____.

9) McCoy places Mira in a _____ _____.

10) The Zetars are composed of the life force of the last _____ of their people.

TRUE/FALSE

1) Mira and Scotty fall in love. _____

2) Mira foretold the disaster at the library. _____

3) Mira's brain wave pattern has been altered. _____

4) The Zetars try to take Spock's body. _____

5) Zetar was destroyed a millenium ago. _____

6) The Zetars are vulnerable to phaser fire. _____

7) The Zetars cannot get through the ship's shields. _____

8) The Zetars are a group intelligence. _____

9) Mira's psychological profile indicates that she has a pliable personality. _____

10) Mira has limited telepathic ability. _____

"Who Mourns for Adonais?"

1) The *Enterprise* is in orbit around
  a. Axanar III   **b.** Babel II
  c. Dollux IV   **d.** Exeon II

2) The *Enterprise* is in the solar system
  a. Epsilon IX   **b.** Beta Geminorum
  c. Alpha Niobe   **d.** Omega Epsilon

3) Apollo calls his home
  a. Asgard   **b.** Helgard
  c. Olympus   **d.** Midgard

4) Apollo compares Spock to
  a. Artemis   **b.** Pan
  c. Thor   **d.** Zeus

5) Apollo's people were
  a. Gods   **b.** Evil
  c. Explorers   **d.** Human

6) Apollo was the God of
  a. Speed   **b.** War
  c. Love   **d.** Light and purity

7) Apollo has an extra organ in his
  a. Chest   **b.** Side
  c. Stomach   **d.** Throat

8) Apollo compares Kirk to
  a. Zeus   **b.** Ares
  c. Agamemnon   **d.** Achilles

9) The first of Apollo's people to return to the cosmos was
  a. Athena   **b.** Hercules
  c. Hera   **d.** Pluto

10) Apollo channels his power through
  a. The Earth   **b.** The sun
  c. His temple   **d.** His arm

FILL-INS

1) In this episode, Chekov is _____ years old.

2) On ancient Earth, Apollo's people were taken for _____.

3) Apollo wants Kirk's people to gather _____ _____.

4) The field surrounding the *Enterprise* is punctured by a concentration of _____.

5) Kirk orders Carolyn to _____ Apollo.

6) Scotty's arm is _____.

7) Apollo tells Kirk that his people's supplies will come from _____ _____.

8) Apollo commits _____.

9) Apollo's people returned to the cosmos on the _____ _____ _____ _____.

10) Apollo is essentially _____ physically.

TRUE/FALSE

1) Kirk tries to appease Apollo. _____

2) Apollo always found Pan interesting company. _____

3) Chekov attacks Apollo several times. _____

4) Chekov introduces himself to Apollo as the Czar of all the Russians. _____

5) Apollo truly wants Kirk's crew to be happy. _____

6) Apollo has the ability to alter his shape. _____

7) Spock remarks that Apollo is rather verbose. _____

8) Apollo expressly asks Spock to beam down to the planet. _____

9) Chekov suggests that Apollo has an independent power source. _____

10) The Cheshire Cat appeared in a Russian fairy tale. _____

_____ "The Immunity Syndrome" _____

1) The *Enterprise* is headed to
   a. Starbase 6   **b.** Starbase 12
   c. Starbase 2   **d.** Starbase 10

2) The *Enterprise* is due for
   a. Reassignment   **b.** Repairs
   c. Rest and recreation   **d.** Crew replacements

3) The *Enterprise* is diverted to sector
   a. 26A   **b.** 39J
   c. 44B   **d.** 51D

4) The *Enterprise* is assigned a
   a. Code blue status   **b.** Rescue priority
   c. War readiness status   **d.** Code yellow status

5) The creature lives off of
   a. Planetary bodies   **b.** Energy
   c. Stars   **d.** Cosmic rays

6) McCoy keeps the crew going with
   a. Masiform D   **b.** Tri-ox
   c. Stimulants   **d.** Vitamins

7) McCoy recommends
   a. Investigating the creature   **b.** Survival
   c. Destroying the creature   **d.** Trying to capture the creature

8) At the moment of their death, the crew of the *Intrepid* felt
   a. Astonishment   **b.** Fear
   c. Curiosity   **d.** Sadness

9) Spock diverts all his secondary power to
   a. Life support   **b.** Engines
   c. Weapons   **d.** Shields

10) The energy readings finally stop dropping at
   a. ¼ power   **b.** Zero power
   c. ¹⁄₁₀ power   **d.** ⅛ power

FILL-INS

1) Spock calls Bones ＿＿＿＿＿＿＿＿ ＿＿＿＿＿＿＿＿.

2) McCoy warns Kirk against too many ＿＿＿＿＿＿＿＿.

3) According to life-monitor readings, the entire crew is ＿＿＿＿＿＿＿＿.

4) McCoy tells Spock that he botched the ＿＿＿＿＿＿＿＿ test.

5) Spock reduces his life support to ＿＿＿＿＿＿＿＿ ＿＿＿＿＿＿＿＿.

6) The cell lives on electronic and ＿＿＿＿＿＿＿＿ energy.

7) Inside the creature's protective shell, all the ship's instruments work ＿＿＿＿＿＿＿＿ ＿＿＿＿＿＿＿＿.

8) The creature's outer layer is studded with space ＿＿＿＿＿＿＿＿.

9) No Vulcan can conceive of a ＿＿＿＿＿＿＿＿.

10) Spock compares the creature with a ＿＿＿＿＿＿＿＿.

TRUE/FALSE

1) McCoy wishes Spock luck. ＿＿＿＿＿＿＿＿

2) The creature is ready to reproduce. ＿＿＿＿＿＿＿＿

3) The first probe sent into the creature is destroyed. ＿＿＿＿＿＿＿＿

4) The creature is 11,000 miles in length.

5) Kirk is looking forward to a new assignment. ＿＿＿＿＿＿＿＿

6) Using phasers on the creature would destroy the *Enterprise* as well. ＿＿＿＿＿＿＿＿

7) McCoy volunteers to go into the creature. ＿＿＿＿＿＿＿＿

8) Spock is better qualified to fly the shuttle craft than Kirk.

   _____

9) The *Intrepid* knew exactly what was killing them.

   _____

10) The creature varies in width between 2,000 and 3,000 miles.

   _____

_____ **"The Alternative Factor"** _____

1) At the beginning of the episode, Kirk orders Leslie to lay in a course for
   a. Starbase 20   **b.** Starbase 30
   c. Starbase 200   **d.** Starbase 10

2) The magnetic field that holds the universe together
   a. Blinks   **b.** Shifts
   c. Intensifies   **d.** Changes polarity

3) The signal for "Invasion Status" is
   a. Code A   **b.** Red Alert
   c. Code 1   **d.** Condition blue

4) Kirk thinks that the magnetic fluctuation could be
   a. Natural   **b.** A prelude to invasion
   c. A Klingon weapon   **d.** An anomaly

5) The officer in charge of reamplifying the ship's dilithium crystals is
   a. Scotty   **b.** Lieutenant Sulu
   c. Lieutenant Masters   **d.** Lieutenant Tomlinson

6) Spock deduces that the evil Lazarus is
   a. Insane   **b.** A liar
   c. A murderer   **d.** A killer

7) The first person to suspect the existence of two Lazaruses is
   a. McCoy   **b.** Spock
   c. Kirk   **d.** Scotty

8) The dimensions are separated by
   a. Time   **b.** A magnetic corridor
   c. Space   **d.** Distance

9) The *Enterprise* is _____ of the effect
    a. In control   **b.** On the edge
    c. Unaware   **d.** At the center

10) Lazarus B is forced into the corridor by
    a. His counterpart   **b.** Kirk
    c. No one   **d.** Spock

FILL-INS

1) Kirk refers to the *Enterprise* as the _____.

2) Spock conducts an investigation of the _____
_____.

3) "Alternative Factor" was first aired during "Star Trek's"
_____ season.

4) Lazarus's ship travels through _____ and
_____.

5) Dilithium crystals are stolen by _____ Lazaruses.

6) Both Lazaruses are trapped in the corridor for
_____.

7) Lazarus starts a fire in the _____ chamber.

8) The good Lazarus is from an _____ universe.

9) Matter and antimatter cancel each other out
_____.

10) The *Enterprise*'s helmsman in this episode is Mr.
_____.

TRUE/FALSE

1) Sensors show humanoid life on the planet's surface.
_____

2) The magnetic effect drains the ship's dilithium crystals.
_____

3) Spock refers to the center of the magnetic effect as a rip in
space. _____

4) McCoy is puzzled when he sees Lazarus without a bandage. _____

5) Lazarus's ship self-destructs. _____

6) It takes 10 minutes for the evil Lazarus to recharge his crystals. _____

7) Spock is accidently transported to the antimatter universe. _____

8) Kirk is almost struck by a falling boulder. _____

9) The evil Lazarus plots to trap both himself and his counterpart in the corridor. _____

10) The magnetic effect knocks out the *Enterprise*'s phasers. _____

_____ **"Turnabout Intruder"** _____

1) The *Enterprise* picks up a distress signal from
    a. Beta Aurigae   **b.** Delta Vega
    c. Epsilon Indi   **d.** Camus II

2) The *Enterprise* was en route to
    a. Beta Aurigae   **b.** Camus II
    c. Delta Vega   **d.** Epsilon Indi

3) The *Enterprise* was to rendezvous with the starship
    a. *Exeter*   **b.** *Potemkin*
    c. *Excalibur*   **d.** *Valiant*

4) The chief medical officer in Janice Lester's research colony is
    a. Dr. Coleman   **b.** Dr. Sanchez
    c. Dr. Reiss   **d.** Dr. Cayton

5) Arthur claims that everyone died from
    a. Zenite poisoning   **b.** Berthold radiation
    c. Celebium radiation   **d.** Gamma Radiation

6) Kirk's body is stolen by
    a. Sargon   **b.** Lester
    c. Coleman   **d.** Henoch

7) Arthur was put out of starfleet for
   a. Murder
   b. Selling drugs
   c. Administrative incompe-
   tence
   d. Desertion

8) The life-entity transfer is
   a. Temporary
   b. Weak
   c. Permanent
   d. Pleasurable

FILL-INS

1) Janice Lester was played by _____
_____.

2) "Turnabout Intruder" was based on a story by
_____ _____.

3) Janice intends to take "Kirk" to the _____ colony.

4) Violation of General Order _____ is the only crime
carrying the death penalty.

5) _____ _____ is played by Harry Land-
ers.

6) McCoy gives Kirk a standard _____ analysis.

7) "Turnabout Intruder" was "Star Trek's" _____
episode.

8) Spock is put on trial for _____.

9) Janice asks Arthur to commit _____.

10) Kirk is defended by _____.

TRUE/FALSE

1) Spock melds minds with Kirk, who is in the body of Janice
Lester. _____

2) Arthur was guilty of flagrant medical blunders.
_____

3) Arthur places his mind in Spock's body. _____

4) Janice and Kirk were once lovers. _____

5) McCoy gives "Kirk" a Robbiani dermal-optic test.
_____

"Return to Tomorrow"

1) Sargon's planet was destroyed
- a. 10 million years ago
- b. 1 million years ago
- c. .5 million years ago
- d. 20 million years ago

2) Six thousand centuries ago, Sargon's people
- a. Colonized the galaxy
- b. Gave up physical form
- c. Went to war
- d. Conquered the galaxy

3) Henoch had been Sargon's
- a. Brother
- b. First officer
- c. Friend
- d. Enemy

4) Henoch plots to kill
- a. Spock
- b. McCoy
- c. Kirk
- d. Sargon

5) Sargon wants to borrow bodies in order to construct
- a. Space ships
- b. New homes
- c. Androids
- d. Computers

6) The first person that Henoch sees upon waking in a new body is
- a. McCoy
- b. Sargon
- c. Chapel
- d. Thalassa

7) When Kirk's body "dies," Sargon flees into
- a. McCoy's body
- b. Space
- c. The ship
- d. Scotty's body

8) Sargon places Spock's consciousness in
- a. Kirk
- b. Chapel
- c. The ship
- d. McCoy

9) Ann Mulhall is a doctor of
- a. Astrophysics
- b. Astrobiology
- c. Psychology
- d. Medicine

10) Sargon and Thalassa depart into
- a. Time
- b. Space
- c. Oblivion
- d. Another dimension

FILL-INS

1) Spock's body is borrowed by _____.

2) Kirk lends his body to _____.

3) Ann's body is taken by _____.

4) Henoch tortures _____.

5) It is possible that Sargon's people visited _____.

6) The decision to help Sargon is _____.

7) When Kirk and Sargon exchange places, they share _____.

8) Thalassa attacks _____.

9) Henoch is injected by _____.

10) The injection given to Henoch was enough to cause _____.

TRUE/FALSE

1) Henoch takes control of Nurse Chapel's mind. _____

2) Sargon refers to the crew of the *Enterprise* as his "children." _____

3) Henoch threatens to make an example of Chekov. _____

4) Sargon's people dared to think of themselves as gods. _____

5) Henoch is tricked by Kirk. _____

6) Thalassa is secretly Henoch's lover. _____

7) Thalassa is frightened by the thought of oblivion. _____

8) When Kirk's body is possessed, his metabolic rate lowers. _____

9) A host body will eventually become adapted to possession. _____

10) Kirk believes that Spock is dead. _____

"Elaan of Troyius"

1) Petri is the ambassador from
    a. Elas
    b. Troyius
    c. The Federation
    d. The Klingon Empire

2) Elaan is the
    a. High Teer of Elas
    b. Ambassador of Troyius
    c. High Priestess of Troyius
    d. Dohlman of Elas

3) Elaan's bodyguards carry
    a. Phasers
    b. Lasers
    c. Nuclear weapons
    d. Disrupters

4) Elaan is addressed as
    a. Your Glory
    b. Your Worship
    c. Your Majesty
    d. Your Highness

5) Petri presents Elaan with a
    a. Medal
    b. Scroll
    c. Ring
    d. Necklace

6) Elasian women control their men
    a. Biochemically
    b. Politically
    c. Through hypnosis
    d. Through drugs

7) Elaan asks Kirk to teach her
    a. Earth customs
    b. How to be liked
    c. Elasian customs
    d. Troyian customs

8) The best-protected part of the ship is
    a. The bridge
    b. Sick bay
    c. Engineering
    d. The transporter room

9) Troyius possesses a wealth of
    a. Gold
    b. Zenite
    c. Pergium
    d. Dilithium crystals

10) Elaan presents Kirk with _____ as a personal memento
    a. A picture
    b. A rose
    c. A dagger
    d. Her necklace

FILL-INS

1) The Klingon spy is _____.
2) The *Enterprise* will explode if she uses her _____ _____.
3) Elasian tears act like a super _____ _____.
4) Elaan finds her quarters _____.
5) Ship's sensors pick up a _____ _____.
6) The wedding will be attended by the Federation _____ _____.
7) Transmissions to the Klingons are being sent from _____.
8) Elaan's necklace is made of _____ _____.
9) The *Enterprise* number _____ shield is damaged.
10) The Klingons take a direct hit _____ _____.

TRUE/FALSE

1) Elas is the inner planet of the star system. _____
2) Petri must teach Elaan manners. _____
3) Elaan likes Petri. _____
4) Elaan's quarters were provided by Yeoman Rand.
5) Kryton and Elaan were to be married. _____
6) Elaan's bodyguards are trained to resist telepathic interrogation techniques. _____
7) There is no antidote for Elasian tears. _____
8) The Klingons order Kirk to turn Elaan over to them. _____
9) The Klingon attack reduces the *Enterprise*'s impulse power by 31%. _____
10) The *Enterprise* destroys the Klingon ship. _____

"The Paradise Syndrome"

1) **Kirk loses his**
   a. Mind
   c. Phaser
   b. Memory
   d. Communicator

2) **The natives make Kirk their**
   a. Chief
   c. Advisor
   b. Priest
   d. Medicine man

3) **Kirk calls himself**
   a. Kirok
   c. Captain of the *Enterprise*
   b. A god
   d. Kraken

4) **Kirk revives an unconscious child with**
   a. CPR
   c. Native supplies
   b. His medikit
   d. Artificial respiration

5) **Salish had once been the tribe's**
   a. Greatest warrior
   c. Priest
   b. Chief
   d. Medicine man

6) **Salish discovers that Kirk**
   a. Is from another planet
   c. Wants to marry Miramanee
   b. Has amnesia
   d. Bleeds

7) **Miramanee's people had been placed on their planet by**
   a. The Preservers
   c. The Creators
   b. The Old Ones
   d. Landru

8) **The chief of the tribe is called**
   a. Salish
   c. Goro
   b. Tonko
   d. Chandra

9) **Under stress, Spock can go for weeks without**
   a. Food
   c. Air
   b. Water
   d. Sleep

10) **Kirk's head was caught in a**
   a. Force bolt
   c. Power relay
   b. Memory beam
   d. Communications beacon

FILL-INS

1) Kirk is mistaken for a _____.

2) Miramanee is the tribe's _____.

3) Kirk teaches the tribe about food _____.

4) Spock tries to split the asteroid using the ship's
_____.

5) Spock deciphers the hieroglyphics with the aid of his
_____.

6) Kirk and Miramanee are _____ at the temple.

7) The obelisk is an _____ _____.

8) Kirk dreams of the _____.

9) Miramanee is going to have a _____.

10) Miramanee had been betrothed to _____.

TRUE/FALSE

1) Kirk knows how to gain access to the obelisk.
_____

2) Spock's exhaustion is brought on by guilt. _____

3) Kirk teaches the tribe the principles of irrigation.
_____

4) The ship's deflectors move the asteroid 00.13%.
_____

5) Spock burns out the ship's warp drive. _____

6) Spock and McCoy must give up their initial search for Kirk.
_____

7) Salish becomes Kirk's friend. _____

8) Kirk is first seen coming out of the obelisk by Salish.
_____

9) Kirk believes that he is a god. _____

10) Spock restores Kirk's memory with the Vulcan mind meld.
_____

_____ "The Corbomite Maneuver" _____

1) The _Enterprise_ encounters a buoy moving at
a. Warp 2
b. Light speed
c. Sublight speed
d. Warp 3

2) Kirk has a physical examination
a. Semiannually
b. Yearly
c. Monthly
d. Quarterly

3) The _Enterprise_ is held motionless by the buoy for
a. 24 hours
b. 15 hours
c. 2 days
d. 18 hours

4) "The Corbomite Maneuver" marks the first appearance of
a. Mr. Scott
b. Yeoman Rand
c. Lieutenant Sulu
d. Lieutenant Riley

5) Bailey reminds Kirk of
a. McCoy
b. Himself
c. Spock
d. Scotty

6) Balok commands the starship
a. _Warhawk_
b. _Vesuvius_
c. _Explorer_
d. _Fesarius_

7) Balok comes from
a. The Tholian Alliance
b. The First Federation
c. The Gorn Empire
d. Orion Space

8) McCoy takes Bailey
a. To the brig
b. To sick bay
c. To his quarters
d. For coffee

9) Balok reminds Spock of
a. Surak
b. Sarek
c. T'Pau
d. Kirk

10) Kirk boards the _Fesarius_ with McCoy and
a. Spock
b. Bailey
c. Sulu
d. Rand

FILL-INS

1) Yeoman Rand heats some coffee with a _____ _____.

2) McCoy puts Kirk on a _____.

3) Bailey _____ on the bridge.

4) The buoy almost destroys the *Enterprise* with _____.

5) Kirk tricks Balok by using the principles found in _____.

6) Yeoman Rand brings Kirk a _____ for supper.

7) Balok destroys a _____ _____.

8) Balok's alter ego is a _____.

9) Balok's pilot craft weighs _____ _____ _____.

10) Bailey plots a _____ course away from the buoy.

TRUE/FALSE

1) Balok was testing Kirk's intentions. _____

2) Kirk orders a series of phaser drills. _____

3) Bailey panics on the bridge. _____

4) Bailey offers to stay aboard the *Fesarius*. _____

5) The buoy weighs 5,000 metric tons. _____

6) Corbomite has been incorporated into the hulls of Earth ships since the early days of space flight. _____

7) The *Enterprise* breaks away from the *Fesarius*'s sensor beam. _____

8) McCoy eats in Kirk's quarters with his captain. _____

9) Balok refers to the dummy as Watson to his Holmes. _____

10) Balok conducts Kirk on a tour of the *Fesarius*. _____

"The Enemy Within"

1) The transporter is damaged by
   a. A power surge   **b.** An ion storm
   c. A magnetic ore   **d.** Sabotage

2) The *Enterprise* is in orbit around
   a. Alpha 177   **b.** Beta 254
   c. Gamma 200   **d.** Delta 279

3) When the evil Kirk first materializes, his command insignia is
   a. Upside down   **b.** On the wrong side
   c. Inverted   **d.** Missing

4) Yeoman Rand's hobby is
   a. Music   **b.** Painting
   c. Writing   **d.** Cooking

5) The evil Kirk knocks out
   a. Fisher   **b.** McCoy
   c. Chekov   **d.** Spock

6) "The Enemy Within" introduces
   a. Yeoman Rand   **b.** The IDIC medallion
   c. The Vulcan nerve pinch   **d.** The Vulcan mind meld

7) Without his negative half, Kirk loses his ability to
   a. Reason   **b.** Command
   c. Feel emotions   **d.** Delegate authority

8) At night, the temperature on the planet's surface reaches
   a. 50 below   **b.** 100 below
   c. 120 below   **d.** 250 below

9) Sulu asks Kirk for
   a. Heating units   **b.** Saurian brandy
   c. Tents   **d.** A pot of coffee

10) Scott repairs the transporter by tapping directly into the ship's
   a. Antimatter pods   **b.** Phaser control units
   c. Warp engines   **d.** Impulse engines

FILL-INS

1) _____ men are stranded on the planet's surface.

2) Scotty requests a _____ meter in order to test the transporter circuits.

3) The negative Kirk orders McCoy to give him _____ _____.

4) The first person to realize that there are two Kirks is _____.

5) Kirk's power of decision comes from his _____ side.

6) Kirk's essential courage comes from his _____ side.

7) In this episode, the ship's navigator is Lieutenant _____.

8) The evil Kirk covers his wounds with _____.

9) The negative Kirk blasts a hole in the ship's main _____ _____.

10) Scotty's repairs on the transporter allow for a 5 point variation in _____ _____.

TRUE/FALSE

1) Scotty's transporter assistant is Technician Wilson._____

2) The transporter's ionizer unit can be repaired in 2 days._____

3) Two members of the landing party die of frostbite._____

4) The alien dog died of shock._____

5) The transporter abort control is intact._____

6) The evil Kirk takes Wilson's phaser._____

7) Search parties are ordered to take whatever steps are necessary in capturing the intruder._____

8) Sulu asks Kirk for some rice wine._____

9) McCoy suggests putting the evil Kirk in the brig._____

10) Communicators are unaffected by extreme low temperatures._____

"Errand of Mercy"

1) Starfleet sends a message to the *Enterprise* in
   a. Code 1   **b.** Code 2
   c. Code 3   **d.** Code 4

2) The *Enterprise* is to prevent the Klingons from using the planet
   a. As a source of natural resources   **b.** As a base
   c. To repair their ships   **d.** As a recreation area

3) The temporary head of the planet's council is
   a. Trefayne   **b.** Baroner
   c. Ayelborne   **d.** Kevis

4) The natives provide Kirk and Spock with
   a. Weapons   **b.** Disguises
   c. Information   **d.** Shelter

5) Spock poses as a Vulcan
   a. Teacher   **b.** Healer
   c. Trader   **d.** Traveler

6) Kirk adopts the name
   a. Ayelborne   **b.** Trefayne
   c. Trillium   **d.** Baroner

7) Kor distrusts people who
   a. Agree too quickly   **b.** Smile too much
   c. Don't talk   **d.** Have no fear

8) Spock is interrogated through
   a. A mind meld   **b.** Hypnosis
   c. Torture   **d.** A mind sifter

9) Kor threatens to have Spock
   a. Tortured   **b.** Executed
   c. Dissected   **d.** Put on trial for espionage

10) Kirk and Spock are freed from prison by
   a. Ayelborne   **b.** Kor
   c. Trefayne   **d.** Baroner

FILL-INS

1) Kor holds the service rank of _____.

2) Kirk steals a Klingon _____ _____.

3) Kor orders public assemblages to be limited to _____ people.

4) There are _____ Klingon _____ around the planet.

5) Kor asks Kirk to reveal the _____ of Starfleet's forces.

6) The war is stopped by the _____.

7) Kor believes that humans and Klingons are _____ _____.

8) Kirk and Spock were watched by _____ guards while in prison.

9) Kor orders his men to kill 200 citizens every _____ _____.

10) Infraction of the smallest Klingon regulations is punishable by _____.

TRUE/FALSE

1) The Klingons issued an ultimatum to the Federation to withdraw from the disputed areas. _____

2) Kirk organizes an underground. _____

3) Kor orders the implementation of special occupation order four. _____

4) Trefayne senses the approach of the Klingon forces. _____

5) Errand of Mercy is the historical beginning of the Organian Peace Treaty. _____

6) Klingon commanders are never kept under surveillance. _____

7) The controls on the *Enterprise* become too hot to handle. _____

8) Kirk is embarrassed by his actions on Organia. _____

9) In the future, the Federation and the Klingon Empire will become allies. _____

10) Kor accuses the Federation of cutting off vital Klingon supply lines. _____

_____ **"Shore Leave"** _____

1) McCoy first sights
 a. Alice
 c. A rabbit
 b. A tiger
 d. A samurai

2) Bones says that the planet reminds him of
 a. The Wizard of Oz
 c. Mother Goose fairy tales
 b) Alice in Wonderland
 d. Grimm's fairy tales

3) Kirk's reaction time is down
 a. 5 to 10%
 c. 9 to 12%
 b. 7 to 9%
 d. 10 to 15%

4) Sulu finds a
 a. .357 magnum
 c. Police special
 b. 9 mm automatic
 d. .44 magnum revolver

5) Kirk meets a former lover named
 a. Ruth
 c. Janice
 b. Edith
 d. Areel

6) McCoy is "killed" by
 a. Don Juan
 c. A tiger
 b. A knight
 d. A fighter plane

7) Rodriguez spots a
 a. WW II fighter
 c. Spitfire
 b. WW I biplane
 d. Messerschmitt

8) Fifteen years ago, Kirk was an academy
 a. Freshman
 c. Junior
 b. Sophomore
 d. Senior

9) Barrows becomes infatuated with
 a. Kirk
 c. McCoy
 b. Spock
 d. Sulu

10) Years ago, Kirk and Finnegan were
 a. Classmates
 c. Friends
 b. Shipmates
 d. Enemies

FILL-INS

1) Rodriguez's first name is _____.

2) Kirk and Spock are stalked by a _____.

3) The planet was intended to be an _____ _____.

4) Sulu is chased by a _____.

5) Kirk is tricked into taking shore leave by _____.

6) Yeoman Barrows finds a _____.

7) The woman with Rodriguez is named _____ _____.

8) The man who attacked Barrows carried a jeweled _____.

9) The more complex the mind, the greater the need for _____.

10) The alien proprietor of the planet calls himself the _____.

TRUE/FALSE

1) Barrows beams down to the planet with McCoy. _____

2) Kirk takes Sulu's gun. _____

3) Initial landing parties found no signs of animal life forms. _____

4) McCoy shows Kirk tiger tracks. _____

5) Finnegan refers to Kirk as a plebe. _____

6) McCoy is killed by a plane making a strafing run. _____

7) At the end of the episode, Kirk decides that the planet is too dangerous to allow shore leave. _____

8) McCoy only peeks in the line of duty. _____

9) McCoy is taken below the surface for repairs. _____

10) Kirk decides to go back to the ship immediately after the emergency is over. _____

"The City on the Edge of Forever"

1) The *Enterprise* is caught in waves of
   a. Space displacement   b. Time displacement
   c. Dimensional displacement   d. Cosmic rays

2) McCoy accidently injects himself with
   a. Ryetalyn   b. Hydronlyn
   c. Tri-ox   d. Cordrazine

3) The time portal has been waiting millions of years for
   a. People   b. Kirk
   c. Time to stop   d. A question

4) Kirk and Spock go back to the year
   a. 1920   b. 1925
   c. 1930   d. 1935

5) Kirk steals some
   a. Money   b. Clothes
   c. Food   d. Tools

6) Kirk and Spock materialize in
   a. An alley   b. A basement
   c. A home   d. A store front

7) Edith runs the _____ mission
   a. 13th Street   b. 21st Street
   c. 12th Street   d. 30th Street

8) Edith offers Kirk and Spock work at
   a. $1 an hour   b. 50¢ an hour
   c. 25¢ an hour   d. 15¢ an hour

9) Edith accurately predicts the coming of
   a. World War II   b. Television
   c. The atomic bomb   d. The space age

10) Kirk's rent is
   a. $5 per week   b. $2 per week
   c. $10 per week   d. $7 per week

FILL-INS

1) Edith asks Kirk if he has a _____ for the night.

2) Spock attempts to construct mnemonic _____ _____.

3) Kirk tells a policeman that Spock's head was caught in a _____ _____ _____.

4) The time portal is both _____ and _____.

5) The screenplay for "City on the Edge of Forever" won the _____ _____ award for 1967–68.

6) This episode won science fiction's coveted _____ award.

7) Edith's occupation is _____ _____.

8) Spock steals some _____.

9) Edith tells Kirk that she can get them 5 hours' work at _____¢ an hour.

10) McCoy wanders into the _____ _____ _____.

TRUE/FALSE

1) Kirk falls in love with Edith. _____

2) Kirk saves Edith's life. _____

3) Sulu suffers some heart flutter. _____

4) Kirk first greets Edith with a lie. _____

5) Edith's tool box is locked with a conventional lock. _____

6) Spock wears a derby. _____

7) Edith observes that Spock belongs at Jim's side. _____

8) Edith would have delayed the United States entry into World War II. _____

"Balance of Terror"

1) The *Enterprise* is in space sector
    a. L5   **b.** Z6
    c. R9   **d.** P11

2) The *Enterprise* loses contact with
    a. Outpost 1   **b.** Outpost 2
    c. Outpost 4   **d.** Outpost 5

3) Robert Tomlinson is to be married to
    a. Tina Lawson   **b.** Ann Mulhall
    c. Angela Mártine   **d.** Marlena Moreau

4) The Romulans destroy Earth Outposts 11, 3, 4 and
    a. 5   **b.** 7
    c. 6   **d.** 8

5) The ship's navigator is Lieutenant
    a. Tomlinson   **b.** Stiles
    c. Bailey   **d.** Farrell

6) Outpost 4 is commanded by
    a. Commodore Mendez   **b.** Captain Kelly
    c. Commander Hanson   **d.** Commodore Stocker

7) Sulu suggests that the *Enterprise* maintain
    a. Red Alert   **b.** Yellow Alert
    c. Security Alert   **d.** War Alert

8) The Romulan's weapon causes metals to
    a. Explode   **b.** Disintegrate
    c. Implode   **d.** Melt

9) Stiles's first assignment was in
    a. Communications   **b.** Navigation
    c. Engineering   **d.** Weapons

10) The only crewman killed in the battle with the Romulans is
    a. Stiles   **b.** Tomlinson
    c. Kyle   **d.** Farrell

FILL-INS

1) Earth Outpost 4 is composed of solid _____.

2) The Romulan weapon is limited in _____.

3) Kirk is visited in his quarters by _____.

4) Stiles shows an intense dislike for _____ _____.

5) The Romulans head for a magnitude 7 _____.

6) The Romulan Commander demotes _____ two steps in rank.

7) The Romulan's power is simple _____.

8) The Romulan Commander damages the *Enterprise* with a _____ _____.

9) The ship's navigator is relieved by Lieutenant _____.

10) McCoy asks Kirk not to destroy the one named _____.

TRUE/FALSE

1) The Romulan Commander is anxious for war. _____

2) The *Enterprise* is faster than the Romulan ship. _____

3) Lieutenant Stiles is saved by Kirk. _____

4) Kirk opts to violate the Neutral Zone. _____

5) The Romulans believe that the *Enterprise* is merely a reflection. _____

6) McCoy tells Kirk that there are 3 million Earthlike planets in our galaxy. _____

7) The seats of Romulan power are the twin planets Romulus and Remus. _____

8) The crew of the *Enterprise* are the first members of the Federation to actually see Romulans. _____

9) The Romulan Commander destroys his own ship. _____

"Is There in Truth No Beauty?"

1) Humans who see a Medusan
  a. Die   **b.** Go insane
  c. Laugh   **d.** Are repulsed

2) Larry Marvick is one of the designers of
  a. Duotronics   **b.** Stratos
  c. The Enterprise   **d.** Starfleet Headquarters

3) At dinner, Kirk offers Miranda
  a. Saurian brandy   **b.** Antarean glow water
  c. Scotch   **d.** Antarean brandy

4) Spock greets Kollos wearing
  a. Dress blues   **b.** An IDIC
  c. Protective goggles   **d.** Gloves

5) Kollos finds the transporter effect
  a. Unsettling   **b.** Interesting
  c. Pleasurable   **d.** Frightening

6) The *Enterprise* is driven to speeds exceeding
  a. Warp 11   **b.** Warp 12.9
  c. Warp 9.5   **d.** Warp 13

7) Medusans have developed _____ to a fine art
  a. Logic   **b.** Mathematics
  c. Physics   **d.** Navigation

8) Miranda hates
  a. Love   **b.** Pity
  c. Fear   **d.** Hate

9) Spock/Kollos observes that humans are
  a. Entertaining   **b.** Brave
  c. Aggressive   **d.** Lonely

10) Spock/Kollos quotes from
  a. Milton   **b.** Byron
  c. Shelly   **d.** Keats

FILL-INS

1) Kirk shows Miranda the ship's _____.

2) Medusan thought patterns are among the most _____ in the universe.

3) Miranda is committed to _____ _____ with Kollos.

4) Miranda gets around with the aid of a _____ _____.

5) Uhura's name means _____.

6) Kirk calls Miranda Spock's _____.

7) Spock's sanity is saved by _____.

8) When Spock dissolves his meld with Kollos, he forgets to put on his _____.

9) Miranda thanks Kirk for allowing her to _____.

10) Before leaving the *Enterprise,* Miranda is given a _____.

TRUE/FALSE

1) Miranda was born on Earth. _____

2) Miranda senses someone thinking about murder. _____

3) Miranda was once in love with Larry Marvick. _____

4) Miranda comes to understand the philosophy of IDIC. _____

5) Miranda is in favor of Spock and Kollos joining minds. _____

6) Spock had been offered the assignment with Kollos. _____

7) Miranda's infirmity is exposed by Spock. _____

8) Kirk attempts to seduce Miranda. _____

9) Kollos is anxious to dissolve his link with Spock. _____

10) McCoy confronts Miranda about her jealousy of Spock.

_____

_____ **"The Empath"** _____

1) The *Enterprise* is in standard orbit around
    a. Antos IV   **b.** Tellus III
    c. Minara II   **d.** Triacus

2) A solar flare forces the *Enterprise* to leave the area for
    a. 72.3 hours   **b.** 74.1 hours
    c. 48.9 hours   **d.** 23.7 hours

3) Gem is given her name by
    a. Kirk   **b.** Spock
    c. McCoy   **d.** Linke

4) Ozaba quotes
    a. Psalm 95 verse 4   **b.** Psalm 50 verse 2
    c. The Lord's Prayer   **d.** Psalm 32 verse 5

5) Before they attack, the sandbats of Maynark IV appear to be
    a. Plants   **b.** Rock crystals
    c. Furry animals   **d.** Tree bark

6) Gem is a functional
    a. Empath   **b.** Telepath
    c. Shape shifter   **d.** Android

7) Gem first uses her abilities on
    a. Kirk   **b.** Spock
    c. McCoy   **d.** Lal

8) If McCoy is taken by the Vians, the probability that he will die is
    a. 100%   **b.** 96%
    c. 93%   **d.** 87%

9) If Spock is taken by the Vians, the probability is quite high that he will
    a. Be crippled   **b.** Die
    c. Suffer brain damage   **d.** Go blind

10) The choice as to who is to go with the Vians is made by
    a. Lot   **b.** McCoy
    c. Kirk   **d.** Spock

FILL-INS

1) Gem learns compassion from _____.

2) Kirk suffers from the _____.

3) Gem learns courage from _____.

4) The Vian control device is powered by _____ _____.

5) Gem is taught sacrifice by _____.

6) McCoy's lungs are _____ after he is tortured.

7) Linke and Ozaba are stored in giant _____ _____.

8) The search party led by Scotty is a _____.

9) McCoy compliments Spock's _____ _____.

10) McCoy is _____ by Gem.

TRUE/FALSE

1) Linke and Ozaba are alive. _____

2) The Vians have the power to save their sun. _____

3) Gem offers her life for McCoy. _____

4) McCoy knocks Spock out with a phaser. _____

5) Gem accompanies Kirk, Spock, and McCoy back to the *Enterprise.* _____

6) Spock is tortured by the Vians. _____

7) Scotty tells Kirk the story of the merchant. _____

8) McCoy suffers heart damage. _____

9) Kirk is the first to break out of the Vian force field. _____

10) Gem is responsible for saving her world. _____

"Operation—Annihilate!"

1) **Sam Kirk's first name is**
   a. Bill
   b. Jim
   c. George
   d. Gregory

2) **Sam's wife is named**
   a. Areel
   b. Aurelan
   c. Anne
   d. Alicia

3) **Jim Kirk's nephew is named**
   a. Paul
   b. Jim
   c. Peter
   d. Charles

4) **Sam Kirk's private transmitter code is**
   a. TDK 538
   b. GSK 783
   c. KGB 564
   d. HYG 674

5) **The first system to fall to the creatures was**
   a. Ingraham B
   b. Beta Portalan
   c. Lavinius V
   d. Alpha Signi

6) **Two hundred years ago, the creatures struck**
   a. Lavinius V
   b. Ingraham B
   c. Beta Portalan
   d. Theta Cygni XII

7) **The creatures invade the human**
   a. Brain
   b. Circulatory system
   c. Respiratory system
   d. Central nervous system

8) **McCoy's K-3 indicator registers a patient's**
   a. Temperature
   b. Pulse rate
   c. Pain level
   d. REM patterns

9) **The creatures can be destroyed by**
   a. Heat
   b. Radiation
   c. Phaser fire
   d. Ultraviolet light

10) **McCoy exposes the creature to**
    a. Berian radiation
    b. Cobalt radiation
    c. Berthold radiation
    d. Gamma radiation

FILL-INS

1) The Denevan who flies into the sun cries out that he is _____.

2) Deneva was colonized _____ years ago.

3) The creatures inflict extreme _____.

4) The creatures are forcing the Denevans to build _____ _____.

5) The creatures make a _____ sound.

6) Each creature resembles a single _____ _____.

7) Spock is held at phaser point by _____.

8) One of the creatures is captured by _____.

9) The treatment that cures Spock temporarily destroys his _____.

10) The alternative to killing the creatures is the destruction of _____.

TRUE/FALSE

1) The creatures have been spreading through the galaxy for hundreds of years. _____

2) The creatures have been traveling in a straight line. _____

3) A creature attaches itself to Kirk. _____

4) The creatures are phaser-resistant. _____

5) Kirk discovers the creatures' weakness. _____

6) The creatures invaded Deneva from Beta Portalan. _____

7) Spock is able to control his pain. _____

8) McCoy blames Kirk for Spock's injury. _____

9) The population of Deneva is over 2 million. _____

10) Kirk's sister-in-law survives. _____

"A Taste of Armageddon"

1) The *Enterprise* is headed to Eminiar VII with orders to
   a. Establish a base
   b. Open diplomatic relations
   c. Negotiate mining rights
   d. Stop a war

2) The *Enterprise* is warned away from Eminiar with code
   a. 710
   b. 97
   c. 107
   d. 79

3) The Eminians have been at war for
   a. 1000 years
   b. 500 years
   c. 200 years
   d. 2000 years

4) Eminiar was first contacted by the Federation
   a. 1 year ago
   b. 10 years ago
   c. 25 years ago
   d. 50 years ago

5) The starship _____ was lost in this quadrant
   a. *Exeter*
   b. *Intrepid*
   c. *Valiant*
   d. *Yorktown*

6) Kirk and his party are led to the Eminian
   a. Detention area
   b. Division of Control
   c. Division of Alien Affairs
   d. Division of War

7) Anan 7 is the leader of the
   a. Military
   b. Civilian authority
   c. High Council
   d. War party

8) The Eminian guards carry
   a. Phaser I
   b. Phaser II
   c. Nuclear weapons
   d. Sonic disrupters

9) The *Enterprise* has been declared
   a. Severely damaged
   b. Destroyed
   c. Invalid
   d. Neutral

10) Kirk orders Scotty to implement General Order
   a. 20
   b. 4
   c. 7
   d. 24

FILL-INS

1) Every year, the war claims _____ to _____ million lives.

2) The *Enterprise* is carrying Ambassador _____ _____.

3) The Ambassador orders Scotty to assume a _____ status.

4) Anan tries to trick Scotty by using a _____ _____.

5) Eminiar attacks the *Enterprise* with _____ _____.

6) The *Enterprise*'s helmsman is Lieutenant _____.

7) Anan's daughter is prevented from leaving her quarters by Yeoman _____.

8) Anan calls Kirk a _____.

9) The victims have _____ hours to report for execution.

10) Eminiar has a direct line to the _____ _____.

TRUE/FALSE

1) The *Valiant* had been declared destroyed by the Eminians. _____

2) The Federation ambassador offers to mediate the dispute. _____

3) Scotty refuses to drop the *Enterprise*'s shields despite Anan's assurances. _____

4) Kirk intends to destroy Emniar's enemies. _____

5) Anan's daughter has been declared exempt from the war. _____

6) Anan's wife had been declared dead recently. _____

7) Spock tells a guard that there is a multilegged creature crawling on his shoulder. _____

8) Kirk and Spock destroy all the disintegration chambers.

_____

9) Kirk is subdued by 3 guards. _____

10) Kirk intended to destroy Eminiar within 2 hours.

_____

_____ **"The Ultimate Computer"** _____

1) At the age of 24, Richard Daystrom developed
- **a.** Duotronics
- **b.** Multitronics
- **c.** Tritronics
- **d.** Warp drive

2) Daystrom is the recipient of the Nobel and _____ prizes
- **a.** Z-Magnees
- **b.** Vulcan science
- **c.** Starfleet Service
- **d.** Federation research

3) For the M-5 tests, the *Enterprise* is to have a crew of
- **a.** 10
- **b.** 20
- **c.** 30
- **d.** 40

4) Bob Wesley is the commander of the Starship
- **a.** *Hood*
- **b.** *Potemkin*
- **c.** *Exeter*
- **d.** *Lexington*

5) The captain of the *Excalibur* is
- **a.** Stocker
- **b.** Tracey
- **c.** Decker
- **d.** Harris

6) The attack force against the *Enterprise* consists of
- **a.** 2 starships
- **b.** 3 starships
- **c.** 4 starships
- **d.** 5 starships

7) M-5 charts and explores the planet
- **a.** Gamma Hydra II
- **b.** Beta Gamma III
- **c.** Retnax four
- **d.** Alpha Carinae II

8) The M-5 destroys the ore freighter
- **a.** *Beagle*
- **b.** *Central*
- **c.** *Woden*
- **d.** *Botany Bay*

9) In the first M-5 drill, the *Enterprise* fires phasers at
  a. $\frac{1}{10}$ power   **b.** $\frac{1}{20}$ power
  c. $\frac{1}{100}$ power   **d.** $\frac{1}{2}$ power

10) The term referring to a part that serves no useful purpose is
  a. Junk   **b.** Nofkis
  c. Thyla   **d.** Dunsel

FILL-INS

1) Wesley sends his regards to Captain _____.

2) Spock points out to Kirk that a starship runs on _____.

3) Spock believes that computers are more _____ than humans.

4) Daystrom programmed M-5 with human _____ _____.

5) M-5 is unlike any other computer because it _____.

6) The *Lexington* suffers _____ dead.

7) M-5 is convinced to shut down by _____.

8) M-5 taps energy from the ship's _____ _____.

9) Daystrom refers to the task force as _____ _____.

10) Daystrom suffers a _____ _____.

TRUE/FALSE

1) Daystrom has found his fame difficult to live with.
  _____

2) Daystrom made his first major breakthrough 25 years ago.
  _____

3) M-1 through M-4 were earlier successful Daystrom designs.
  _____

4) Kirk and M-5 are in agreement as to landing party personnel. _____

5) McCoy brings Kirk a martini. _____

6) McCoy's bartending skills are famous from here to Orion. _____

7) M-5 protects itself with phasers._____

8) M-5 shuts down power on Decks 1 through 11. _____

9) An *Enterprise* engineer is killed by M-5. _____

10) Spock thinks it would be amusing to pattern a computer after McCoy. _____

_____ "Metamorphosis" _____

1) Nancy Hedford was assigned to prevent a war on
   a. Saurogi III   **b.** Alpha Epsilon II
   c. Epsilon Canaris III   **d.** Delta Vega

2) The shuttle craft is taken to
   a. Delta Oragi   **b.** Gamma Omega III
   c. Psi 2000   **d.** Gamma Canaris N

3) Nancy contracts
   a. Sakuro's disease   **b.** Kodos's disease
   c. Sythococcus Novae   **d.** Rigellian fever

4) The Companion is made up of ionized
   a. Hydrogen   **b.** Helium
   c. Argon   **d.** Krypton

5) The temperature on the Companion's planet is a constant
   a. 76 degrees   **b.** 69 degrees
   c. 72 degrees   **d.** 70 degrees

6) Cochrane has been on the Companion's planet for
   a. 100 years   **b.** 150 years
   c. 200 years   **d.** 50 years

7) Cochrane is the discoverer of
    a. Dimensional space space   **b.** Subspace drive
    c. Hyperspace drive   **d.** Space warp drive

8) The Companion is
    a. Genderless   **b.** Male
    c. Female   **d.** Bisexual

9) The Companion renders Spock unconscious with
    a. A force bolt   **b.** An electric shock
    c. Sound   **d.** Gas

10) The Companion thinks of Cochrane as a
    a. Pet   **b.** Friend
    c. Prisoner   **d.** Lover

FILL-INS

1) Kirk asks Spock to explain their methods of _____ to Cochrane.

2) Spock tries to _____-_____ the Companion.

3) Cochrane communicates with the Companion _____.

4) The Companion calls Cochrane the _____.

5) Cochrane's apparent age is _____.

6) The Companion joins with _____.

7) The shuttle was supposed to rendezvous with _____.

8) The planet generates a general _____ _____ field.

9) Kirk communicates with the Companion _____.

10) When the Companion becomes human, it gives up _____.

TRUE/FALSE

1) Cochrane was dying of loneliness. _____

2) Nancy's disease causes coma. _____

3) Cochrane refers to himself as a Judas goat. _____

4) If the Companion leaves the planet for an extended length of time it will die. _____

5) Cochrane leaves the Companion. _____

6) Nancy is saved by McCoy. _____

7) Cochrane and the Companion share a symbiotic relationship. _____

8) McCoy points out that Kirk was trained as a diplomat.
_____

9) A large part of the Companion's makeup is simple electricity. _____

10) Spock convinces the Companion to let them go.
_____

"Mirror, Mirror"

1) The *Enterprise* is caught in
    a. A dimensional vortex   **b.** Waves of time displacement
    c. An Ion storm   **d.** A meteor storm

2) Spock II asks Kyle for
    a. His phaser   **b.** His agonizer
    c. His punisher   **d.** His communicator

3) Our Kirk, McCoy, Scotty, and Uhura find themselves aboard the
    a. O.S.S. *Enterprise*   **b.** U.S.S. *Enterprise*
    c. H.M.S. *Enterprise*   **d.** I.S.S. *Enterprise*

4) The I.S.S. *Enterprise* security chief is
    a. Kenner II   **b.** Sulu II
    c. Chekov II   **d.** Farrell II

5) The leader of the Halkans is
a. Tharn   b. Lal
c. Balok   d. Akaar

6) Kirk orders Scotty to short out the
a. Main phaser couplings   b. Warp engines
c. Deflectors   d. Computer

7) An attempt is made on Kirk II's life by
a. Spock   b. Farrell
c. Chekov   d. Marlena

8) Kirk II's personal guard is
a. Commander Kenner   b. Lieutenant Kyle
c. Chief Farrell   d. Mr. Lesley

9) Marlena Moreau is a
a. Chemist   b. Nurse
c. Biologist   d. Physicist

10) Spock II warns Kirk I of
a. Sulu's plans   b. Chekov's plans
c. Starfleet's orders   d. An attempt on his life

FILL-INS

1) The Empire's symbol is a planet speared by a
   _____.

2) Marlena is the captain's _____.

3) Kirk II's greatest weapon is the _____ field.

4) McCoy recognizes an _____ burn in sick bay.

5) Kirk II became the captain through the murder of
   _____.

6) Kirk II's first act as captain of his *Enterprise* was the suppression of the _____ uprising.

7) Sulu II is distracted from his security board by
   _____.

8) The third officer of the alternate *Enterprise* is
   _____.

9) Spock II mind melds with _____.

10) Kirk has always suspected that Spock was a bit of a
_____ at heart.

TRUE/FALSE

1) Chekov II spends some time in an agony booth.
_____

2) Chief Farrell has offered to take Marlena temporarily.
_____

3) Spock II's life is saved by Kirk. _____

4) Sulu II's attack is foiled by Marlena. _____

5) Spock II vows to overthrow the Empire. _____

6) McCoy points out to Spock II the illogic of waste.
_____

7) Spock II is ordered to kill Kirk unless he destroys the Halkans. _____

8) Kirk II killed 5,000 colonists on Vega IX. _____

9) Scotty offers to stay behind in the parallel universe.
_____

"Wolf in the Fold"

1) **Scotty is taken to the planet Argelius II for**
   a. Medical care
   b. An engineer's convention
   c. Reeducation
   d. Therapeutic shore leave

2) **Scotty recently suffered a**
   a. Stroke
   b. Concussion
   c. Back injury
   d. Heart attack

3) **Kirk, McCoy, and Scotty are entertained by an Argelian belly dancer named**
   a. Natira
   b. Sybo
   c. Kara
   d. Shanna

4) **Argelians applaud with**
   a. Wooden paddles
   b. Horns
   c. Flashing lights
   d. Bells

5) Hengist is a native of
    a. Regulus II   **b.** Canopus IV
    c. Sarpeidon   **d.** Rigel IV

6) The chief administrator of Argelius is
    a. Hengist   **b.** Moorla
    c. Jaris   **d.** Karob

7) The number one suspect in the murders on Argelius is
    a. Hengist   **b.** Moorla
    c. Scotty   **d.** Jaris

8) The Prefect of Argelius is
    a. Hengist   **b.** Moorla
    c. Jaris   **d.** Karob

9) The Great Awakening of Argelius occurred
    a. 50 years ago   **b.** 500 years ago
    c. 100 years ago   **d.** 200 years ago

10) Kesla was the name given to the mass murderer of women on the planet
    a. Rigel IV   **b.** Deneb II
    c. Zetar   **d.** Alpha Centauri III

FILL-INS

1) The entity was known on Earth as _____ _____ _____.

2) Sybo is murdered by _____.

3) The entity flees into the ship's _____.

4) The murder weapon was produced by the hill people of _____ _____.

5) The entity comes from the planet _____.

6) Scotty's serial number is _____.

7) The law of Argelius is _____.

8) _____ was to marry the Argelian belly dancer.

9) Scotty did not black out when _____ was killed.

10) Psycho-tricorder technician _____ _____ is murdered.

———————————— TRUE/FALSE ————————————

1) Sybo was a sensitive. ———————

2) McCoy believes that Scotty might resent women because of a recent injury. ———————

3) The entity came to Argelius from Daran 5. ———————

4) Hengist is dead. ———————

5) The entity last struck 1 solar year ago. ———————

6) Spock drives the entity from the ship's computer.
———————

7) The entity takes Spock over. ———————

8) The entity cuts the ship's warp drive. ———————

9) The entity cuts off communication with Starfleet.
———————

10) Scotty is given an Argelian truth serum. ———————

——— "Where No Man Has Gone Before" ———

1) The *Valiant* was lost
 a. 5 years ago
 c. 200 years ago
 b. 10 years ago
 d. 50 years ago

2) The captain of the *Valiant* was frantically searching for information concerning
 a. Telepathy
 c. Life energy transfer
 b. ESP
 d. Shape shifters

3) The *Enterprise*'s helmsman in this episode is
 a. Sulu
 c. Lee Kelso
 b. Gary Mitchell
 d. Montgomery Scott

4) Dr. Dehner joined the *Enterprise* at
 a. Starbase 2
 c. The Aldebaran Colony
 b. The Canopus Colony
 d. The Omicron Colony

5) At the edge of the galaxy, the *Enterprise* encounters
 a. Intelligent life
 c. A planet killer
 b. An energy barrier
 d. Mutated humans

6) When Kirk visits Gary in sick bay, Mitchell is reading
   a. Kant   **b.** Sartre
   c. Spinoza   **d.** Plato

7) The *Enterprise* doctor is
   a. Mark Piper   **b.** Philip Boyce
   c. John Cayton   **d.** Karl Rotwang

8) Delta Vega has a
   a. Repair center   **b.** Medical center
   c. Lithium cracking plant   **d.** Mining operation

9) Gary Mitchell's service rank is
   a. Lieutenant commander   **b.** Lieutenant
   c. Chief   **d.** Commander

10) Dimorus is populated by intelligent
   a. Cats   **b.** Rodents
   c. Lizards   **d.** Plants

FILL-INS

1) On Delta Vega, Gary creates an _____.

2) Gary compares humans to _____.

3) Mitchell becomes immune to _____ _____.

4) The *Enterprise* burns out her _____ _____.

5) Gary knew a "real nova" on the planet _____ _____.

6) Gary quotes "_____ Woman."

7) The starboard impulse packs decay to _____.

8) The barrier has a _____ charge.

9) The chief physicist on board the *Enterprise* is _____.

10) Dr. Dehner's first name is _____.

TRUE/FALSE

1) Kirk's tombstone reads "James T. Kirk." _____

2) Gary always favored Kaferian apples. _____

3) Kirk lists Gary as missing. _____

4) Gary once took a poison dart aimed at Spock.
_____

5) In the last scene, Kirk has a cast on his wrist.
_____

6) Kirk orders the *Enterprise* to leave orbit in 18 hours.
_____

7) Gary is killed by a rockfall. _____

8) Gary's power grows gradually. _____

9) Kirk and Gary have known each other for 15 years.
_____

10) Delta Vega is slightly larger than Earth. _____

"This Side of Paradise"

1) **The colony on Omicron Ceti III has a population of**
   a. 400   b. 50
   c. 302   d. 150

2) **Berthold rays destroy**
   a. Plant life   b. The soil
   c. Animal life   d. The ozone layer

3) **Spock and Leila met on**
   a. Vulcan   b. Rigel
   c. Earth   d. Starbase 2

4) **Spock and Leila knew each other**
   a. 10 years ago   b. 5 years ago
   c. 6 years ago   d. 8 years ago

5) The first member of the *Enterprise* crew to come in contact with the spores is

   a. Sulu   **b.** Spock

   c. Kirk   **d.** McCoy

6) The leader of the colony is

   a. John Desalle   **b.** Elias Sandoval

   c. David Merick   **d.** David Reiss

7) The colonists are to be taken to

   a. Earth   **b.** Rigel II

   c. Starbase 27   **d.** Starbase 11

8) Spock has seen dragons on

   a. Cheron   **b.** Daraen V

   c. Ekos III   **d.** Berengaria VII

9) The spores' effect can be destroyed by

   a. Alcohol   **b.** Lexorin

   c. Violent emotions   **d.** Vulcan mind techniques

10) Spock's mother is a

   a. Scientist   **b.** Teacher

   c. Doctor   **d.** Diplomat

FILL-INS

1) At first, Spock finds the effect of the spores _____.

2) Kirk has orders to _____ the colony.

3) As a child, Sandoval had _____ _____.

4) McCoy sits under a tree, drinking a _____ _____.

5) Kirk places Spock in _____ custody.

6) Spock's father is a _____.

7) Spock has never stopped to look at _____.

8) The colony has no _____.

9) Leila's last name is _____.

10) Leila is played by _____ _____.

TRUE/FALSE

1) Unprotected, a man can survive exposure to Berthold rays for about a week. _____

2) When Sandoval was a child, he contracted polio. _____

3) McCoy once had 3 broken ribs. _____

4) Sulu is something of an expert on the subject of farming. _____

5) Kirk finds Spock hanging upside down from a tree. _____

6) McCoy threatens to put Sandoval in a hospital. _____

7) Under the influence of the spores, the entire crew commits mutiny. _____

8) Uhura shorts out the subspace radio. _____

9) Kirk and Spock initiate a brawl among the colonists and crew with the aid of a subsonic transmitter. _____

10) Scotty does not appear in this episode. _____

"Space Seed"

1) **Uhura picks up a signal in**
   a. Binary code
   c. Standard code
   b. Morse code
   d. English

2) **The ship is called the**
   a. *Grissom*
   c. *Botany Bay*
   b. *Elba*
   d. *St. Helen*

3) **The ship is class**
   a. DY-200
   c. DY-300
   b. DY-100
   d. DY-400

4) **The ship was built in the late**
   a. 21st century
   c. 22d century
   b. 1980s
   d. 1990s

5) Marla's hobby is
- **a.** Writing
- **b.** Sculpting
- **c.** Painting
- **d.** Singing

6) Warp drive was discovered in
- **a.** 2126
- **b.** 2285
- **c.** 2001
- **d.** 2018

7) Marla holds the service rank of
- **a.** Ensign
- **b.** Lieutenant
- **c.** Lieutenant commander
- **d.** Yeoman

8) Khan held power on earth
- **a.** From 1990–1995
- **b.** From 1992–1996
- **c.** From 1997–2000
- **d.** From 1998–2001

9) Khan is exiled to
- **a.** Ceti Alpha V
- **b.** Ceti Alpha VI
- **c.** Alpha Ceti V
- **d.** Alpha Ceti VI

10) Khan asks Kirk if he's ever read
- **a.** Milton
- **b.** Dumas
- **c.** Sartre
- **d.** Shakespeare

FILL-INS

1) Khan's full name is _____ _____ _____.

2) Khan controlled Asia through the _____.

3) Khan is the product of _____ _____.

4) Kirk orders all decks flooded with _____ gas.

5) Khan requests access to the ship's _____ _____.

6) McCoy tells Kirk that he would have made a fair _____.

7) Khan cuts off the ship's _____ _____ systems.

8) Khan's first words upon awakening in his ship were, _____ _____.

9) Khan places Kirk in a _____ _____.

10) Kirk is set free by _____.

_____ **TRUE/FALSE** _____

1) Khan takes over engineering after he takes the bridge. _____

2) Marla did a portrait of Napoleon. _____

3) Kirk is jealous of Khan's attentions toward Marla. _____

4) Kirk defeats Khan bare-handed. _____

5) Kirk drops the charges against Khan. _____

6) Khan has a crew of 50. _____

7) Khan's ship was named for a penal colony off the coast of France. _____

8) Khan confesses to Marla his plan to take over the *Enterprise.* _____

9) Khan believes that social occasions are merely warfare concealed. _____

10) Marla stays on board the *Enterprise* to face charges of mutiny. _____

_____ **"Friday's Child"** _____

1) **The leader of the Ten Tribes is**
    a. Kras   **b.** Haan
    c. Akaar   **d.** Akuta

2) **Maab strikes a deal with**
    a. Kirk   **b.** Keel
    c. Kras   **d.** Haan

3) **Kirk is offered a chance for ritual combat by**
    a. Duur   **b.** Keel
    c. Deem   **d.** Kras

4) The Capellans use a boomerang-like weapon called a
- **a.** Redjac
- **b.** Kligat
- **c.** Lirpa
- **d.** Roscoe

5) The Klingons attempt to lure the *Enterprise* away from Capella with a false distress signal from the
- **a.** *Exeter*
- **b.** *Kobayashi Maru*
- **c.** *Yorktown*
- **d.** *Dierdre*

6) Eleen's baby is delivered by
- **a.** Maab
- **b.** McCoy
- **c.** Keel
- **d.** Duur

7) Topaline is used in
- **a.** Phasers
- **b.** Warp engines
- **c.** Computers
- **d.** Life-support systems

8) Under the laws of her people, Eleen must
- **a.** Give up her child
- **b.** Die
- **c.** Be exiled
- **d.** Marry the new ruler

9) Kras is killed by
- **a.** Maab
- **b.** Akaar
- **c.** Kirk
- **d.** Keel

10) Maab is killed by
- **a.** Kirk
- **b.** Spock
- **c.** Kras
- **d.** Keel

FILL-INS

1) Eleen gives birth to a baby _____.

2) Eleen's baby is the new _____ _____.

3) The baby is named _____ _____ _____.

4) Kirk uses _____ _____ _____ to light the cave.

5) Eleen is played by _____ _____.

6) Kirk and Spock create an explosion using _____.

7) Kras is portrayed by _____ _____.

8) Kirk and Spock use _____ and _____
against the Capellan warriors.

9) Capellans have little use for the _____ arts.

10) The rescue party is lead by _____.

_____ **TRUE/FALSE** _____

1) Eleen is anxious to have her baby. _____

2) McCoy slaps Eleen. _____

3) Kirk leaves Sulu in command of the *Enterprise.*
_____

4) Cura is a Capellan deity. _____

5) Eleen is fascinated by McCoy. _____

6) McCoy hands the baby to Spock. _____

7) Eleen names her child after Spock. _____

8) Touching the wife of a Capellan ruler is punishable by death.
_____

9) Eleen knocks Kirk unconscious. _____

10) Eleen burns her leg. _____

_____ **"The Apple"** _____

1) The *Enterprise* is in orbit around
   a. Delta Gamma IV   **b.** Gamma Trianguli VI
   c. Beta Oragi IV   **d.** Robus Glaesi IV

2) Hendorff is killed by a(n)
   a. Lightning bolt   **b.** Poisonous plant
   c. Exploding rock   **d.** Native

3) The planet has an average mean temperature of
   a. 65 degrees   **b.** 80 degrees
   c. 70 degrees   **d.** 76 degrees

4) Starfleet has invested 122,220-plus credits in
   a. Spock   **b.** Kirk
   c. McCoy   **d.** Scotty

5) Vaal is a
a. Man
b. God
c. Computer
d. Robot

6) Vaal tries to destroy the *Enterprise* by
a. Overloading the warp engines
b. Using heat beams
c. Cutting off life support
d. Draining the antimatter pods

7) Akuta is known as the
a. Eyes of Vaal
b. God Servant
c. Hands of Vaal
d. Mouth of Vaal

8) Vaal requires almost constant
a. Worship
b. Repairs
c. Cleaning
d. Feeding

9) The plant poison is 1,000 times stronger than
a. Therigan
b. Saplin
c. Alkaloid
d. Arsenic

10) Kirk destroys Vaal with
a. Phasers
b. Logic
c. Antimatter
d. Photon torpedoes

FILL-INS

1) Akuta has antennae protruding from his _____.

2) Akuta is played by _____ _____.

3) Makora is portrayed by _____ _____.

4) The people of Vaal are forever _____.

5) Kaplan is killed by a _____ _____.

6) Makora and Sayana observe Chekov and Landon _____.

7) Yeoman Landon's first name is _____.

8) Chekov insists that Eden was in _____.

9) McCoy injects Spock with _____.

10) The exploding rocks are easily _____.

TRUE/FALSE

1) Mallory is killed by a lightning bolt. _____

2) Kirk takes a chest full of poison thorns. _____

3) The landing party prevents the natives from feeding Vaal.
_____

4) Yeoman Landon is infatuated with Spock. _____

5) Spock saves Kirk's life. _____

6) Vaal can control the weather. _____

7) The exploding rocks contain uranite. _____

8) "The Apple" was written by Gene Roddenberry.
_____

9) Kirk tries to explain "children" to the people of Vaal.
_____

10) Without Vaal, the people will grow old. _____

"I, Mudd"

1) **The *Enterprise* is taken to the planet**
   a. Mudd   **b.** Stella
   c. Gamma III   **d.** Eve

2) **Harry has a wife named**
   a. Alice   **b.** Stella
   c. Trudy   **d.** Annabelle

3) **Every time Harry thinks about his wife, he**
   a. Laughs   **b.** Cries
   c. Sighs   **d.** Goes farther out into
                                space

4) **Mudd was arrested on**
   a. Alpha VI   **b.** Darlan II
   c. Deneb V   **d.** Hrubes III

5) **Harry tried to sell all the rights to**
   a. The *Enterprise*   **b.** Starfleet Headquarters
   c. A pergium mine   **d.** A Vulcan fuel synthesizer

6) The android's master computer is called
   a. Norman
   b. Herman
   c. Control central
   d. Landru

7) The androids were created by the
   a. Old Ones
   b. Providers
   c. Ancient Ones
   d. Makers

8) Mudd's planet is type
   a. K
   b. L
   c. M
   d. N

9) Kirk and Spock "kill"
   a. Harry
   b. Chekov
   c. McCoy
   d. Scotty

10) Kirk leaves Harry with 500
   a. Alices
   b. Trudys
   c. Stellas
   d. Annabelles

FILL-INS

1) Spock and Harry pretend to set off a _____.

2) Norman is played by _____ _____.

3) The androids are defeated by _____.

4) Spock describes logic as a _____ _____
_____ _____ _____ smell bad.

5) There is only _____ Norman.

6) When the androids commune with the master computer,
their _____ glow.

7) Kirk tells Alice that the *Enterprise* is a _____
_____.

8) Kirk and Spock direct their attack at _____.

9) Harry tells Norman that he is telling a _____.

10) The androids intend to take the _____.

TRUE/FALSE

1) Chekov has never met Harry before. _____

2) The androids are 1,743,912 years old. _____

3) No android body has ever worn out. _____

4) Spock tells a "Barbara" that he loves her. _____

5) Harry helps Kirk defeat the androids. _____

6) The androids recognize that Harry is flawed.
_____

7) The androids wish to serve mankind. _____

8) McCoy injects Harry with a stimulant. _____

9) Norman is destroyed. _____

10) Spock takes an android back to the *Enterprise* for study.
_____

"The Trouble with Tribbles"

1) The *Enterprise* is diverted to space station
   a. B-9   **b.** K-7
   c. L-111   **d.** 7-112

2) The space station is near
   a. Wrigley's Planet   **b.** Tinker's Planet
   c. Leo's Planet   **d.** Sherman's Planet

3) Kirk is ordered to guard a shipment of
   a. Pergium   **b.** Quadrotriticale
   c. Monochromium   **d.** Zenite

4) Nilz Baris is an undersecretary
   a. Of the Federation   **b.** Of Interplanetary Affairs
   c. Of Starfleet   **d.** Of Agricultural Affairs

5) Tribbles have no
   a. Hearts   **b.** Fur
   c. Mouths   **d.** Teeth

6) Cyrano offers to sell tribbles at
    a. 5 credits each   **b.** 10 credits each
    c. 2 credits each   **d.** 6 credits each

7) The Klingon commander is
    a. Koloth   **b.** Kang
    c. Kras   **d.** Kor

8) Korax calls Kirk
    a. A fool   **b.** A Maynark sandbat
    c. A Vegan slug   **d.** A Denebian slime devil

9) The first punch in the barroom brawl is thrown by
    a. Chekov   **b.** Korax
    c. Scotty   **d.** Kirk

10) The Chief Astronomer at the Royal Academy of Great Britain was
    a. Ivan Burkoff   **b.** John Burke
    c. Randolph Burke   **d.** Woodrow Long

FILL-INS

1) Kirk takes great pleasure in insulting _____ _____.

2) Cyrano Jones sells _____ _____ gems.

3) Nilz Baris is played by _____ _____.

4) Scotty gives the tribbles to the _____.

5) Korax compares the *Enterprise* to a _____ _____.

6) Cyrano Jones is played by _____ _____.

7) Chekov refers to Klingons as _____.

8) According to Chekov, scotch was invented by a little old lady from _____.

9) Baris contacts the *Enterprise* on channel _____.

10) Kirk finds himself buried in _____.

TRUE/FALSE

1) Cyrano Jones sells Antarean glow water. _____

2) Arne Darvin is a Federation agent. _____

3) Scotty's favorite pastime is reading technical journals.
_____

4) Scotty and Chekov are insulted by Koloth. _____

5) Twenty-three years ago, a battle was fought on Donatu V.
_____

6) The Klingons request R&R on the Space Station.
_____

7) Scotty calls Vodka a man's drink. _____

8) Regulan blood worms are soft and shapeless.
_____

9) "The Trouble with Tribbles" was written by David Gerrold.
_____

10) It will take Jones 17.9 years to clean all the tribbles out of
the space station. _____

"The Gamesters of Triskelion"

1) Triskelion is in the star system
   a. B-34 Delta   **b.** M-24 Alpha
   c. H-31 Beta   **d.** J-35 Gamma

2) Triskelion has a
   a. Trinary star   **b.** Binary star
   c. Yellow sun   **d.** Red sun

3) The master drill thrall is
   a. Shahna   **b.** Lars
   c. Tamoon   **d.** Galt

4) Chekov's drill thrall is
   a. Tamoon   **b.** Shahna
   c. Lars   **d.** Keela

5) The *Enterprise* had been on a mission to the planetoid
   a. Megan III   **b.** Beta Iotia
   c. Gamma II   **d.** Delta Vega

6) Spock tracks the landing party
   a. 11.630 light years   **b.** 15.937 light years
   c. 50.003 light years   **d.** 20.332 light years

7) Kirk's drill thrall is
   a. Galt   **b.** Tamoon
   c. Deela   **d.** Shanna

8) Kirk offers to fight
   a. 2 thralls   **b.** 4 thralls
   c. 6 thralls   **d.** 3 thralls

9) Kloog comes from
   a. Rigel VII   **b.** Eminiar VII
   c. Anon VII   **d.** Aldebaran VII

10) Kirk's final opponent is
   a. Lars   **b.** Galt
   c. Shanna   **d.** Tamoon

FILL-INS

1) Shanna is played by _____ _____.

2) Shanna's mother was killed in a _____

_____.

3) Kirk offers the Providers a _____.

4) Triskelion's currency is referred to as _____.

5) A _____ is a Triskelion unit of time.

6) _____ _____ portrays Tamoon.

7) The Providers agree to _____ the thralls.

8) Uhura is "chosen" for _____.

9) Chekov's relief navigator is _____

_____.

10) Kloog is played by _____ _____.

TRUE/FALSE

1) Chekov is infatuated with his drill thrall. ⎯⎯⎯⎯⎯⎯

2) The Providers intend to use the landing party as breeding stock. ⎯⎯⎯⎯⎯

3) "The Gamesters of Triskelion" was a third-season "Star Trek" episode. ⎯⎯⎯⎯⎯

4) Shanna was born on Triskelion. ⎯⎯⎯⎯⎯

5) Shanna stays behind on Triskelion. ⎯⎯⎯⎯⎯

6) The Providers are unimpressed with Kirk's fighting spirit. ⎯⎯⎯⎯⎯

7) Uhura is taken with her drill thrall. ⎯⎯⎯⎯⎯

8) Kirk tells Shanna about the stars. ⎯⎯⎯⎯⎯

9) Shanna refuses to fight with Kirk. ⎯⎯⎯⎯⎯

10) "The Gamesters of Triskelion" was directed by Gene Roddenberry. ⎯⎯⎯⎯⎯

"A Piece of the Action"

1) The *Enterprise* visits the planet
- **a.** Cheron
- **b.** Ekos
- **c.** Zion
- **d.** Iota

2) A hundred years ago, the planet was visited by the U.S.S.
- **a.** *Beagle*
- **b.** *Valiant*
- **c.** *Horizon*
- **d.** *King*

3) The boss of the planet's largest territory is
- **a.** Jojo Krako
- **b.** Tepo
- **c.** Bela Oxmyx
- **d.** Kunio

4) "The Book" is titled
- **a.** *Chicago Mobs of the Twenties*
- **b.** *Underworld*
- **c.** *Capone*
- **d.** *The Roaring Twenties*

5) "The Book" was published in
- **a.** 2020
- **b.** 1984
- **c.** 1992
- **d.** 2015

6) Bela's chief adversary is
   a. Cirl the Knife   **b.** Tepo
   c. Kalo   **d.** Krako

7) A half fizzbin is
   a. Two jacks   **b.** Two queens
   c. Two aces   **d.** Two kings

8) Kirk puts the bag on
   a. Tepo   **b.** Krako
   c. Cirl   **d.** Bela

9) Three Jacks is a
   a. Fizzbin   **b.** Kronk
   c. Full fizzbin   **d.** Sralk

10) The basic component in almost every piece of Starfleet equipment is the
   a. Transcoder   **b.** Transtator
   c. Transvexer   **d.** Transponder

FILL-INS

1) Bela Oxmyx is played by _____ _____.

2) "The Book" was left on the planet by the crew of the
_____.

3) McCoy loses his _____.

4) A _____ fizzbin cannot be beat.

5) Tepo is played by _____ _____.

6) Kirk cuts the Federation in for a _____
_____ _____ _____.

7) _____ is left in charge of the planet.

8) Bela wants Kirk to help him _____ the other
bosses.

9) Scotty offers Krako a pair of _____
_____.

10) Krapo is portrayed by _____ - _____.

TRUE/FALSE

1) Kirk takes over the planet. _____

2) Krako puts the bag on Spock. _____

3) Bela likes to play fizzbin. _____

4) In order to complete a fizzbin, you need a king or a deuce, except at night when you need a queen or a four.
_____

5) Krako is taken aboard the *Enterprise*. _____

6) In fizzbin, everyone gets six cards. _____

7) Bela offers Kirk a cut. _____

8) In fizzbin, the second card goes up, except on Tuesday.
_____

9) Fizzbin is a real game. _____

10) Kirk has all the bosses beamed into Oxmyx's office.
_____

"By Any Other Name"

1) Rojan's home planet is
   a. Kelva   **b.** Orkon
   c. Kendra   **d.** Ovion

2) Rojan's people have been in space for
   a. 100 years   **b.** 200 years
   c. 300 years   **d.** 400 years

3) Spock is supposedly subject to recurring bouts of
   a. Rigellian kassaba fever   **b.** Sythococcus novae
   c. Selek's disease   **d.** Krasbak fever

4) Rojan puts Drea in charge of
   a. Engineering   **b.** Life Support
   c. Sick bay   **d.** Auxiliary Control

5) Rojan's second in command is
   a. Kelinda   **b.** Tomar
   c. Hanar   **d.** Drea

6) Scotty's "green" liquor comes from
    a. Titan   **b.** Io
    c. Pluto   **d.** Ganymede

7) McCoy injects Hanar with
    a. Stokaline   **b.** Cordrazine
    c. Masiform-D   **d.** Formazine

8) McCoy injects Spock with
    a. Stokaline   **b.** Cordrazine
    c. Masiform-D   **d.** Formazine

9) Kelinda compares flowers with her native
    a. Kleer   **b.** Krasa
    c. Sahsheer   **d.** Ahn-woon

10) Rojan freezes Kirk with a
    a. Neural field   **b.** Neural neutralizer
    c. Neural dampener   **d.** Neural stimulator

FILL-INS

1) Kirk makes Rojan jealous by seducing _____.

2) Scotty gives Tomar some very old _____.

3) Rojan's people are a race of _____.

4) Rojan is played by _____ _____.

5) Tomar is in charge of _____.

6) Kirk offers to help Rojan find a _____.

7) Rojan kills Yeoman _____.

8) Most of the crew is reduced to _____.

9) _____ _____ plays Kelinda.

10) Rojan was born _____ _____.

TRUE/FALSE

1) Kirk seduces Drea. _____

2) Rojan's people are humanoid by nature. _____

3) Spock helps Kirk push Rojan into a rage. _____

4) Rojan is one link in a generations-old chain. _____

5) Scotty passes out from too much liquor. _____

6) Scotty and Tomar start out on Saurian brandy.
_____

7) Kirk steals one of Rojan's control devices. _____

8) Rojan wears his control device on his wrist. _____

9) Kelinda is in love with Spock. _____

10) Drea is in love with Kirk. _____

"The Tholian Web"

1) The entire crew of the *Defiant*
  a. Went insane   **b.** Deserted
  c. Committed mutiny   **d.** Committed treason

2) Kirk is caught in
  a. Time   **b.** Space
  c. Spacial interphase **d.** A dimensional corridor

3) Tholians do not tolerate
  a. Lateness   **b.** Aliens
  c. Humanoids   **d.** Deceit

4) Tholians are known for their
  a. Logic   **b.** Punctuality
  c. Compassion   **d.** Brutality

5) The commander of the Tholian ship is
  a. Trinine   **b.** Varkine
  c. Loskene   **d.** Pontene

6) The antidote to the space madness is a
    a. Theragen derivative   **b.** Hydronlin derivative
    c. Cobalt derivative   **d.** Masiform derivative

7) McCoy's antidote is a dilute form of
    a. Romulan truth serum   **b.** Klingon nerve gas
    c. Tholian nerve gas   **d.** Gorn truth serum

8) The first person to see Kirk's "ghost" is
    a. Sulu   **b.** Scotty
    c. Uhura   **d.** Chekov

9) Chekov goes insane
    a. In the mess hall   **b.** On the *Defiant*
    c. On the bridge   **d.** In his quarters

10) Spock calls McCoy
    a. Doc   **b.** Leonard
    c. Bones   **d.** Friend

FILL-INS

1) Spock and McCoy view _____ _____ _____.

2) McCoy injects Kirk with _____ _____.

3) There has never been a _____ aboard a Federation starship.

4) The fabric of space is _____ by the Tholians.

5) The ruling body of the Tholian people is called the _____.

6) "The Tholian Web" was directed by _____ _____.

7) McCoy dilutes the antidote with _____.

8) The space sector causes the _____ to malfunction.

9) The landing party wears _____ _____ on the *Defiant*.

10) _____ delivers Kirk's eulogy.

TRUE/FALSE

1) Spock disables a Tholian ship._____

2) McCoy believes that Kirk is dead._____

3) McCoy and Spock thank Kirk for his last orders._____

4) Spock believes that Jim is dead._____

5) Kirk's "ghost" appears in engineering._____

6) Kirk is thrown clear of the *Defiant.*_____

7) Uhura is the first crewman to go insane._____

8) The Tholians offer to help rescue Kirk._____

9) The Tholians have annexed this space sector._____

10) "The Tholian Web" won an Emmy Award._____

"Whom Gods Destroy"

1) The *Enterprise* is in orbit around
  a. Ardana   **b.** Elba II
  c. Excalbia   **d.** Exenar III

2) The chief administrator of the asylum is Governor
  a. Cory   **b.** Kodos
  c. Adams   **d.** Van Gelder

3) Garth is from the planet
  a. Ekos   **b.** Antos
  c. Izar   **d.** Triskelion

4) Garth held the rank of
  a. Captain   **b.** Admiral
  c. Commodore   **d.** Starship Fleet Captain

5) Garth's consort is
  a. Marta   **b.** Vina
  c. Shahna   **d.** Isis

6) The response to "Queen to Queen's level three" is
  a. King's Rook to Pawn level two
  b. Queen to King's level one
  c. King to Knight's level three
  d. Knight to Bishop four

7) Garth learned cellular transmutation on
  a. Izar
  b. Orion
  c. Antos IV
  d. Ekos

8) The Cochrane deceleration is a
  a. Law of physics
  b. Military tactic
  c. Myth
  d. School of engineering thought

9) Garth won a great victory on
  a. Axanar
  b. Ekos
  c. Izar
  d. Antos IV

10) There was a famous Romulan/Federation battle at
  a. Beta Trianguli
  b. Antos IV
  c. Tau Ceti
  d. Gamma Orion

_____ FILL-INS _____

1) Garth is played by _____ _____.

2) Garth makes Kirk his _____ _____.

3) _____ is played by Yvonne Craig.

4) Garth's crew committed _____.

5) Cory is portrayed by _____ _____.

_____ TRUE/FALSE _____

1) Garth transforms himself into Spock._____

2) The atmosphere of Elba II is poisonous._____

3) Marta is cured of her insanity._____

4) Marta tries to kill Spock._____

5) The *Enterprise* was bringing a revolutionary new drug to the asylum._____

—————— "The Way to Eden" ——————

1) Doctor Sevrin comes from the planet
- **a.** Elba II
- **b.** Tiburon
- **c.** Antos IV
- **d.** Daran V

2) Sevrin carries
- **a.** Choriomeningitis
- **b.** Rigellian Fever
- **c.** Falconschitzitis
- **d.** Sythococcus novae

3) Sevrin's people are looking for the planet
- **a.** Eden
- **b.** Adan
- **c.** Yonada
- **d.** Cheron

4) Chekov's first name is
- **a.** Sergi
- **b.** Alexi
- **c.** Egon
- **d.** Pavel

5) Sevrin's people follow the philosophy of
- **a.** IDIC
- **b.** One
- **c.** Nome
- **d.** Katra

6) Sevrin's people stole the spaceship
- **a.** *Paradise*
- **b.** *Le-lak*
- **c.** *Aurora*
- **d.** *Beagle*

7) Irini knew Chekov
- **a.** As a child
- **b.** At the Academy
- **c.** Aboard the *Reliant*
- **d.** On Omicron Ceti III

8) Adam is a gifted
- **a.** Writer
- **b.** Painter
- **c.** Poet
- **d.** Singer

9) Tongo Rad is interested in
- **a.** Fencing
- **b.** Botany
- **c.** Old weapons
- **d.** Books

10) Adam calls Kirk
- **a.** Captain
- **b.** Baby
- **c.** Dunsel
- **d.** Herbert

FILL-INS

1) Adam is played by _____ _____.

2) McCoy compares Sevrin to _____
_____.

3) Tongo Rad comes from the planet _____.

4) Rad's father is an _____.

5) Sevrin is an expert in _____.

6) Sevrin is portrayed by _____ _____.

7) The symbol of Adam's philosophy is an _____.

8) Sevrin knocks out the crew of the *Enterprise* by using
_____.

9) _____ is located in _____ space.

10) Chekov tells Irini to be _____ occasionally.

TRUE/FALSE

1) Sevrin is insane. _____

2) Spock sits in on a "session" with Sevrin's people.
_____

3) Kirk is sympathetic to Adam's goals. _____

4) Sevrin steals an *Enterprise* shuttle craft. _____

5) Irini dies from eating a poisonous plant. _____

"For the World Is Hollow
_____ and I Have Touched the Sky" _____

1) Natira's world is called
  a. Ardana
  c. Yonada

  b. Odona
  d. Shandara

2) McCoy contracts
  a. Sythococcus novae
  c. Xenopolycythemia

  b. Rigellian fever
  d. Choriomeningitis

3) Daran V has a population of
  a. 523,265,000
  c. 3,724,000,000

  b. 332,764,000
  d. 4,567,000,000

4) Natira falls in love with
  a. Kirk
  c. Spock

  b. Scotty
  d. McCoy

5) Natira's world will collide with Daran V within
  a. 360 days
  c. 396 days

  b. 325 days
  d. 365 days

6) Natira's people have been in flight for
  a. 10,000 years
  c. 5,000 years

  b. 2,000 years
  d. 7,000 years

7) McCoy's disease causes the production of
  a. Antigens
  c. A virus

  b. Excess red blood cells
  d. Excess white blood cells

8) The *Enterprise* is ordered away from Natira's world by
  a. Admiral Westerliet
  c. Commodore Stone

  b. Admiral Komack
  d. Commodore Stocker

9) Natira gives Kirk, Spock, and McCoy a powder made of
  a. Chemical compounds
  c. Herb derivatives

  b. Vegetables
  d. Dried fruit

10) The first person to know of McCoy's disease is
  a. M'Benga
  c. Kirk

  b. Chapel
  d. Spock

FILL-INS

1) McCoy is cured by the knowledge of the _____.

2) Natira and McCoy are _____.

3) _____ _____ plays Natira.

4) Natira's world is put back on course by _____.

5) Natira is the _____ _____ of her people.

TRUE/FALSE

1) Natira proposes to McCoy. _____

2) McCoy intends to stay with Natira. _____

3) Natira's people do not believe in hiding their feelings. _____

4) Natira's world is two hundred miles in diameter. _____

5) Spock supervises McCoy's cure. _____

"And the Children Shall Lead"

1) The *Enterprise* visits the planet
  a. Triacus
  b. Ardana
  c. Tau Epsilon
  d. Sarpeidon

2) The leader of the Federation scientific expedition was
  a. Prof. Wilson
  b. Prof. Daystrom
  c. Prof. Starnes
  d. Prof. Pearson

3) The last adult alive on the colony was
  a. Starnes
  b. Lee Yang
  c. Daystrom
  d. Pearson

4) Some of the members took
  a. Slyothin
  b. Cyalodin
  c. Tetralubisol
  d. Borgiathin

5) The children call the Gorgan
  a. The guardian   b. The friend
  c. Master   d. The Friendly Angel

6) The colony is located in the star system
  a. Tau Omega   b. Epsilon Indi
  c. Alpha Gamma   d. Delta Vega

7) McCoy is concerned about the children's
  a. Parents   b. Physical condition
  c. Lack of appetite   d. Psychological condition

8) The Gorgan intends to take over the planet
  a. Triacus   b. Ardana
  c. Marcos XII   d. Daran V

9) The children are suffering from
  a. Hysterical amnesia   b. Lacunar amnesia
  c. Psychotic delusions   d. Hypnotic suggestion

10) Kirk intends to take the children to
  a. Starbase 1   b. Starbase 2
  c. Starbase 3   d. Starbase 4

FILL-INS

1) Tommy is played by _____ _____.

2) The Gorgan's people made war in the _____ _____ system.

3) The children summon the Gorgan with a _____.

4) Kirk eats a small portion of _____ _____.

5) Lawyer _____ _____ played the Gorgan.

6) The Gorgan cannot survive without the _____.

7) The Gorgan manipulates the children's _____.

8) _____ sees daggers on the main view screen.

9) Starnes refers to the Gorgan as the _____ _____.

10) Kirk shows the children pictures of their _____.

TRUE/FALSE

1) The Gorgan is exposed by Spock. _____

2) The Gorgan can control a person's emotions. _____

3) The Gorgan enables the children to create illusions. _____

4) The children's parents all committed suicide. _____

5) Tommy's mother survived the Gorgan's attack. _____

"Day of the Dove"

1) Kirk and Kang meet on
  a. Delta Vega   **b.** The *Enterprise*
  c. Beta XIIA   **d.** Orion

2) Chekov claims to have a brother named
  a. Pavel   **b.** Piotr
  c. Sergi   **d.** Alexi

3) Chekov claims that his brother was killed
  a. In battle with a Klingon warship   **b.** In a laboratory accident
  c. In a Klingon prison camp   **d.** In a Klingon raid

4) The creature feeds off
  a. Energy   **b.** Hate
  c. Envy   **d.** Greed

5) Kang's science officer is
  a. Korax   **b.** Mara
  c. Koloth   **d.** Kahless

6) Kang has an agonizer used on
  a. Kirk   **b.** Spock
  c. McCoy   **d.** Chekov

7) The Klingons take over
  a. Sick bay   **b.** Weapons control
  c. Engineering   **d.** The bridge

8) The Klingons have no
   a. God
   c. Moses
   b. Jesus
   d. Satan

9) All the weapons on the *Enterprise* are converted into
   a. Swords
   c. Clubs
   b. Dust
   d. Guns

10) Scotty carries a
   a. .357 magnum
   c. Claymore
   b. Fencing foil
   d. Broadsword

FILL-INS

1) Mara is played by _____ _____.

2) Mara is attacked by _____.

3) The truce is arranged by _____.

4) Kang is played by _____ _____.

5) The final backup system on the *Enterprise* is _____ _____ _____.

6) Scotty attacks _____ out of racial hatred.

7) McCoy tells Kirk and Spock to act like _____ men.

8) The creature glows _____ when it feeds.

9) The creature will not allow anyone to _____.

10) Kang cuts off _____ _____ to the bridge.

TRUE/FALSE

1) The creature is driven off by goodwill. _____

2) The Klingons recently destroyed a Federation outpost. _____

3) Kirk has the Klingons suspended in transit. _____

4) Kirk has the Klingons put in the brig. _____

5) Mara is Kang's wife. _____

"Wink of an Eye"

1) The *Enterprise* is lured to Scalos by
   a. A space probe
   b. An invitation
   c. False life readings
   d. A distress signal

2) The Scalosians suffer from
   a. Psychosis
   b. Hyperacceleration
   c. Slowed metabolism
   d. Rapid aging

3) In their diseased state, Scalosians sound like
   a. Bells
   b. Tones
   c. Insects
   d. The wind

4) The queen of the Scalosians is
   a. Deela
   b. Drea
   c. Droxine
   d. Odona

5) The Scalosian disease is transmitted through
   a. The water
   b. The soil
   c. Food
   d. Perspiration

6) Scalos recently experienced
   a. An Ion storm
   b. Earthquakes
   c. Volcanic eruptions
   d. Tidal waves

7) The scientific leader of the Scalosians is
   a. Rojan
   b. Redjac
   c. Krako
   d. Rael

8) Scalos rates 7 on the
   a. Industrial scale
   b. Evolutionary scale
   c. Richter scale
   d. Intelligence scale

9) Rael is assisted by
   a. Deela
   b. Droxine
   c. Drea
   d. Ekor

10) The *Enterprise* is repaired by
   a. Spock
   b. Kirk
   c. Drea
   d. Droxine

FILL-INS

1) _____ is played by Kathie Brown.

2) The disease causes aliens to become _____ in nature.

3) The disease is caused by _____ released into the Scalosian ecological chain.

4) Rael is played by _____ _____.

5) The Scalosians intend to turn the *Enterprise* into a giant _____ _____.

TRUE/FALSE

1) Deela's weapon is faster than a phaser. _____

2) The Federation will quarantine Scalos until a cure for its people can be found. _____

3) Rael is jealous of Spock. _____

4) The Scalosians intend to use the *Enterprise* men as breeding stock. _____

5) The children of Scalos were immune to the disease. _____

6) "Wink of an Eye" aired during "Star Trek's" second season. _____

7) The Scalosian men are sterile. _____

8) McCoy is able to cure the Scalosians. _____

9) Aliens contracting the disease burn out rapidly. _____

10) The controls on the hangar deck are frozen. _____

"That Which Survives"

1) Losira's planet is
   a. Class D
   b. Class M
   c. Class F
   d. Class K

2) D'Amato is the ship's
   a. Botanist
   b. Geologist
   c. Security chief
   d. Archaeologist

3) Losira hurls the *Enterprise*
   a. 570 light-years away
   b. 325 light-years away
   c. 990.7 light-years away
   d. 765.9 light-years away

4) Losira kills Ensign
   a. Sanders
   b. Davis
   c. Bryson
   d. Wyatt

5) Losira's people came from
   a. Rigel
   b. Orion
   c. Sandara
   d. Kalanda

6) "That Which Survives" is
   a. Losira
   b. Kirk
   c. Beauty
   d. Hate

7) M'Benga also appears in the "Star Trek" episode entitled
   a. "Miri"
   b. "A Private Little War"
   c. "Friday's Child"
   d. "Bread and Circuses"

8) Losira damages the ship's
   a. Impulse engines
   b. Life support
   c. Matter antimatter inte-
      grator bypass control
   d. Dilithium regeneration
      chamber

9) Losira injures
   a. Kirk
   b. Spock
   c. McCoy
   d. Sulu

10) Sulu's relief helmsman is
   a. Lieutenant Glaeser
   b. Lieutenant Rahda
   c. Lieutenant Garetti
   d. Lieutenant Gray

FILL-INS

1) Losira is played by _____ _____.
2) Losira is a _____ _____.
3) The landing party believes that Losira may be a _____-based life form.
4) Spock hits his head against the _____ _____.
5) The *Enterprise* takes _____ hours to return to Losira's planet.

TRUE/FALSE

1) Losira cannot hurt a person she has not specifically come for. _____
2) Losira injures Kirk. _____
3) Spock has Uhura update her subspace report. _____
4) The autopsy on Wyatt is done by M'Benga. _____
5) Scotty stabilizes the ship's magnetic flow. _____

"The Cloud Minders"

1) The *Enterprise* must stop a plague on
   a. New Paris   b. Merak II
   c. Pison III   d. Deneb III

2) The plague affects
   a. Humans   b. Fish
   c. Warm blooded livestock   d. Plants

3) The *Enterprise* goes to the planet
   a. Ardana   b. Yonada
   c. Sandara   d. Sarpeidon

4) Plasus lives in the city of
- **a.** Cantos
- **c.** Stratos
- **b.** Ariel
- **d.** Ionos

5) The *Enterprise* has come for a shipment of
- **a.** Zienite
- **c.** Curanide
- **b.** Ryetalyn
- **d.** Pergium

6) The planet's high advisor is
- **a.** Droxine
- **c.** Vanna
- **b.** Plasus
- **d.** Anan 7

7) The cloud city is kept aloft by
- **a.** Rockets
- **c.** Updrafts
- **b.** Turbines
- **d.** Antigravity elevation

8) Plasus tortures
- **a.** Kirk
- **c.** Vanna
- **b.** Droxine
- **d.** Spock

9) Kirk offers to give the miners
- **a.** Money
- **c.** Protective clothing
- **b.** Filter masks
- **d.** Transportation

10) The members of the miners' underground are called
- **a.** Devastators
- **c.** Disruptors
- **b.** Destroyers
- **d.** Disharmonors

FILL-INS

1) The miners use hand weapons called _____.

2) The miners use throwing weapons called _____.

3) Plasus is played by _____ _____.

4) Vanna is the leader of the _____.

5) _____ is attracted to Spock.

6) Kirk kidnaps _____.

7) Vanna is played by _____ _____.

8) The miners suffer from mental _____.

9) Kirk tries to kill _____.

10) _____ _____ portrays Droxine.

TRUE/FALSE

1) Droxine decides to live among the Troglytes. _____

2) Vanna attempts to kidnap Spock. _____

3) The Troglytes are sensitive to sunlight. _____

4) Plasus orders Kirk to stay off the planet. _____

5) Troglytes can enter the cloud city at will. _____

"Requiem for Methuselah"

1) Rigellian fever resembles
   a. Legionnaire's disease   **b.** Vulcan plague
   c. Bubonic plague   **d.** Romulan plague

2) The only cure for Rigellian fever is
   a. Ryetalyn   **b.** Zienite
   c. Kironide   **d.** Pergium

3) Flint's planet is in the
   a. Alpha system   **b.** Beta system
   c. Delta System   **d.** Omega System

4) Reena has the equivalent of
   a. 5 university degrees   **b.** 11 university degrees
   c. 13 university degrees   **d.** 17 university degrees

5) Reena is adept at
   a. Eight-ball   **b.** Nine-ball
   c. Chicago   **d.** Billiards

6) Spock plays a waltz by
   a. Mozart   **b.** Brahms
   c. Bach   **d.** Wagner

7) Flint was the painter
   a. Van Gogh   **b.** Da Vinci
   c. Picasso   **d.** Kreelas

8) Flint purchased his planet under the name of
   a. Lazarus   **b.** Flint
   c. Brack   **d.** Kapec

9) Flint is over
    a. 3,000 years old   **b.** 6,000 years old
    c. 9,000 years old   **d.** 12,000 years old

10) Taranallus was born on
    a. Rigel IV   **b.** Tiburon
    c. Earth   **d.** Centauri VII

FILL-INS

1) Reena is a(n) _____.

2) Flint has a(n) _____ Bible.

3) Flint knew the astronomer _____.

4) Flint is played by _____ _____.

5) Spock helps Kirk _____.

6) Reena is killed by _____ _____.

7) Reena falls in love with _____.

8) Reena is played by _____ _____.

9) _____ is rendered inert by irillium.

10) The artist Sten comes from _____ _____.

TRUE/FALSE

1) Flint knew Moses. _____

2) Flint is now near death. _____

3) Flint's planet is called Holberg 917G. _____

4) Flint's screens give the planet the illusion of lifelessness. _____

5) Flint was Tycho Brahe. _____

6) Flint owns a Shakespeare First Folio. _____

7) Kirk blames Spock for Reena's death. _____

8) Reena is biologically human. _____

9) Kirk teaches Reena to feel. _____

10) Flint returns to Earth. _____

"The Savage Curtain"

1) The *Enterprise* visits Excalbia to investigate rumors that it
   a. Is about to explode
   b. Contains dilithium crystals
   c. Has life
   d. Is falling into its sun

2) The natives of Excalbia are made of
   a. Rock
   b. Crystal
   c. Steel
   d. Flesh

3) Lincoln was a hero of
   a. Sulu's
   b. Uhura's
   c. Kirk's
   d. Scotty's

4) The Excalbian native is named
   a. Selek
   b. Yarnek
   c. Kryton
   d. Cruton

5) The Excalbian creates an arena of
   a. 500 meters
   b. 700 meters
   c. 900 meters
   d. 1000 meters

6) Colonel Green led a genocidal war circa
   a. 1990–2000
   b. 2000–2100
   c. 2300–2325
   d. 1600–1650

7) Lincoln asks Kirk if he drinks
   a. Gin
   b. Bourbon
   c. Scotch
   d. Whiskey

8) On Excalbia, Spock meets the Vulcan philosopher
   a. Sarek
   b. Surak
   c. Seetar
   d. Sonak

9) The "evil" side is led by
   a. Green
   b. Zora
   c. Genghis Khan
   d. Kahless

10) The *Enterprise* is orbiting at around
   a. 763 miles
   b. 987 miles
   c. 643 miles
   d. 1,000 miles

FILL-INS

1) Zora experimented on subject tribes on _____.

2) Kahless lures Lincoln by imitating _____.

3) Nome is a philosophy meaning _____.

4) Green is played by _____ _____.

5) Lincoln is played by _____ _____.

TRUE/FALSE

1) The Excalbians wish to study the concept of good and evil. _____

2) The Excalbians are carbon-cycle life forms. _____

3) Kirk goes after Surak. _____

4) Lincoln attempts to make peace with the "evil" side. _____

5) Lincoln is delighted to find that he can still wrestle. _____

"The *Enterprise* Incident"

1) In his medical log, McCoy states that Kirk is suffering extreme
   a. Pain
   b. Exhaustion
   c. Lethargy
   d. Tension

2) Kirk resists McCoy's attempts to conduct a
   a. Physical examination
   b. Psychological profile
   c. Psycho simulator test
   d. Psychotricorder test

3) The Romulan flagship sends the *Enterprise* a
   a. Code 1 directive
   b. Class 2 signal
   c. Class 4 interrogative
   d. Code 6 message

4) Tal holds the rank of
   a. Praetor
   b. Centurion
   c. Commander
   d. Subcommander

5) The Romulan commander accuses Kirk of
    a. Creating an interstellar war
    b. Espionage
    c. Treason
    d. Murder

6) A subspace message from the neutral zone would reach Starfleet in about
    a. 1 month
    b. 3 weeks
    c. 2 weeks
    d. 1 week

7) Kirk is "betrayed" by
    a. McCoy
    b. Sulu
    c. Starfleet
    d. Spock

8) Kirk crossed the neutral zone on
    a. Orders from Starfleet
    b. Orders from the Federation Council
    c. His own
    d. Receiving a distress signal

9) Kirk disguises himself as a Romulan
    a. Commander
    b. Subcommander
    c. Centurion
    d. Lieutenant

10) The Romulan commander offers Spock
    a. Immunity
    b. His own ship
    c. Information
    d. Lunch

FILL-INS

1) Kirk orders Sulu to cross the _____ _____.

2) The Romulans have knowledge of certain Starfleet _____.

3) The Commander invites Spock to _____.

4) The cloaking device is stolen by _____.

5) McCoy revives Kirk with a _____ _____.

6) Spock demands the Romulan _____ _____ _____.

7) Scotty installs the cloaking device in the _____ control unit.

8) The *Enterprise* breaks away from the Romulan task force at warp _____.

9) Spock pleads guilty to _____.

10) It is said that a Vulcan cannot _____.

TRUE/FALSE

1) Kirk is having a breakdown. _____

2) McCoy knows Kirk's plans from the beginning.
_____

3) Scotty threatens to kill his Romulan guests. _____

4) Spock seduces the Romulan commander. _____

5) The Vulcan death grip is an ancient form of execution.
_____

6) Kirk runs into a force field. _____

7) Ship's stores produce a Romulan uniform for Kirk.
_____

8) Kirk gives Scotty 5 minutes to install the cloaking device.
_____

9) Tal is second officer on board the Romulan flagship.
_____

10) Romulan interrogation techniques would be ineffective against Kirk. _____

"Patterns of Force"

1) **John Gill is a famous**
   a. Scientist
   c. Historian
   b. Doctor
   d. Anthropologist

2) **At Starfleet Academy Gill instructed**
   a. Spock
   c. Scotty
   b. Kirk
   d. McCoy

3) **Gill has been out of touch with the Federation for**
   a. 6 months
   c. 2 years
   b. 1 year
   d. 9 months

4) Kirk and Spock are equipped with
   a. Psycho tricorders
   c. Phaser II
   b. A medi-kit
   d. A subcutaneous transponder

5) John Gill was sent by the Federation as a(n)
   a. Cultural observer
   c. Ambassador
   b. Scientific advisor
   d. Military attaché

6) The power behind the throne on Ekos is
   a. Eneg
   c. Melakon
   b. Daras
   d. Gill

7) II Daras is awarded the Iron Cross
   a. First class
   c. Third class
   b. Second class
   d. Fourth class

8) The dictator of Ekos is
   a. Eneg
   c. Melakon
   b. John Gill
   d. Davod

9) The leader of the Zeon underground is
   a. Isak
   c. Abram
   b. Davod
   d. Micha

10) Isak was to marry a woman named
   a. Dion
   c. Daras
   b. Uletta
   d. Sheba**

FILL-INS

1) Daras betrayed her _____.

2) Gill denounces _____ as a traitor.

3) McCoy poses as a Gestapo _____.

4) Kirk and Spock use _____ crystals to make a crude laser.

5) _____ is working with the Zeon underground.

6) Kirk steals a _____ uniform.

7) Gill is killed by _____.

8) The Enterprise is in _____ orbit around
   _____.

9) _____ was shot down in the street.

10) Zeons are, by nature, extremely _____.

_____ TRUE/FALSE _____

1) Spock uses Kirk's back as a platform. _____

2) Kirk and Spock are interrogated by a Nazi major.
   _____

3) McCoy has trouble putting on his tunic. _____

4) Daras is a "traitor" to the Party. _____

5) Ekosians are advanced technologically. _____

6) Eneg is the minister of propaganda. _____

7) Gill was drugged by Eneg. _____

8) Zeon is technologically backward. _____

9) Zeons find killing repulsive. _____

10) McCoy injects Gill with a general stimulant. _____

_____ "Plato's Stepchildren" _____

1) **The food on Platonius contains**
   a. Ryetalyn
   b. Pergium
   c. Kironide
   d. Zienite

2) **Parmen suffers a massive infection brought on by**
   a. A fractured leg
   b. Frostbite
   c. A broken tooth
   d. A scratch

3) **Platonians have the power of**
   a. Psychokinesis
   b. Illusion
   c. Telepathy
   d. Matter transmutation

4) **Parmen's slave is named**
   a. Decius
   b. Cracus
   c. Alexander
   d. Flavius

5) **Parmen's home world was the planet**
   a. Ardana
   b. Sandara
   c. Sarpeidon
   d. Cheron

6) Philana stopped aging at
   a. 30   **b.** 25
   c. 20   **d.** 35

7) The Platonian's power comes from
   a. Zienite   **b.** Ryetalyn
   c. Solar energy   **d.** Kironide

8) Parmen presents Kirk with a
   a. Sword   **b.** Shield
   c. Lyre   **d.** Scroll

9) Parmen gives Spock a
   a. Scroll   **b.** Flute
   c. Lyre   **d.** Shield

10) Philana is
   a. 2,000 years old   **b.** 2,100 years old
   c. 2,200 years old   **d.** 2,300 years old

FILL-INS

1) Parmen wants to keep _____ on Platonius permanently.

2) McCoy is presented with a scroll penned by _____.

3) Parmen is played by _____ _____.

4) Parmen forces Kirk to quote the poet, _____.

5) Alexander is portrayed by _____ _____.

TRUE/FALSE

1) Parmen is the leader of Platonius. _____

2) Kirk defeats Parmen in a psychokinetic duel. _____

3) Spock is immune to the Platonians' power. _____

4) Philana is Parmen's sister. _____

5) Parmen forces Spock to exhibit emotions. _____

PHOTO QUIZ

1) Where does Kirk say Spock comes from?

2) Name this creature's planet.

3) Name McCoy's opponent.

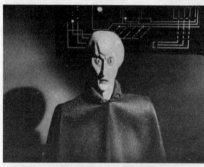

4) Name this character's alter ego.

5) What planet is Spock on?

6) What weapon is Spock holding?

7) Where are Kirk and Spock?

8) Name the episode.

9) Where are they?

10) Name the episode.

11) What is Spock's musical instrument called?

12) What is Nurse Chapel preparing?

13) McCoy's devices are really exotic _____ .

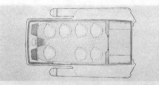

14) The *Galileo* was destroyed in which episode?

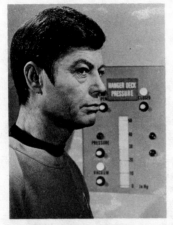

15) Give McCoy's location.

16) Kirk's next move should have been _____.

17) What space station is Kirk on?

18) In which episode does Kirk first wear dress blues?

19) In which episode did Kirk use a phasefire?

20) Where are Spock and McCoy?

21) What is Kirk's serial number?

22) Name this episode.

23) Where is Spock?

24) Identify this episode.

25) What is Scotty's favorite pastime?

26) Name this episode.

27) Sulu is first seen in which episode?

28) In "Amok Time," Kirk risks his career to take Spock to which planet?

29) What is the maximum safe cruising speed of the U.S.S. *Enterprise*?

30) What is Chekov's rank in this episode?

STAR TREK—THE MOTION PICTURE

1) V'ger is first approached by
   a. Three Klingon warships   **b.** An unmanned probe
   c. The *Enterprise*   **d.** Romulan ships

2) V'ger's destination is
   a. Vulcan   **b.** Rigel
   c. Eminiar   **d.** Earth

3) The first Federation outpost to monitor V'ger is
   a. Starbase 12   **b.** Earth Outpost 4
   c. Epsilon 9   **d.** Earth Colony 3

4) V'ger fires bolts composed of
   a. Fire   **b.** Plasma energy
   c. Light   **d.** Solar radiation

5) At the beginning of the film, Spock is on
   a. The *Enterprise*   **b.** Vulcan
   c. Epsilon IX   **d.** Leave

6) Spock is undergoing
   a. Retraining
   b. The Kahs-wan
   c. The Kohlinahr
   d. The Pon farr

7) The Klingon flagship is called
   a. *Amar*
   b. *Hunter*
   c. *Denar*
   d. *Striker*

8) *Star Trek—The Motion Picture* was directed by
   a. Harve Bennett
   b. Robert Wise
   c. Leonard Nimoy
   d. Gene Roddenberry

9) *Star Trek—The Motion Picture* introduces
   a. Persis Khambatta
   b. Kirstie Alley
   c. Robin Curtis
   d. Steve Collins

10) Spock's mind is touched by
   a. Kirk
   b. Sarek
   c. V'ger
   d. Ilia

11) Starfleet Headquarters is in
   a. New York
   b. San Francisco
   c. Chicago
   d. Houston

12) Kirk goes to Starfleet Headquarters to see Admiral
   a. Nagura
   b. Komack
   c. Winters
   d. Giovanni

13) The *Enterprise* must leave Earth within
   a. 24 hours
   b. 2 days
   c. 12 hours
   d. 1 week

14) The *Enterprise* refit took
   a. 5 years
   b. 7 months
   c. 2 years
   d. 18 months

15) The new captain of the *Enterprise* was to have been
   a. Sulu
   b. Decker
   c. Scotty
   d. Spock

16) The *Enterprise* must intercept V'ger within
   a. 5 days
   b. 3 days
   c. 4 days
   d. 1 day

17) Kirk refers to the command chair as
  a. Home
  b. Luxurious
  c. The center seat
  d. Uncomfortable

18) Decker takes a temporary grade reduction to
  a. Lieutenant
  b. Commander
  c. Lieutenant commander
  d. Chief

19) For a short time, Decker functions as the ship's
  a. Engineering officer
  b. Security chief
  c. Science officer
  d. Helmsman

20) Decker is Kirk's
  a. Executive officer
  b. Nephew
  c. Protégé
  d. Weapons officer

21) Upon reaching the *Enterprise,* Kirk goes directly to
  a. See Decker
  b. Sick bay
  c. The bridge
  d. His quarters

22) Sonak is killed in
  a. A V'ger attack
  b. A transporter accident
  c. A fight
  d. His sleep

23) Kirk orders the entire ship's crew to be assembled at
  a. 0400 hours
  b. 1200 hours
  c. 0800 hours
  d. 1100 hours

24) The *Enterprise* transporter chief is
  a. Lieutenant Kyle
  b. Janice Rand
  c. Chief DiFalco
  d. Chekov

25) Chekov is the ship's
  a. Transporter chief
  b. Weapons chief
  c. Navigator
  d. Helmsman

26) V'ger's powerfield is _____ in diameter
  a. 3 parsecs
  b. 25 A.U.s
  c. 82 A.U.s
  d. 5 parsecs

27) Ilia comes from the planet
  a. Delta IV
  b. Organia
  c. Orion
  d. Andoria

28) Before Ilia can enter Starfleet, she has to file an oath of
 a. Allegiance
 b. Loyalty
 c. Celibacy
 d. Obedience

29) When McCoy boards the *Enterprise,* he is wearing
 a. A uniform
 b. A hat
 c. A beard
 d. Dress blues

30) Phaser power is channeled through the ship's
 a. Deflector units
 b. Impulse engines
 c. Computer
 d. Warp engines

31) Kirk has not logged a single star hour in
 a. 6 months
 b. 5½ years
 c. 1 year,
 3 months
 d. 2½ years

32) Spock is greeted on the hangar deck by
 a. Kirk
 b. Sulu
 c. Decker
 d. Chekov

33) Chapel is now a
 a. Research biologist
 b. Doctor
 c. Surgical nurse
 d. Chief medical officer

34) The ship's warp engines are repaired by
 a. Scotty
 b. Decker
 c. Spock
 d. Sonak

35) V'ger generates
 a. Twelfth-level energy
 b. Fifth-level energy
 c. Tenth-level energy
 d. Unlimited energy

36) *Star Trek—The Motion Picture* was produced by
 a. Robert Wise
 b. Harve Bennett
 c. Gene Roddenberry
 d. Howard B. Sowards

37) All sensors directed at V'ger are
 a. Analyzed
 b. Reflected back
 c. Absorbed
 d. Ignored

38) V'ger sends a probe to the *Enterprise* in the form of
 a. Ilia
 b. Decker
 c. Kirk
 d. Spock

39) V'ger kills
  a. Sonak
  c. Sulu
  b. Nogura
  d. Ilia

40) V'ger tries to communicate with the *Enterprise* on a frequency of
  a. MHZ 25,000
  c. MHZ 1 million
  b. MHZ 300,000
  d. MHZ 6 million

FILL-INS

1) McCoy refuses to get into the _____.

2) The transporter breaks down because of a _____ _____.

3) Jim is first taken over to the *Enterprise* by Commander _____.

4) When the ship's engines go into antimatter imbalance, a _____ may result.

5) Will Decker is played by _____ _____.

6) Spock's shuttle has a grade _____ priority.

7) Ilia is replaced by _____ _____.

8) V'ger is searching for its _____.

9) V'ger intends to reduce the crew of the *Enterprise* to _____ _____.

10) V'ger was originally the NASA probe _____ _____.

11) Spock steals a _____ _____.

12) V'ger's first probe is composed of _____ _____.

13) The *Enterprise* is drawn inside V'ger by a _____ _____.

14) Spock compares V'ger to a _____.

15) Spock attempts to mind meld with the _____ _____.

16) McCoy complains that engineers love to _____
_____.

17) Kirk meets Commander _____ at Starfleet Headquarters.

18) Sonak's family can be reached through the _____
_____.

19) Chekov's pain is eased by _____.

20) Kirk lists Decker and Ilia as _____.

TRUE/FALSE

---

1) Klingons use a D-7 class battle cruiser to approach V'ger.
_____

2) Kirk does not want to return as captain of the *Enterprise*.
_____

3) Spock does not complete the Kohlinahr. _____

4) Ilia has empathic powers. _____

5) Spock weeps for V'ger. _____

6) V'ger wishes to destroy its creator. _____

7) V'ger signals Earth by subspace radio. _____

8) Decker joins with V'ger through the Ilia probe.
_____

9) A thruster suit's burn duration is 30 seconds.
_____

10) Spock suggests that Kirk treat V'ger like a child.
_____

11) The *Enterprise* passes to within 500 meters of V'ger.
_____

12) V'ger destroys a space station. _____

13) The entire ship's crew is assembled on the Recreation Deck.
_____

14) The Kohlinahr is the discipline that teaches Vulcans to live
with their emotions. _____

15) Decker is in love with Ilia. _____

16) V'ger asks: "Is this all that I am?" _____

17) Scotty rigs the *Enterprise* to self-destruct. _____

18) Admiral Nogura approaches Kirk about resuming command of the *Enterprise*. _____

19) Kirk has been chief of Starfleet Operations for 2 years. _____

20) The *Enterprise* shields withstand 2 of V'ger's force bolts. _____

21) Chekov destroys the asteroid in the wormhole with the ship's phasers. _____

22) V'ger originally came from Earth. _____

23) The *Enterprise* comes back from her mission completely intact. _____

24) Spock decides to return to Vulcan. _____

STAR TREK II: THE WRATH OF KHAN

1) *Star Trek II* **takes place in the**
    a. 21st century   **b.** 22d century
    c. 23d century   **d.** 25th century

2) *Star Trek II* **introduces**
    a. Kirstie Alley   **b.** Persis Khambatta
    c. Robin Curtis   **d.** Bibi Besch

3) **The "no win scenario" is also known as**
    a. The Murasaki effect   **b.** The Kobayashi Maru
    c. The Mutara nebula   **d.** Final exams

4) **The only cadet ever to beat the no win scenario was**
    a. Spock   **b.** Saavik
    c. Kirk   **d.** Pike

5) **Spock gives Kirk a book for**
    a. His anniversary as captain   **b.** His retirement
    c. No reason   **d.** His birthday

6) **The title of the book is**
    a. *Hamlet*   **b.** *Wuthering Heights*
    c. *War and Peace*   **d.** *A Tale of Two Cities*

7) The *Enterprise* is scheduled for
    a. Refitting   **b.** A training cruise
    c. War games   **d.** Routine maintenance

8) Kirk attempted the no win scenario
    a. 1 time   **b.** 2 times
    c. 3 times   **d.** 4 times

9) At the beginning of *Star Trek II*, the captain of the *Enterprise* is
    a. Kirk   **b.** Spock
    c. Sulu   **d.** Decker

10) Kirk is visited in his apartment by
    a. McCoy   **b.** Spock
    c. Saavik   **d.** Carol

11) Kirk is allergic to
    a. Tri-ox   **b.** Retinax 5
    c. Ryetalyn   **d.** Entulin

12) McCoy gives Kirk a bottle of
    a. Saurian brandy   **b.** Jack Daniels
    c. Klingon scotch   **d.** Romulan ale

13) Saavik observes that Kirk is very
    a. Stubborn   **b.** Handsome
    c. Tired   **d.** Human

14) The first officer of the *Reliant* is
    a. Kyle   **b.** Stonn
    c. Terrell   **d.** Chekov

15) The serial number on the primary hull of *Reliant* is
    a. NCC-1702   **b.** NCC-1864
    c. NCC-007   **d.** NCC-1812

16) The *Reliant* is en route to
    a. Ceti Alpha V   **b.** Alpha Ceti V
    c. Ceti Alpha VI   **d.** Alpha Ceti VI

17) The *Reliant* is searching for a test site for
    a. A new starship   **b.** A new weapon
    c. The Armageddon device   **d.** The Genesis device

18) Chekov and Terrell are captured by
   a. Joachim
   c. Khan
   b. David
   d. Kirk

19) Khan's wife was killed by
   a. Hostile natives
   c. Kirk
   b. A Ceti eel
   d. An earthquake

20) The Botany Bay was lost in space (No pun intended) in the year
   a. 2020
   c. 1996
   b. 2135
   d. 2283

21) Six month's after Khan's people were set down on Ceti Alpha V, Ceti Alpha VI
   a. Exploded
   c. Collided with a meteor
   b. Fell into her sun
   d. Shifted her orbit

22) Khan's wife was former Starfleet Lieutenant
   a. Helen Noel
   c. Areel Shaw
   b. Marla McGivers
   d. Caroline Palamas

23) Ceti eels enter the body through the
   a. Blood
   c. Ears
   b. Mouth
   d. Nose

24) Once inside the body, the eels wrap themselves around
   a. The medulla
   c. Spinal cord
   b. The cerebral cortex
   d. Heart

25) Scotty has recently had a wee bout of
   a. Scotch
   c. Heart trouble
   b. Shore leave
   d. Flu

26) The *Enterprise* is piloted out of space dock by
   a. Spock
   c. Chekov
   b. Kirk
   d. Saavik

27) Saavik is half Vulcan, half
   a. Human
   c. Romulan
   b. Klingon
   d. Orion

28) Saavik is addressed as
   a. Miss
   c. Ms.
   b. Mr.
   d. Mrs.

29) Khan's second in command is
   a. Avram   **b.** Marla
   c. Joachim   **d.** Ari

30) Khan is fond of quoting from
   a. *Moby Dick*   **b.** Shakespeare
   c. Dickens   **d.** *Tale of Two Cities*

31) Khan and his people were marooned for
   a. 10 years   **b.** 20 years
   c. 15 years   **d.** 25 years

32) Starfleet has kept the peace for
   a. 50 years   **b.** 100 years
   c. 200 years   **d.** 300 years

33) Jim Kirk is David's
   a. Commander   **b.** Friend
   c. Father   **d.** Uncle

34) *Star Trek II* was directed by
   a. Leonard Nimoy   **b.** Harve Bennett
   c. Jack B. Sowards **d.** Nicholas Meyer

35) *Reliant*'s prefix code is
   a. 111-007   **b.** 16309
   c. 402   **d.** -999 765

36) The young cadet killed during *Reliant*'s first attack on the *Enterprise* is
   a. Peter Preston   **b.** Paul Winfield
   c. John Cayton   **d.** Phil Potter

37) Regula is a class _____ planet
   a. M   **b.** C
   c. D   **d.** 7

38) The closing narration of *Star Trek II* is read by
   a. William Shatner   **b.** Leonard Nimoy
   c. DeForest Kelly   **d.** Gene Roddenberry

39) Carol observes that David and Kirk are
   a. Completely different   **b.** A lot alike
   c. Never going to get along **d.** Competing with each
                               other

40) Terrell kills
a. Khan
b. The Regula scientists
c. Joachim
d. Himself

41) Kirk and Khan take their battle into
a. Other dimensions
b. The Neutral Zone
c. Klingon space
d. The Mutara nebula

42) Spock dies of
a. Radiation poisoning
b. Phaser wounds
c. A progressive disease
d. Gas inhalation

43) Kirk doesn't like
a. David
b. Saavik
c. To lose
d. Waiting

44) From the time it is armed, the Genesis device takes
_____ **to detonate**
a. 30 seconds
b. 2 minutes
c. 4 minutes
d. 10 minutes

45) At the end of *Star Trek II*, **Kirk feels**
a. Depressed
b. Young
c. Old
d. Angry

_____ **Fill-Ins** _____

1) Spock believes that there are always _____.

2) The _____ of the _____ outweigh the
_____ of the _____.

3) Carol Marcus is played by _____ _____.

4) The head of Project Genesis is _____
_____.

5) McCoy gives Kirk a pair of _____.

6) "I have been and always shall be your _____."

7) Spock mind melds with _____.

8) Ceti eels killed _____ of Khan's people.

9) Two hundred years ago, Khan was a _____.

10) Ceti eels render the victim susceptible to _____.

11) Kirk originally found Khan in a state of _____
_____.

12) Khan orders Terrell to kill _____.

13) Kirk tells McCoy that the first order of business is
_____.

14) Kirk uses the prefix code to make *Reliant* _____
_____ _____.

15) Khan swears to avenge _____.

16) The Genesis planet forms using matter from the
_____ _____.

17) At Spock's funeral, Scotty plays _____
_____.

18) In his quarters, Kirk offers David a _____.

19) Chekov's first name is _____.

20) *Star Trek II* was written by _____ _____.

TRUE/FALSE

1) In this movie Khan and Kirk never meet face to face.
_____

2) Once activated, the Genesis device can be disarmed.
_____

3) Carol Marcus was Kirk's wife. _____

4) David has never trusted Starfleet. _____

5) David refers to Kirk as an overgrown Boy Scout.
_____

6) McCoy thinks that Kirk should retire. _____

7) Chekov blames Kirk for Terrell's death. _____

8) Khan steals the Genesis device. _____

9) Khan finally makes peace with Kirk. _____

10) There is enough food in the Genesis cave to last a lifetime.
_____

11) The second phase of the Genesis experiment was to take
place on the surface of a dead planet. _____

12) General Order 4 states that no flag officer may enter a hazardous area without an armed escort. _____

13) There is a Klingon proverb, "Revenge is a dish best served cold." _____

14) Carol and Jim rekindle their affair. _____

15) David never reconciles with his father. _____

16) Kirk beat the no win scenario by changing the simulator program. _____

17) Khan has two-dimensional thought patterns. _____

18) The *Enterprise* first approaches *Reliant* with her shields raised. _____

19) Peter Preston stayed at his post. _____

20) Peter Preston is brought to the bridge by Saavik. _____

STAR TREK III: THE SEARCH FOR SPOCK

1) At the beginning of the film, the *Enterprise* is headed for
   a. Starbase 12   b. Starbase 9
   c. Earth   d. Vulcan

2) Spock's quarters are on
   a. D deck   b. C deck
   c. H deck   d. A deck

3) David and Saavik are on
   a. Earth   b. Starbase 9
   c. The *Excelsior*   d. The *Grissom*

4) The intruder in Spock's quarters is
   a. McCoy   b. Chekov
   c. David   d. Kirk

5) The Vulcan spirit is called
   a. Mantra   b. Kata
   c. Katra   d. Bodan

6) Spock placed his spirit in
   a. Kirk   b. McCoy
   c. Saavik   d. Sarek

7) Kirk is visited in his apartment by
a. Nogura
b. Morrow
c. Sarek
d. Amanda

8) The *Enterprise* should take _____ to refit
a. 2 weeks
b. 3 weeks
c. 8 weeks
d. 7 weeks

9) Scotty tells Kirk that he can refit the *Enterprise* in
a. 5 weeks
b. 4 weeks
c. 3 weeks
d. 2 weeks

10) The *Enterprise* is due to be
a. Overhauled
b. Decommissioned
c. Redesigned
d. Turned into a museum

11) McCoy begs Kirk to take him to
a. Mount Seleya
b. Sick bay
c. Earth
d. A bar

12) Sarek mind melds with
a. Spock
b. McCoy
c. Kirk
d. Saavik

13) A prime ingredient in the Genesis planet is
a. Protomatter
b. Antimatter
c. Dilithium
d. Corbomite

14) Kruge receives the Genesis tape from
a. A Starfleet informer
b. Maltz
c. Torg
d. Valkris

15) The *Grissom*'s sensors detect
a. No life on Genesis
b. Plant life on Genesis
c. Animal life on Genesis
d. Aquatic life on Genesis

16) The *Enterprise* is visited by
a. Komack
b. Nogura
c. Morrow
d. J. T. Esteban

17) The *Grissom* is a
a. Scout ship
b. Constitution class starship
c. Destroyer
d. Scientific research vessel

18) The *Grissom* is commanded by
    a. J. T. Esteban
    c. Commander Kyle
    b. Commander Morrow
    d. Captain Terrell

19) The Genesis planet is located in the
    a. Ceti Alpha sector
    c. Murasaki sector
    b. Mutara region
    d. Inchon region

20) The Genesis planet is
    a. Class M
    c. Perfect
    b. Class D
    d. Unstable

21) Spock's casket is
    a. 7 meters long
    c. 4 meters long
    b. 3 meters long
    d. 5 meters long

22) Sarek accuses Kirk of denying Spock his
    a. Life
    c. Family
    b. Past
    d. Future

23) The Genesis planet is subject to
    a. Rapid aging
    c. Floods
    b. Rapid shrinkage
    d. Rotation shifts

24) Kruge commands a Klingon
    a. Destroyer
    c. D-7 class starship
    b. Scout
    d. Bird of Prey

25) Kruge holds the rank of
    a. Captain
    c. Lord
    b. Commander
    d. Subcommander

26) The *Excelsior* is equipped with
    a. Cryotubes
    c. Multitronics
    b. 12 shuttle craft
    d. Transwarp drive

27) The *Excelsior* is commanded by
    a. Sulu
    c. Captain Styles
    b. Morrow
    d. J. T. Esteban

28) Morrow holds the service rank of
    a. Captain
    c. Admiral
    b. Commander, Starfleet
    d. Commissioner

29) Genesis is declared
  a. An open world
  b. Off limits
  c. An anomaly
  d. A success

30) Scotty is assigned to
  a. The *Enterprise*
  b. The *Grissom*
  c. The *Excelsior*
  d. Starfleet Headquarters

31) Kirk's apartment is in
  a. New York
  b. San Francisco
  c. Chicago
  d. Dallas

32) In Spock's casket, Saavik and David find
  a. Spock
  b. A tricorder
  c. Nothing
  d. A burial robe

33) Scotty sabotages the *Excelsior*'s
  a. Transwarp engines
  b. Transwarp computer
  c. Dilithium converter
  d. Antimatter control

34) Kirk pleads with Morrow to
  a. Get him a new ship
  b. Take him to Vulcan
  c. Restore the *Enterprise* immediately
  d. Let him go to Genesis

35) McCoy goes to an Earth
  a. Doctor
  b. Night club
  c. Chapel
  d. Port

36) McCoy likes to drink
  a. Scotch
  b. Vodka
  c. Antarian bourbon
  d. Altair water

37) Saavik and David are caught in
  a. A sandstorm
  b. A hurricane
  c. A blizzard
  d. A tornado

38) Spock's death occurred on stardate
  a. 8128.9
  b. 8128.53
  c. 8128.78
  d. 8128.67

39) The Vulcan child cannot
  a. Walk
  b. Think
  c. Speak
  d. See

40) The *Grissom* hails Starfleet Command on subspace coded channel
    a. 91.1   **b.** 95.5
    c. 98.8   **d.** 90.9

41) The Klingon ship has a crew of
    a. 20   **b.** 12
    c. 10   **d.** 18

42) Sulu doesn't like to be called
    a. Sir   **b.** Captain
    c. Inept   **d.** Tiny

43) Kirk injects McCoy with
    a. Tri-ox   **b.** Lexorin
    c. Hyronolin   **d.** Retinax

44) Kirk injects McCoy in the
    a. Gluteus maximus   **b.** Arm
    c. Neck   **d.** Thumb

45) Scotty rigs a control center to the *Enterprise*'s
    a. Command chair   **b.** Navigation station
    c. Communications station   **d.** Library computer

46) The adolescent Spock suffers from
    a. Pon farr   **b.** Fal tor pan
    c. Tal Shaya   **d.** Kal if far

47) The High Priestess on Vulcan is
    a. T'Pau   **b.** T'Pring
    c. T'Lar   **d.** T'Wan

48) After starting the ship's destruct sequence, Kirk and his people must evacuate within
    a. 2 minutes   **b.** 1 minute
    c. 3 minutes   **d.** 5 minutes

49) Kirk tells McCoy that he is the victim of
    a. Plak tow   **b.** A Vulcan mind meld
    c. A practical joke   **d.** A nervous breakdown

50) David is killed with a
    a. Phaser   **b.** Disruptor
    c. Dagger   **d.** Sword

FILL-INS

1) Kirk's first destruct sequence is _____.

2) Chekov's destruct sequence is _____.

3) Scotty's destruct sequence is _____.

4) The final destruct sequence is _____.

5) _____ is considered to be unstable.

6) Spock is subject to rapid _____.

7) Valkris and Kruge were _____.

8) The *Enterprise* is chased by the U.S.S. _____.

9) The Starfleet transporter room is manned by _____.

10) Kruge executes his ship's _____.

11) _____ conditions on Genesis are unstable.

12) The refusion takes a Vulcan _____.

13) Kruge is played by _____ _____.

14) Sarek believes that Spock joined with _____.

15) Sarek is portrayed by _____ _____.

16) Kirk toasts _____ _____.

17) The Vulcan High Priestess is played by _____ _____.

18) Kruge's first officer is _____.

19) McCoy is set free by _____.

TRUE/FALSE

1) The Genesis planet cannot survive. _____

2) Kruge is killed by Spock. _____

3) Kirk receives word that no charges will be pressed against him. _____

4) Kruge wanted to take prisoners from the *Grissom*. _____

5) From 5 to 0, no order in the universe can countermand the destruct order. _____

6) Kirk takes David's body back to Earth. _____

7) Kirk brings the Bird of Prey back intact. _____

8) Spock calls Jim by name. _____

9) Kirk believes that the needs of the one outweighed the needs of the many. _____

10) The refusion is not dangerous. _____

11) Sarek takes part in the refusion. _____

12) Sarek admits to emotions where Spock is concerned. _____

13) The refusion is only partially successful. _____

14) Kirk detects the Klingon ship through an energy distortion. _____

15) Kirk tries to save Kruge's life. _____

FOR THE EXPERTS

Identify the episode and the speaker associated with each of the following quotes:

1) "Don't you think I know that?"
2) "I have killed my Captain . . . and my friend."
3) "Beware Romulans bearing gifts."
4) "I never will understand the medical mind."
5) "It would have been glorious."
6) "I found one quite sufficient."
7) "I would advise youse to shut up and keep dialin'."
8) "It is said thy Vulcan blood is thin."
9) "I never get involved with older women."
10) "Are thee human, or are thee Vulcan?"
11) "I will render Kathleen . . . One . . . More . . . Time!!"
12) "How can you be deaf with ears like those."
13) "Don't call me tiny."
14) "This'll be your big chance to get away from it all."
15) "The play's the thing wherein we'll catch the conscience of the king."
16) "You couldn't pronounce it."
17) "You are the Creator."

18) "All of Vulcan in one package."
19) "See what you've done to me."
20) "I'm taking the center seat."
21) "You have been called the best first officer in the fleet."
22) "He is mad . . . Or I am. It depends on your point of view."
23) "She must have been a pearl of great price."
24) "Have you read Milton, Captain?"
25) "Regards to Captain Dunsel."
26) "You never told me your first name, Mr. Spock."
27) "The result was a wrecked ship and a dead crew."
28) "We could have roamed the stars together."
29) "You'll never understand the things that love can drive some-one to."
30) "There are a million things in this universe you can have, and a million things you can't have."
31) "All I ask is a tall ship and a star to steer her by."
32) "The man is the center of all things."
33) "It should be hauled away . . . as garbage."
34) "It seemed like the logical thing to do."
35) "The child is yours."
36) "You don't run a starship with your hands, you run it with your head."
37) "Shut up Spock. We're rescuing you."
38) "I want more of these Kirk . . . Many more."
39) "I'm stimulating him."
40) "Pray you die easily."
41) "You either believe in yourself, or you don't."
42) "It's hard to believe a man could die of loneliness."
43) "Welcome to Olympus, Captain Kirk."
44) "She'll kill you if you love her."
45) "We are much alike, Captain, you and I."
46) "Brain and brain! What is brain."
47) "I'm not going to kill . . . today."
48) "He killed my father . . . and my mother."
49) "Let bloody vengeance take its final course."
50) "I'm putting the bag on Krako."
51) "It is a thing to do. Like feeding Val."
52) "Behold the God who bleeds."
53) "This is how I define unwarranted."
54) "I am for you James Kirk."
55) "Androids don't eat Miss Chapel."
56) "Madness has no purpose."
57) "He's my lover and I have to kill him."

58) "Love and compassion are dead in you. You're nothing but intellect."

59) "This . . . unit . . . must . . . die!"

60) "Spock, you're alive."

61) "Scotty doesn't believe in gods."

62) "The needs of the few outweigh the needs of the many."

63) "I owe him my life a dozen times over. Isn't that worth a career?"

64) "I'm putting you gentlemen on the hot seat with me."

65) "Melakon is a traitor to his own people."

66) "And can nothing disturb this cycle?"

67) "You must have your own ship."

68) "No . . . Kill . . . I."

69) "If I were human . . . there could be . . . joining?"

70) "My friend James Kirk."

71) "We'll do it without your help, this time, Vulcan."

72) "Go. Or stay, but do it because it is what you wish to do."

73) "They don't like Klingons!"

74) "Oh, our friend Trefayne is quite intuitive."

75) "Oblivion together doesn't frighten me."

Answer the following mind-buster multiple-choice questions:

1) Tyree's wife is called
   a. Elieen   **b.** Nona
   c. Shanna   **d.** Daras

2) The original title of "A Piece Of The Action" was
   a. "The Chicago Of Space"   **b.** "Assignment Feds"
   c. "Mission To Chaos"   **d.** "The Fizzbin Caper"

3) Vegan Choriomeningitis is fatal within
   a. Six hours   **b.** Twelve hours
   c. Twenty-four hours   **d.** Thirty-six hours

4) Nomad was launched in the month of
   a. August   **b.** January
   c. March   **d.** April

5) Robert Johnson's wife was called
   a. Sharon   **b.** Elaine
   c. Donna   **d.** Joanna

6) Amanda's maiden name is
- **a.** Gray
- **b.** Kent
- **c.** Parker
- **d.** Grayson

7) The archeological dig on the planet M-113 is headed by
- **a.** Robert Crater
- **b.** Roger Corby
- **c.** Robert Johnson
- **d.** James Hanley

8) "Mudd's Women" was directed by
- **a.** Gene Coon
- **b.** Robert Falcone
- **c.** Harvey Hart
- **d.** D. C. Fontana

9) Miri is played by
- **a.** Tracy Pearson
- **b.** Susan Oliver
- **c.** Kim Darby
- **d.** Jeanne Bal

10) The only person ever to turn down a seat on the Federation Council was
- **a.** Garth of Izar
- **b.** Sarek of Vulcan
- **c.** Cochrane of Izar
- **d.** T'Pau of Vulcan

11) Commodore Travers is well-known for his
- **a.** Military record
- **b.** Closed-mindedness
- **c.** Hospitality
- **d.** Administrative talents

12) The primary industry on Janus Six is
- **a.** Mining
- **b.** Construction
- **c.** Recreation
- **d.** Agriculture

13) "The Gamesters of Triskelion" was originally entitled
- **a.** "The Gamesters of Rigel"
- **b.** "The Gamesters"
- **c.** "The Gamesters of Pentathlan"
- **d.** "The Gamesters of Andromeda"

14) The U.S.S. _Exeter_ was commanded by
- **a.** Matt Decker
- **b.** Bob Wesley
- **c.** Ron Tracey
- **d.** Robert Merik

15) Sam Cogley has a great love for
- **a.** Opera
- **b.** Old books
- **c.** Gin
- **d.** Paintings

16) Space sector 904 is a
    a. Globular cluster   **b.** Star chamber
    c. Magnetic anomaly   **d.** Star desert

17) Gary Seven tells Roberta Lincoln that he works for
    a. Her Majesty's Secret Ser-   **b.** Interpol
        vice
    c. The F.B.I.   **d.** The C.I.A.

18) The *Enterprise* is sent to star system 6-11 to investigate the disappearance of the
    a. *Beagle*   **b.** *Archon*
    c. *Cronos*   **d.** *Valiant*

19) The *Intrepid* was lost in the
    a. Gamma 7-A system   **b.** Delta 5-A system
    c. Omega 5-B system   **d.** Beta 4-B system

20) The ruling body of Elas is called the
    a. Council of Nobles   **b.** Council of Ten
    c. Royal Council   **d.** Council

21) Balok loves to drink
    a. Romulan ale   **b.** Antarian nectar
    c. Tranya   **d.** Vegan brandy

22) There is a planetary amusement park in the _____ **region**
    a. Alpha Ceti   **b.** Mutara
    c. Murasaki   **d.** Omicron Delta

23) In large doses, cordrazine causes
    a. Paranoia   **b.** Coma
    c. Psychotic tendencies   **d.** Depression

24) Kollos is a
    a. Tellerite   **b.** Rigellian
    c. Vulcan   **d.** Medusan

25) Private transmissions to Deneva are received over
    a. Subspace frequency one   **b.** Subspace frequency two
    c. Subspace frequency three   **d.** Subspace frequency four

ANSWERS

"Star Trek" History

Multiple Choice: 1) b   2) a   3) c   4) c   5) a   6) b   7) d   8) a
9) c   10) b   11) c   12) b   13) d   14) c   15) d   16) a   17) c
18) a   19) b   20) d   21) b   22) c   23) c   24) b   25) d   26) a
27) c   28) b   29) c   30) b   31) b   32) c   33) c   34) d   35) b
36) b   37) c   38) d   39) d   40) a   41) b   42) c   43) b   44) b
45) c   46) a   47) a   48) c   49) b   50) a

"Star Trek" Technology

Multiple Choice: 1) c   2) a   3) b   4) d   5) d   6) b   7) a   8) d
9) b   10) d   11) b   12) d   13) b   14) b   15) c   16) d   17) a
18) c   19) d   20) b   21) b   22) a

Matching: 1) l   2) k   3) m   4) j   5) d   6) b   7) c   8) e   9) i
10) f   11) a

Fill-Ins: 1) Seq. 2 Code 1–1A–2B   2) 710   3) M113   4) Earth
5) Gamma 400   6) 40   7) 1990s   8) 2000s   9) 24   10) 11

Matching II: 1) g   2) a   3) e   4) f   5) d   6) c

Alien Life Forms in the "Star Trek" Universe

Multiple Choice: 1) d   2) a   3) b   4) d   5) b   6) c   7) b   8) a
9) a   10) b   11) d   12) a   13) d   14) b   15) d   16) c   17) b
18) a   19) c   20) a   21) b   22) d   23) b   24) c   25) d   26) c
27) d   28) a   29) c   30) d   31) d   32) d   33) b   34) b   35) d
36) b   37) c   38) d   39) b   40) b   41) d   42) c   43) b   44) a
45) d   46) c   47) d   48) d   49) a   50) a   51) c   52) a   53) c
54) a   55) c   56) c   57) d   58) c   59) c   60) b   61) c   62) b
63) a   64) a   65) d   66) b   67) d   68) c   69) d   70) b   71) c
72) a   73) b   74) d   75) a   76) c   77) d   78) b   79) d   80) b
81) c   82) b   83) a   84) c   85) d   86) c   87) b   88) c   89) d
90) c   91) c   92) a   93) d   94) c   95) b   96) c   97) d   98) a
99) c   100) b   101) b

Matching: 1) i   2) h   3) f   4) j   5) k   6) a   7) c   8) m   9) l
10) d   11) b   12) n   13) q   14) s   15) t   16) e   17) o   18) p
19) r   20) w

James T. Kirk

Multiple Choice: 1) b   2) c   3) b   4) a   5) d   6) c   7) b   8) a
9) d   10) c   11) c   12) b   13) d   14) a   15) b
Matching: 1) d   2) c   3) m   4) a   5) h   6) i   7) n   8) k   9) l
10) u   11) 0   12) b   13) s   14) t   15) p   16) v   17) r   18) q
19) f   20) e

William Shatner

Multiple Choice: 1) c   2) b   3) c   4) b   5) c   6) a   7) c   8) d
9) a   10) b   11) c   12) d   13) a   14) c   15) b

Mr. Spock

Multiple Choice: 1) a   2) d   3) c   4) b   5) b   6) c   7) a   8) d
9) c   10) d   11) a   12) c   13) a   14) c   15) b
Matching: 1) e   2) c   3) g   4) j   5) d   6) i   7) b   8) a   9) h
10) k

Leonard Nimoy

Multiple Choice: 1) b   2) c   3) d   4) c   5) a   6) b   7) c   8) b
9) c   10) b   11) d   12) a   13) b   14) c   15) d

The Crew of the U.S.S. *Enterprise*

Multiple Choice: 1) a   2) b   3) c   4) d   5) b   6) b   7) a   8) b
9) c   10) d   11) b   12) c   13) d   14) a   15) c   16) d   17) b
18) a   19) c   20) d   21) c   22) d   23) a   24) c   25) a

Series Regulars

Multiple Choice: 1) d   2) a   3) b   4) c   5) d   6) a   7) c   8) d
9) c   10) a   11) c   12) b   13) a   14) c   15) c

The Episodes

"Obsession"

Multiple Choice: 1) c 2) c 3) c 4) a 5) d 6) b 7) a 8) a
9) b 10) b

Fill-Ins: 1) unstable 2) di-kironium 3) himself 4) freezes
5) sweet 6) impulse vent 7) size 8) antimatter 9) Spock
10) fission

True/False: 1) True 2) False—Captain 3) True 4) True
5) False 6) True 7) True 8) False 9) True 10) True

"A Private Little War"

Multiple Choice: 1) b 2) a 3) d 4) b 5) c 6) a 7) d 8) d
9) b 10) d

Fill-Ins: 1) Vulcan ward 2) McCoy 3) phaser 4) Tyree
5) Nona 6) woman 7) Michael Whitney 8) slapped
9) Booker Marshall 10) Yutan

True/False: 1) False—Organian Peace Treaty 2) True 3) False—
M'Benga 4) False—Nona 5) True 6) True 7) False
8) True 9) True 10) False

"The Mark of Gideon"

Multiple Choice: 1) c 2) c 3) d 4) a 5) b 6) b 7) c 8) c
9) b 10) d

Fill-Ins: 1) David Hurst 2) prolong a crisis 3) Hodin's 4) people 5) Fitzgerald 6) immortal 7) repairman 8) Sharon
Acker 9) Krodak 10) her memory

True/False: 1) True 2) True 3) False 4) True 5) True
6) True 7) True 8) False 9) False 10) False

"The Changeling"

Multiple Choice: 1) a 2) d 3) c 4) b 5) d 6) c 7) c 8) c
9) b 10) d

Fill-Ins: 1) eight 2) Kirk 3) biological 4) plague 5) interplanetary code 6) Omega Cygni 7) Singh 8) Jackson Roykirk
9) warp 11 10) Vic Perrin

True/False: 1) True 2) True 3) False—Nomad 4) True
5) False—Lieutenant 6) True 7) True 8) True 9) True
10) False

"The Deadly Years"

Multiple Choice: 1) d 2) d 3) c 4) a 5) b 6) b 7) b 8) c 9) b 10) c

Fill-Ins: 1) Theodore Wallace 2) biologist 3) extraordinary competency 4) Code 3 5) Aldebaran III 6) Gamma Hydra II 7) arthritis 8) Charles Drake 9) cold 10) neutral zone

True/False: 1) True 2) True 3) False—Corbomite Maneuver 4) False 5) True 6) False 7) True 8) False—to Spock 9) False 10) True

"Journey to Babel"

Multiple Choice: 1) c 2) d 3) d 4) c 5) d 6) a 7) a 8) c 9) b 10) a

Fill-Ins: 1) Benjisidrine 2) Jane Wyatt 3) Mark Lenard 4) Orion 5) Thelev 6) Gav 7) blood pressure 8) Orion 9) sehlats 10) teddy bear

True/False: 1) True 2) True 3) False 4) False 5) True 6) False—on Vulcan 7) False 8) True 9) True 10) True

"Spock's Brain"

Multiple Choice: 1) b 2) a 3) a 4) b 5) c 6) d 7) c 8) c 9) b 10) c

Fill-Ins: 1) teacher 2) controller 3) 10,000 4) communicator 5) waists 6) Spock 7) Spock 8) Mary Dusay 9) Glacial 10) 3

True/False: 1) True 2) False—a trilaser connector 3) True 4) False—he stuns Luma 5) False 6) True 7) False—ion power 8) True 9) False 10) True

"Conscience of the King"

Multiple Choice: 1) b 2) c 3) b 4) d 5) a 6) b 7) b 8) a 9) a 10) a

Fill-Ins: 1) Arnold Moss 2) Galactic Cultural Exchange *Program* 3) tetralubisol 4) 20 5) Kirk, Riley 6) Hamlet's father/the ghost 7) mad 8) Lenore 9) March 10) observation

True/False: False 2) False—Lenore did 3) False 4) True 5) True 6) True 7) True 8) False 9) True 10) True

"The Naked Time"

Multiple Choice: 1) b   2) a   3) c   4) d   5) b   6) a   7) d   8) b
9) c   10) b

Fill-Ins: 1) Marc Daniels   2) sword   3) "I'll Take You Home Again Kathleen"   4) Baker Two   5) woman   6) perspiration   7) Christine   8) time   9) Kevin Riley   10) Kevin Riley

True/False: 1) True   2) False—it has never been done   3) False
4) True   5) True

"Let This Be Your Last Battlefield"

Multiple Choice: 1) d   2) a   3) c   4) b   5) b   6) b   7) b   8) b
9) d   10) a

Fill-Ins: 1) political traitors   2) right   3) left   4) extradition, Cheron   5) bridge   6) destroy   7) directional   8) invisible
9) force   shields   10) inferior

True/False: 1) False   2) True   3) True   4) True   5) False
6) False—from 5 to 0   7) True   8) True   9) True   10) False

"All Our Yesterdays"

Multiple Choice: 1) a   2) b   3) c   4) d   5) a   6) d   7) c   8) b
9) d   10) a

Fill-Ins: 1) duplicates   2) Library   3) prosecutor   4) hot springs
5) exposure   6) 5,000   7) lying   8) together   9) Zor Khan
10) arm

True/False: 1) True   2) True   3) False   4) True   5) False
6) True   7) True   8) True   9) True   10) False—he uses it on Kirk

"Charlie X"

Multiple Choice: 1) d   2) a   3) c   4) b   5) d   6) d   7) a   8) d
9) b   10) c

Fill-Ins: 1) phasers   2) shock   3) recite poetry   4) bottle of perfume   5) Tina Lawton   6) subspace frequency 3   7) D. C. Fontana   8) 3   9) Robert Walker, Jr.   10) 2

True/False: 1) True   2) False—it is destroyed by Charlie   3) True
4) False—he changes them to pictures of Janice Rand   5) False

"Dagger of the Mind"

Multiple Choice: 1) a   2) c   3) d   4) b   5) c   6) b   7) c   8) d
9) a   10) c

Fill-Ins: 1) James Gregory   2) ventilator shaft   3) fall in love
4) loneliness   5) therapist   6) communication, transport   7) Vincent McEveety   8) dismantle the neural neutralizer   9) remember   10) penology

True/False: 1) True   2) False   3) True   4) True   5) False—Kirk is a great admirer of Adams

"Man Trap"

Multiple Choice: 1) b   2) a   3) c   4) d   5) b   6) c   7) b   8) d
9) a   10) b   11) d

Fill-Ins: 1) a bellyache   2) chase an asteroid   3) Sulu   4) salt
5) buffalo   6) mottling   7) paralyzes   8) GQ Four   9) ineffective   10) McCoy

True/False: 1) True   2) True   3) False—first season   4) False
5) True   6) False—McCoy kills the creature   7) False—Swahili
8) True   9) True   10) False

"Mudd's Women"

Multiple Choice: 1) a   2) a   3) b   4) c   5) a   6) c   7) b   8) c
9) b   10) b

Fill-Ins: 1) Eve, Ruth, and Magda   2) Herm Gossett   3) lie detector   4) subspace radio   5) placebo   6) 6   7) Mudd's women
8) hanging them out in the wind   9) mattress   10) character witness

True/False: 1) True   2) False   3) True   4) True   5) False—39
6) False—double jack   7) True   8) True   9) False   10) True

"Miri"

Multiple Choice: 1) d   2) a   3) c   4) b   5) d   6) d   7) a   8) a
9) c   10) b

Fill-Ins: 1) closet   2) Michael J. Pollard   3) 24   4) biocomputer
5) carrier   6) nitrogen cycle   7) puberty   8) legs   9) insanity
10) 6 months

True/False: 1) True   2) False   3) True   4) False—McCoy tests the vaccine   5) False—she sharpens pencils   6) True   7) True
8) False—Vincent McEveety   9) True   10) True

"Amok Time"

Multiple Choice: 1) b   2) c   3) a   4) a   5) d   6) d   7) a   8) a
9) c   10) d

Fill-Ins: 1) killed   2) death   3) Arlene Martel   4) thinner   5) die
6) prosper   7) closest friends   8) blood fever   9) Komack
10) logically

True/False: 1) False   2) True   3) True   4) True   5) False
6) True   7) False—it simulates death   8) True   9) False   10) True

"Arena"

Multiple Choice: 1) c   2) a   3) b   4) d   5) c   6) d   7) c   8) b
9) c   10) d   11) d

Fill-Ins. 1) lizard   2) humanoids   3) cannon   4) leg, rock slide
5) sulfur   6) diamonds   7) winner   8) kill   9) Carole Shayne
10) fast

True/False: 1) True   2) False   3) False   4) True   5) False—he
uses burning cloth   6) True   7) False   8) False—it is DePaul
9) True   10) True

"Tomorrow Is Yesterday"

Multiple Choice: 1) b   2) a   3) d   4) c   5) a   6) c   7) b   8) b
9) c   10) d

Fill-Ins: 1) computer   2) blackjack   3) history   4) tractor beam
5) slingshot   6) astronaut   7) gravitational pull   8) Colonel
9) Fellini   10) astronaut

True/False: 1) False   2) True   3) True   4) False   5) False—he
doesn't remember it   6) True   7) False—chicken noodle
8) True   9) True   10) True

"Catspaw"

Multiple Choice: 1) c   2) d   3) b   4) d   5) b   6) c   7) c   8) d
9) c   10) b

Fill-Ins: 1) Kirk   2) Theo Marcuse   3) Robert Bloch   4) door
5) Antoinette Bower   6) castle   7) 10   8) mental power   9) dungeon   10) dies

True/False: 1) True   2) False   3) False—Korob does   4) False
5) True   6) True   7) True   8) True   9) False—they die
10) False

"The Doomsday Machine"

Multiple Choice: 1) b   2) a   3) b   4) b   5) d   6) a   7) c   8) d   9) d   10) c

Fill-Ins: 1) NCC-1017   2) explode   3) solar day   4) Spock   5) Matt   6) third   7) neutronium   8) bluff   9) sick bay   10) *Moby Dick*

True/False: 1) True   2) False   3) True   4) True   5) True   6) False   7) False   8) True   9) False   10) True

"Devil in the Dark"

Multiple Choice: 1) b   2) d   3) b   4) a   5) b   6) d   7) c   8) d   9) a   10) c

Fill-Ins: 1) Giotto   2) mother   3) tunnel   4) Vandemberg   5) big, shaggy   6) pain   7) taste   8) bricklayer   9) Appel   10) bandage

True/False: 1) True   2) False   3) False   4) True   5) True   6) True   7) True   8) False—there were 100 people   9) True   10) True

"The Menagerie"

Multiple Choice: 1) d   2) b   3) c   4) c   5) a   6) c   7) b   8) d   9) b   10) c   11) d   12) c   13) a   14) b   15) b   16) c   17) c   18) b   19) a   20) c   21) a

Fill-Ins: 1) Gene Roddenberry   2) two-part   3) Hugo   4) illusion   5) Vina   6) Orion slave girl   7) smiled   8) adaptable   9) underground   10) narcotic   11) breeding stock   12) 203   13) guilty   14) limited   15) Majel Barrett   16) captivity   17) Lieutenant   18) war   19) experience   20) overload

True/False: 1) False   2) False—it was an illusion   3) False—it was an illusion   4) False   5) False   6) False—a high protein concentrate   7) True   8) True   9) True   10) False   11) False—he has him confined to quarters   12) True   13) True   14) True   15) False   16) True   17) False   18) False—it means yes   19) True   20) True

"What Are Little Girls Made Of?"

Multiple Choice: 1) b   2) a   3) c   4) d   5) a   6) c   7) b   8) b   9) c   10) d

Fill-Ins: 1) half-breed   2) suicide   3) Pasteur   4) Chapel's   5) programming   6) surprise   7) Ted Cassidy   8) Rok   9) hand   10) Spock

True/False: 1) False—she loves Korby   2) False   3) False
4) True   5) True   6) False—they were destroyed by the androids
7) True   8) False   9) False   10) True

"The Galileo Seven"

Multiple Choice: 1) c   2) d   3) b   4) d   5) c   6) d   7) a   8) c
9) b

Fill-Ins: 1) 24   2) first   3) space normal   4) luck   5) phaser
power   6) Gaetano's   7) alternatives   8) re-entry   9) radiation
10) 5

True/False: 1) False   2) False   3) True   4) False—class M
5) False   6) True   7) False   8) True   9) False—Boma survives
10) True

"Bread and Circuses"

Multiple Choice: 1) b   2) d   3) a   4) c   5) d   6) b   7) a   8) c
9) b

Fill-Ins: 1) psychosimulator   2) 47   3) of God   4) sun worshippers   5) commendation   6) Empire TV   7) 400   8) Drusilla
9) televised   10) You Name the Winner

True/False: 1) False   2) True   3) False   4) True   5) False
6) True   7) False   8) False   9) True   10) False

"Omega Glory"

Multiple Choice: 1) b   2) a   3) c   4) b   5) a   6) c   7) b   8) a
9) b   10) d

Fill-Ins: 1) year of the red bird   2) prime directive   3) Y3X point
004   4) common cold   5) phaser packs   6) Yankees   7) natural
8) worship word   9) heart

True/False: 1) False—Constitution   2) True   3) False—Sulu
4) True   5) True   6) False   7) False   8) True   9) True
10) True

"Spectre of the Gun"

Multiple Choice: 1) b   2) a   3) c   4) d   5) c   6) b   7) c   8) d
9) b   10) c

Fill-Ins: 1) Morgan Earp   2) bushwhack   3) force field   4) be
changed   5) ineffective   6) telepathically   7) Billy Clanton
8) Doc Holliday   9) Chekov   10) real

True/False: 1) True   2) False   3) True   4) False   5) False
6) True   7) True   8) False   9) True   10) True

"Court-martial"

Multiple Choice: 1) b 2) b 3) c 4) d 5) c 6) a 7) d 8) c
9) a 10) c

Fill-Ins: 1) prosecution 2) Lieutenant 3) Elisha Cook, Jr.
4) Martian colonies 5) ground 6) Axanar Peace Mission
7) Sam Cogley 8) Kirk 9) Vulcan Scientific Legion of Honor
10) dead

True/False: 1) True 2) True 3) False 4) True 5) True
6) True 7) True 8) False 9) True 10) True

"The Squire of Gothos"

Multiple Choice: 1) c 2) b 3) a 4) a 5) d 6) a 7) b 8) d
9) c 10) d

Fill-Ins: 1) Vincent 2) William Campbell 3) toxic 4) Kirk
5) supplies, Beta VI 6) geologist 7) Lieutenant 8) control device 9) James Doohan 10) reigns, conquest

True/False: 1) True 2) False—Helen of Troy 3) False—it's lead by McCoy 4) True 5) True 6) True 7) False 8) False—pistols
9) False 10) True

"Assignment: Earth"

Multiple Choice: 1) b 2) b 3) d 4) c 5) b 6) c 7) b 8) d
9) c 10) c

Fill-Ins: 1) one 2) deflectors 3) Isis 4) Robert Lansing 5) 20
6) euphoria 7) servo 8) Teri Garr 9) light speed breakaway
10) Brooklyn

True/False: 1) True 2) False—it's behind the bar 3) True
4) True 5) True 6) False—Mr. Cromwell 7) True 8) True
9) True 10) True

"Return of the Archons"

Multiple Choice: 1) b 2) c 3) b 4) d 5) d 6) c 7) b 8) b
9) b 10) c

Fill-Ins: 1) O'Neil 2) Body 3) 3 4) 6,000 5) Charles
Macauley 6) heat beams 7) man 8) absorption 9) Marplon
10) Kirk

True/False: 1) True 2) False 3) False 4) True 5) True
6) False 7) False 8) False 9) True 10) True

"The Lights of Zetar"

Multiple Choice: 1) c   2) b   3) d   4) c   5) b   6) c   7) c   8) b   9) b   10) c

Fill-Ins: 1) dead   2) shields   3) first   4) Memory Alpha   5) Jan Shutan   6) Steinman   7) neural   8) speak   9) pressure chamber   10) 100

True/False: 1) True   2) True   3) True   4) False—Mira's body   5) True   6) True   7) False   8) True   9) True   10) False

"Who Mourns for Adonais?"

Multiple Choice: 1) c   2) b   3) c   4) b   5) c   6) d   7) a   8) c   9) c   10) c

Fill-Ins: 1) 22   2) gods   3) laurel leaves   4) energy   5) spurn   6) paralyzed   7) the *Enterprise*   8) suicide   9) wings of the wind   10) human

True/False: 1) False   2) False   3) False   4) True   5) True   6) False—he can alter his size   7) True   8) False   9) True   10) False

"The Immunity Syndrome"

Multiple Choice: 1) a   2) c   3) b   4) b   5) b   6) c   7) b   8) a   9) d   10) b

Fill-Ins: 1) Captain McCoy   2) stimulants   3) dying   4) acetylcholine   5) bare minimum   6) biological   7) in reverse   8) debris   9) conqueror   10) virus

True/False: 1) False   2) True   3) True   4) True   5) False   6) True   7) True   8) False   9) False   10) True

"The Alternative Factor"

Multiple Choice: 1) c   2) a   3) c   4) b   5) c   6) b   7) c   8) b   9) d   10) b

Fill-Ins: 1) bait   2) the planet's surface   3) first   4) time, space   5) both   6) eternity   7) experimentation   8) antimatter   9) violently   10) Lesli

True/False: 1) True   2) True   3) True   4) True   5) False   6) True   7) False—Kirk is   8) True   9) False   10) False

"Turnabout Intruder"

Multiple Choice: 1) d 2) a 3) b 4) a 5) c 6) b 7) c 8) a

Fill-Ins: 1) Sandra Smith 2) Gene Roddenberry 3) Benecia
4) 7 5) Arthur Coleman 6) Steinman 7) last 8) mutiny
9) murder 10) Spock

True/False: 1) True 2) True 3) False 4) True 5) True

"Return to Tomorrow"

Multiple Choice: 1) c 2) a 3) d 4) d 5) c 6) c 7) c 8) b
9) b 10) c

Fill-Ins: 1) Henoch 2) Sargon 3) Thalassa 4) Uhura 5) Vulcan 6) unanimous 7) consciousness 8) McCoy 9) Chapel
10) unconsciousness

True/False: 1) True 2) True 3) False—he threatens Sulu
4) True 5) False—he is tricked by Sargon 6) False 7) False
8) False—it accelerates 9) True 10) True

"Elaan of Troyius"

Multiple Choice: 1) b 2) d 3) c 4) a 5) d 6) a 7) b 8) b
9) d 10) c

Fill-Ins: 1) Kryton 2) warp engines 3) love potion 4) unsatisfac-
tory 5) Klingon transmission 6) High Commissioner 7) engineering 8) dilithium crystals 9) 4 10) amidships

True/False: 1) True 2) True 3) False 4) False—they are provided
by Lieutenant Uhura 5) False 6) False—they can resist physical
torture 7) True 8) False—they order complete surrender
9) True 10) False

"The Paradise Syndrome"

Multiple Choice: 1) b 2) d 3) a 4) d 5) d 6) d 7) a 8) c
9) d 10) b

Fill-Ins: 1) god 2) priestess 3) preservation 4) phasers 5) lyrette 6) stoned 7) asteroid deflector 8) *Enterprise* 9) baby
10) Salish

True/False: 1) False 2) True 3) True 4) True 5) True
6) True 7) False 8) False—he is seen by Miramanee 9) False
10) True

"The Corbomite Maneuver"

Multiple Choice: 1) b   2) d   3) d   4) b   5) b   6) d   7) b   8) c   9) b   10) b

Fill-Ins: 1) hard phaser   2) diet   3) panics   4) radiation   5) poker   6) salad   7) recorder marker   8) dummy   9) 2000 metric tons   10) spiral

True/False: 1) True   2) True   3) True   4) True   5) False—11,000 metric tons   6) False   7) True   8) False   9) False—Jekyll to his Hyde   10) True

"The Enemy Within"

Multiple Choice: 1) c   2) a   3) d   4) b   5) a   6) c   7) b   8) d   9) d   10) d

Fill-Ins: 1) 4   2) synchronic   3) Saurian brandy   4) Spock   5) negative   6) positive   7) Farrell   8) makeup   9) transporter circuit   10) velocity balance

True/False: 1) True   2) False—it will take a week   3) False   4) True   5) False   6) True   7) False—they are ordered not to hurt the intruder   8) True   9) False   10) False

"Errand of Mercy"

Multiple Choice: 1) a   2) b   3) c   4) b   5) c   6) d   7) b   8) d   9) c   10) a

Fill-Ins: 1) commander   2) sonic grenade   3) 3   4) 8, battleships   5) disposition   6) Organians   7) much alike   8) 10   9) 2 hours   10) death

True/False: 1) True   2) False   3) True   4) True   5) True   6) False   7) True   8) True   9) True   10) True

"Shore Leave"

Multiple Choice: 1) c   2) b   3) c   4) c   5) a   6) b   7) a   8) a   9) c   10) d

Fill-Ins: 1) Esteban   2) tiger   3) amusement park   4) samurai   5) Spock   6) gown   7) Angela   8) dagger   9) play   10) caretaker

True/False: 1) False—she beams down with Kirk   2) True   3) True   4) False—he shows Kirk rabbit tracks   5) True   6) False—he is killed by a knight   7) False   8) False   9) True   10) False

"The City on the Edge of Forever"

Multiple Choice: 1) b   2) d   3) d   4) c   5) b   6) a   7) b   8) d   9) d   10) b

Fill-Ins: 1) flop   2) memory circuit   3) mechanical rice picker   4) machine, being   5) Writers Guild   6) Hugo   7) social worker   8) tools   9) 22   10) 21st Street Mission

True/False: 1) True   2) False   3) True   4) True   5) False—combination lock   6) False   7) True   8) True

"Balance of Terror"

Multiple Choice: 1) b   2) c   3) c   4) d   5) b   6) c   7) c   8) c   9) d   10) b

Fill-Ins: 1) iron   2) range   3) McCoy (or Rand)   4) Mr. Spock   5) comet   6) Decius   7) impulse   8) nuclear warhead   9) Uhura   10) Kirk

True/False: 1) False   2) True   3) False—he is saved by Spock   4) True   5) True   6) True   7) True   8) True   9) True

"Is There in Truth No Beauty?"

Multiple Choice: 1) b   2) c   3) d   4) c   5) a   6) c   7) d   8) b   9) d   10) b

Fill-Ins: 1) garden   2) sublime   3) mind meld   4) sensor web   5) freedom   6) rival   7) Miranda   8) goggles   9) see   10) rose

True/False: 1) False   2) True   3) False   4) True   5) False   6) True   7) False—by McCoy   8) True   9) False   10) False—Kirk confronts Miranda

"The Empath"

Multiple Choice: 1) c   2) b   3) c   4) a   5) b   6) a   7) a   8) d   9) c   10) b

Fill-Ins: 1) Spock   2) bends   3) Kirk   4) thought patterns   5) McCoy   6) congested   7) test tubes   8) mirage   9) bedside manner   10) awed

True/False: 1) False   2) False   3) True   4) False—with an injection   5) False   6) False   7) True   8) True   9) False—Spock is   10) True

"Operation—Annihilate!"

Multiple Choice: 1) c 2) b 3) c 4) b 5) b 6) a 7) d 8) c
9) d 10) a

Fill-Ins: 1) free 2) 100 ·3) pain 4) spaceships 5) buzzing
6) brain cell 7) Scotty 8) Spock 9) sight 10) Deneva

True/False: 1) True 2) True 3) False—to Spock 4) True
5) True 6) False—they invaded from Ingraam B 7) True
8) False 9) False—it is about one million 10) False

"A Taste of Armageddon"

Multiple Choice: 1) b 2) a 3) b 4) d 5) c 6) c 7) c 8) d
9) a 10) d

Fill-Ins: 1) 1, 3 2) Robert Fox 3) peaceful 4) voice duplicator
5) disruptors 6) DePaul 7) Tamura 8) barbarian 9) 24
10) Vendikan council

True/False: 1) True 2) True 3) True 4) False 5) False
6) True 7) True 8) False 9) False—2 guards 10) True

"The Ultimate Computer"

Multiple Choice: 1) a 2) a 3) b 4) d 5) d 6) c 7) d 8) c
9) c 10) d

Fill-Ins: 1) Dunsel 2) loyalty 3) efficient 4) engrams 5) thinks
6) 53 7) Kirk 8) antimatter pods 9) 4 toys 10) nervous
breakdown

True/False: 1) True 2) True 3) False 4) False 5) False—a
Finagle's Folly 6) True 7) False—a force shield 8) False—4 and
6 only 9) True 10) True

"Metamorphosis"

Multiple Choice: 1) c 2) d 3) a 4) a 5) c 6) b 7) d 8) c
9) b 10) d

Fill-Ins: 1) propulsion 2) short circuit 3) telepathically 4) Man
5) 35 6) Nancy 7) the *Enterprise* 8) energy dampening
9) verbally 10) immortality

True/False: 1) True 2) False—it causes death 3) True 4) True
5) False 6) False—she is saved by the Companion 7) True
8) True 9) True 10) False—Kirk convinces the Companion to let
them go

"Mirror, Mirror"

Multiple Choice: 1) c 2) b 3) d 4) b 5) a 6) a 7) c 8) a 9) a 10) c

Fill-Ins: 1) dagger 2) woman 3) tantalus 4) acid 5) Captain Pike 6) Gorlan 7) Uhura 8) Sulu 9) McCoy 10) pirate

True/False: 1) True 2) False—Commander Kenner has 3) False—by McCoy 4) True 5) False—he will consider it 6) False—Kirk does 7) True 8) True 9) True

"Wolf in the Fold"

Multiple Choice: 1) d 2) b 3) c 4) c 5) d 6) a 7) c 8) c 9) d 10) b

Fill-Ins: 1) Jack the Ripper 2) Hengist 3) computer 4) Rigel IV 5) Earth 6) SE 197-514 7) love 8) Morla 9) Sybo 10) Karen Tracy

True/False: 1) True 2) True 3) False—from Rigel IV 4) True 5) True 6) True 7) False 8) False—it cuts life support 9) False 10) False

"Where No Man Has Gone Before"

Multiple Choice: 1) c 2) b 3) c 4) c 5) b 6) c 7) a 8) c 9) a 10) b

Fill-Ins: 1) oasis 2) insects 3) phaser fire 4) warp engines 5) Deneb IV 6) Nightingale 7) lead 8) negative 9) Sulu 10) Elizabeth

True/False: 1) False—it reads James R. Kirk 2) True 3) False—killed in the line of duty 4) False—it was aimed at Kirk 5) True 6) False—12 hours 7) True 8) False—it grows geometrically 9) True 10) False—smaller

"This Side of Paradise"

Multiple Choice: 1) d 2) c 3) c 4) c 5) b 6) b 7) c 8) d 9) c 10) b

Fill-Ins: 1) painful 2) evacuate 3) lobar pneumonia 4) mint julep 5) Sulu's 6) diplomat 7) rainbows 8) animals 9) Kalomi 10) Jill Ireland

True/False: 1) True 2) False 3) True 4) False 5) True 6) True 7) True 8) True 9) True 10) True

"Space Seed"

Multiple Choice: 1) b 2) c 3) b 4) d 5) c 6) d 7) b 8) b 9) a 10) a

Fill-Ins: 1) Khan Noonian Singh 2) Middle East 3) selective breeding 4) neural 5) technical manuals 6) psychologist 7) life support 8) "How long?" 9) decompression chamber 10) Marla

True/False: 1) False 2) True 3) False 4) False—he uses a metal club 5) True 6) False—72 7) False—the coast of Australia 8) True 9) True 10) False—she goes with Khan

"Friday's Child"

Multiple Choice: 1) c 2) c 3) a 4) b 5) d 6) b 7) d 8) b 9) d 10) c

Fill-Ins: 1) boy 2) High Teer 3) Leonard James Akaar 4) magnesite-nitron tablets 5) Julie Newmar 6) communicators 7) Tige Andrews 8) bow, arrows 9) medical 10) Scotty

True/False: 1) False 2) True 3) False 4) False—it is a Capellan insult 5) True 6) True 7) False—she names it after Kirk and McCoy 8) True 9) False—she knocks McCoy unconscious 10) False—her arm

"The Apple"

Multiple Choice: 1) b 2) b 3) d 4) a 5) c 6) d 7) a 8) d 9) b 10) a

Fill-Ins: 1) neck 2) Keith Andes 3) David Soul 4) young 5) lightning bolt 6) kissing 7) Martha 8) Russia 9) Masiform-D 10) broken

True/False: 1) False-an exploding rock 2) False—Spock does 3) True 4) False—with Chekov 5) True 6) True 7) True 8) False—Max Erlich and Gene Coon 9) True 10) True

"I, Mudd"

Multiple Choice: 1) a 2) b 3) d 4) c 5) d 6) c 7) d 8) a 9) d 10) c

Fill Ins: 1) bomb 2) Richard Tatro 3) illogic 4) wreath of pretty flowers that smell bad 5) one 6) badges 7) beautiful woman 8) Norman 9) a lie 10)) *Enterprise*

True/False: 1) True   2) True   3) True   4) False—an "Alice"
5) True   6) True   7) True   8) False—he knocks Harry out
9) False—he is rendered harmless   10) False

"The Trouble with Tribbles"

Multiple Choice: 1) b   2) d   3) b   4) d   5) d   6) b   7) a   8) d
9) c   10) b

Fill-Ins: 1) Mr. Baris   2) Spican flame   3) William Schallert
4) Klingons   5) garbage scow   6) Stanley Adams   7) Cossacks
8) Leningrad   9) E   10) tribbles

True/False: 1) True   2) False—he's a Klingon spy   3) True
4) False—by Korax   5) True   6) True   7) False—he compares it to
milk   8) True   9) True   10) True

"The Gamesters of Triskelion"

Multiple Choice: 1) b   2) a   3) d   4) a   5) c   6) a   7) d   8) d
9) a   10) c

Fill-Ins: 1) Angelique Pettyjohn   2) free-style match   3) wager
4) quatloos   5) trisec   6) Jane Ross   7) educate   8) Lars
9) Jana Haines   10) Mickey Morton

True/False: 1) False   2) True   3) True   4) True   5) True
6) False   7) False   8) True   9) False—she thinks Kirk has lied to
her   10) False—Gene Nelson

"A Piece of the Action"

Multiple Choice: 1) d   2) c   3) c   4) a   5) c   6) d   7) a   8) b
9) d   10) b

Fill-Ins: 1) Anthony Caruso   2)) *Horizon*   3) communicator
4) Royal   5) John Harmon   6) piece of the action   7) Oxmyx
8) hit   9) concrete galoshes   10) Vic Tayback

True/False: 1) True   2) False   3) False—he's never heard of it
4) True   5) True   6) False—the man to the dealer's right gets
seven   7) True   8) True   9) False—Kirk made it up   10)True

"By Any Other Name"

Multiple Choice: 1) a   2) c   3) a   4) b   5) c   6) d   7) d   8) a
9) c   10) a

Fill-Ins: 1) Kelinda   2) Scotch   3) conquerors   4) Warren Stevens   5) engineering   6) home   7) Thompson   8) blocks 9) Barbara Bouchet   10) in space

True/False: 1) False   2) False—they are tentacled non-humanoids 3) True   4) True   5) True   6) True   7) False   8) False—on his belt   9) False   10) False

"The Tholian Web"

Multiple Choice: 1) a   2) c   3) d   4) b   5) c   6) a   7) b   8) c 9) c   10) c

Fill-Ins: 1) Kirk's last orders   2) tri-ox compound   3) mutiny 4) disturbed   5) Tholian Assembly   6) Ralph Senensky   7) alcohol   8) transporter   9) pressure suits   10) Spock

True/False: 1) True   2) True   3) False—they deny having seen them   4) False   5) True   6) True   7) False—Chekov is 8) False   9) True   10) True

"Whom Gods Destroy"

Multiple Choice: 1) b   2) a   3) c   4) d   5) a   6) b   7) c   8) b 9) a   10) c

Fill-Ins: 1) Steve Ihnat   2) heir apparent   3) Marta   4) mutiny 5) Keye Luke

True/False: 1) True   2) True   3) False   4) False—she tries to kill Kirk   5) True

"The Way to Eden"

Multiple Choice: 1) b   2) d   3) a   4) d   5) b   6) c   7) b   8) d 9) b   10) d

Fill-Ins: 1) Charles Napier   2) Typhoid Mary   3) Catulla   4) ambassador   5) acoustics   6) Skip Homeier   7) egg   8) sound 9) Eden, Romulan   10) correct

True/False: 1) True   2) True   3) False—Spock is   4) True 5) False

"For the World Is Hollow and I Have Touched the Sky"

Multiple Choice: 1) c   2) c   3) c   4) d   5) c   6) a   7) b   8) a 9) c   10) b

Fill-Ins: 1) Fabrini   2) married   3) Kate Woodville   4) Spock 5) high priestess

True/False: 1) True   2) True—until he is cured   3) True   4) True
5) True

"And the Children Shall Lead"

Multiple Choice: 1) a   2) c   3) a   4) b   5) b   6) b   7) d   8) c
9) b   10) d

Fill-Ins: 1) Craig Hundley   2) Epsilon Indi   3) chant   4) ice
cream   5) Melvin Belli   6) children   7) emotions   8) Sulu
9) enemy within   10) parents

True/False: 1) False—by Kirk   2) True   3) True   4) True   5) False

"Day of the Dove"

Multiple Choice: 1) c   2) b   3) d   4) b   5) b   6) d   7) c   8) d
9) a   10) c

Fill-Ins: 1) Susan Johnson   2) Chekov   3) Mara   4) Michael Ansara   5) emergency manual control   6) Spock   7) military
8) red   9) die   10) life-support

True/False: 1) True   2) False   3) True   4) False—they are put in
the lounge   5) True

"Wink of an Eye"

Multiple Choice: 1) d   2) b   3) c   4) a   5) a   6) c   7) d   8) a
9) d   10) a

Fill-Ins: 1) Deela   2) docile   3) radiation   4) Jason Evers   5) deep
freeze

True/False: 1) True   2) True   3) False—he's jealous of Kirk
4) True   5) False—they all died   6) False—third season
7) True   8) False   9) True   10) True

"That Which Survives"

Multiple Choice: 1) b   2) b   3) c   4) d   5) d   6) c   7) b   8) c
9) d   10) b

Fill-Ins: 1) Lee Meriwether   2) computer projection   3) silicon
4) command chair   5) 11.33

True/False: 1) True   2) False   3) True   4) False—Dr. Sanchez
5) True

"The Cloud Minders"

Multiple Choice: 1) b 2) d 3) a 4) c 5) a 6) b 7) d 8) c
9) b 10) c

Fill-Ins: 1) mortae 2) thongs 3) Jeff Corey 4) Disruptors
5) Droxine 6) Plasus 7) Charlene Polite 8) retardation
9) Plasus 10) Diana Ewing

True/False: 1) True 2) False—she tries to kidnap Kirk 3) True
4) True 5) False—they require a transport pass

"Requiem for Methuselah"

Multiple Choice: 1) c 2) a 3) d 4) d 5) d 6) b 7) b 8) c
9) b 10) d

Fill-Ins: 1) android 2) Gutenberg 3) Galileo 4) James Daly
5) forget Reena 6) her emotions 7) Kirk 8) Louise Sorel
9) Ryetalyn 10) Marcus II

True/False: 1) True 2) True 3) True 4) True 5) False
6) True 7) False 8) True 9) True 10) False

"The Savage Curtain"

Multiple Choice: 1) c 2) a 3) c 4) b 5) d 6) b 7) d 8) b
9) a 10) c

Fill-Ins: 1) Tiburon 2) Surak 3) All 4) Phillip Pine 5) Lee Berger

True/False: 1) True 2) True 3) False—Lincoln does 4) False—Surak does 5) True

"The *Enterprise* Incident"

Multiple Choice: 1) d 2) b 3) b 4) d 5) b 6) b 7) d 8) a
9) c 10) b

Fill-Ins: 1) neutral zone 2) officers 3) dinner 4) Kirk 5) physiostimulator 6) right of statement 7) deflector 8) 9 9) espionage 10) lie

True/False: 1) False 2) False 3) False 4) True 5) False—it does not exist 6) True 7) False—he gets them from the Romulan hostages 8) False—15 minutes 9) False—First Officer
10) True

"Patterns of Force"

Multiple Choice: 1) c 2) b 3) a 4) d 5) a 6) c 7) b 8) b
9) c 10) b

Fill-Ins: 1) Father 2) Melakon 3) Colonel 4) rubindium
5) Daras 6) Gestapo 7) Melakon 8) maximum, Ekos
9) Uletta 10) peaceful

True/False: 1) True 2) True 3) False—his boots 4) True
5) False 6) False—he is the party chairman 7) False—
by Melakon 8) False 9) True 10) True

"Plato's Stepchildren"

Multiple Choice: 1) c 2) d 3) a 4) c 5) b 6) a 7) d 8) b
9) c 10) d

Fill-Ins: 1) McCoy 2) Hippocrates 3) Liam Sullivan 4) Shakespeare 5) Michael Dunn

True/False: 1) True 2) True 3) False 4) False—his wife 5) True

Photo Quiz

1) China 2) Tellar 3) Flavius 4) Balok 5) Sarpedion
6) Lirpa 7) In Sylvia and Korob's dungeon 8) "Alternative
Factor" 9) In engineering 10) "The Tholian Web"
11) Lyrette 12) A Number One 13) Salt shakers
14) "The *Galileo* 7" 15) On the hangar deck 16) The rook
17) K-7 18) "The Menagerie" 19) "Where No Man Has
Gone Before" 20) In the turbolift 21) SC 937-0176 CEC
22) "All Our Yesterdays" 23) The shuttle craft 24) "Patterns
of Force" 25) Reading technical manuals 26) "Plato's
Stepchildren" 27) "Where No Man Has Gone Before"
28) Vulcan 29) Warp six 30) Commander

Star Trek—The Motion Picture

Multiple Choice: 1) a   2) d   3) c   4) b   5) b   6) c   7) a   8) b
9) a   10) c   11) b   12) a   13) c   14) d   15) b   16) b   17) c
18) b   19) c   20) c   21) c   22) b   23) a   24) b   25) b   26) c
27) a   28) c   29) c   30) d   31) d   32) d   33) b   34) c   35) a
36) c   37) b   38) a   39) d   40) c

Fill-Ins: 1) transporter   2) faulty module   3) Scott   4) wormhole
5) Stephen Collins   6) one   7) Chief DiFalco   8) creator
9) data   patterns   10) Voyager Six   11) thruster suit   12) plasma
energy   13) tractor beam   14) child   15) The Ilia probe
16) change things   17) Sonak   18) Vulcan Embassy   19) Ilia
20) missing

True/False: 1) True   2) False   3) True   4) True   5) True
6) False—V'ger wishes to join with its creator   7) False—by radio
8) True   9) False—10 seconds   10) True   11) True   12) True
13) True   14) False—it purges all emotions   15) True   16) True
17) True   18) False   19) False—2½ years   20) False
21) False—photon torpedoes   22) True   23) True   24) False

Star Trek II: The Wrath of Khan

Multiple Choice: 1) c   2) a   3) b   4) c   5) d   6) d   7) b   8) c
9) b   10) a   11) b   12) d   13) d   14) d   15) b   16) c   17) d
18) c   19) b   20) c   21) a   22) b   23) c   24) b   25) b   26) d
27) c   28) b   29) c   30) a   31) c   32) b   33) c   34) d   35) b
36) a   37) c   38) b   39) b   40) d   41) d   42) a   43) c   44) c
45) b

Fill-Ins: 1) possibilities   2) needs, many, needs, few   3) Bibi
Besch   4) Carol Marcus   5) glasses   6) friend   7) McCoy
8) 20   9) prince   10) suggestion   11) suspended animation
12) Kirk   13) survival   14) lower her shields   15) Joachim
16) Mutara nebula   17) Amazing Grace   18) drink   19) Pavel
20) Jack B. Sowards

True/False: 1) True   2) False   3) False   4) True   5) True
6) False   7) False—he blames Khan   8) True   9) False
10) True   11) False—underground   12) False—G.O. 15
13) True   14) False   15) False   16) True   17) True   18) False
19) True   20) False—by Scotty

Star Trek III: The Search for Spock

Multiple Choice: 1) c 2) b 3) d 4) a 5) c 6) b 7) c 8) c 9) d 10) b 11) a 12) c 13) a 14) d 15) c 16) c 17) d 18) a 19) b 20) d 21) a 22) d 23) a 24) d 25) b 26) d 27) c 28) b 29) b 30) c 31) b 32) d 33) b 34) d 35) b 36) d 37) c 38) c 39) c 40) c 41) b 42) d 43) b 44) d 45) b 46) a 47) c 48) b 49) b 50) c

Fill-Ins: 1) 1-code 1-1-A 2) 2-code 1-1A-2B 3) 3-code 1B-2B-3 4) Code 0-0-0 destruct-0 5) protomatter 6) aging 7) lovers 8) *Excelsior* 9) Uhura 10) gunner 11) Weather 12) day 13) Christopher Lloyd 14) Kirk 15) Mark Lenard 16) absent friends 17) Judith Anderson 18) Torg 19) Kirk

True/False: 1) True 2) False 3) False 4) True 5) True 6) False 7) True 8) True 9) True 10) False 11) False 12) True 13) False 14) True 15) True

For the Experts

Quotations: 1) Decker, Doomsday Machine 2) Spock, Amok Time 3) McCoy, Star Trek II 4) Spock, Miri 5) Kor, Errand of Mercy 6) Kirk, Doomsday Machine 7) Spock, A Piece of the Action 8) T'Pau, Amok Time 9) Kirk, Miri 10) T'Pau, Amok Time 11) Riley, Naked Time 12) McCoy, Star Trek III 13) Sulu, Star Trek III 14) Kirk, Star Trek II 15) Lenore, Conscience of the King 16) Spock, This Side of Paradise 17) Nomad, Changeling 18) Kirk, Amok Time 19) Apollo, Who Mourns For Adonais? 20) Kirk, ST-TMP 21) Kirk, Amok Time 22) Lazarus, Alternative Factor 23) Scotty, Empath 24) Khan, Space Seed 25) Wesley, Ultimate Computer 26) Leila, This Side of Paradise 27) Spock, Doomsday Machine 28) Lester, Turnabout Intruder 29) McCoy, Requiem for Methuselah 30) Kirk, Charlie X 31) Kirk, Ultimate Computer 32) Companion, Metamorphosis 33) Korax, Trouble with Tribbles 34) Sarek, Journey to Babel 35) Eleen, Friday's Child 36) Kirk, Deadly Years 37) McCoy, Immunity Syndrome 38) Tyree, Private Little War 39) Kirk, By Any Other Name 40) Gary, Where No Man Has Gone Before 41) Kirk, Mudd's Women 42) McCoy, Dagger of the Mind 43) Apollo, Who Mourns for Adonais? 44) Marvick, Is There in Truth No Beauty 45) Balok, Corbomite Maneuver 46) Kara, Spock's

ain   47) Kirk, Taste of Armageddon   48) Riley, Conscience of
 King   49) Kodos, Conscience of the King   50) Kirk, Piece of
 Action   51) Akuta, Apple   52) Salish, Paradise Syndrome
) Decker, ST—TMP   54) Losira, That Which Survives
 5) "Kirk," What Are Little Girls Made Of?   56) Spock, Alterna-
ive Factor   57) Mara, Whom Gods Destroy   58) Kirk, Empath
59) M-5, Ultimate Computer   60) Kirk, Immunity Syndrome
61) McCoy, Who Mourns for Adonais?   62) Kirk, Star Trek III
63) Kirk, Amok Time   64) Kirk, Operation—Annihilate!   65) Gill,
Patterns of Force   66) Droxine, Cloud Minders   67) Romulan
Commander, *Enterprise* Incident   68) Horta, Devil in the dark
69) Companion, Metamorphosis   70) Gary, Where No Man Has
Gone Before   71) Stiles, Balance of Terror   72) Khan, Space
Seed   73) Kirk, Trouble with Tribbles   74) Ayleborne, Errand of
Mercy   75) Thalassa, Return to Tomorrow

Multiple Choice

1) b   2) c   3) c   4) a   5) b   6) d   7) a   8) c   9) c   10) d
11) c   12) a   13) c   14) c   15) b   16) d   17) d   18) b   19) a
20) a   21) c   22) d   23) a   24) d   25) c

BIBLIOGRAPHY

Asherman, Allan: *The Star Trek Compendium*
Gerrold, David: *The World of Star Trek,* revised edition. Bluejay
    Books, 1984.
Joseph, Franz: *Starfleet Technical Manual,* Ballantine Books,
    1975.
Trimble, Bjo: *Star Trek Concordance,* Ballantine Books, 1976.
Whitefield, Stephen E., and Roddenberry, Gene: *The Making of
    Star Trek,* Ballantine Books, 1968.